SWERVE

A Boosted Hearts Novel

by Sherilee Gray

Dedication:

For Max and Bella. Dream big.

Acknowledgements:

Thanks to my family for always being so supportive and believing in me. To fellow author Tracey Alvarez for answering all my questions and being my co-dependent sprint buddy. Don't ever stop kicking my ass! As always to Nicola Davidson, my critique partner and friend - it would take another book to list the reasons. To my beta readers Mel and Kelly. You guys totally rock. To Lillie at Lillie's Literary Services for the excellent proofread. And last but not least, to my editor Jill Noelle Noble. Thanks for helping me whip this baby into shape!

Contents

Chapter One

Shay Freestone cursed her ridiculous, flimsily made Poison Ivy costume for the gazillionth time when Batman stepped in front of her, blocking her exit and fingered one of her leaves. She slapped away the creep's hand.

Kayla owed Shay big time for this. Her best friend had shoved her into the embarrassing ensemble two hours ago, quoting Section Two, Item Four of their Best Friends' Handbook, drafted when they were in the seventh grade, after Shay refused to go to the school dance—which meant they both didn't go—and in her friend's absence, Rob Dunkirk, the love of Kayla's life, had danced with April Gunson the entire night. The section in question stated that Shay Freestone and Kayla Green agreed to do whatever necessary, *whenever* required, in the pursuit of securing love for either of the aforementioned.

But *this*, this was going above and beyond.

Batman moved closer, a bead of sweat sliding down his temple from under his now askew black mask. "Come on, Ivy. Don't go yet. The party's just getting started."

Gag. She tried to slip by, but he kept coming until his protruding belly—which was straining his utility belt dangerously—bumped into her, forcing her back a step.

"I really have to go."

1

He licked his fleshy, cherry-red lips and leaned in. "First, I need to find out if your kiss really is poisonous."

Is this cretin for real? She leaned back farther. Why on earth had she let Kayla drag her to this ridiculous party? Best Friends' Handbook, be damned. So what if Shay'd been a hermit the last few months? That was preferable to standing in a corner by herself the whole night, feeling like a complete idiot, while her traitorous friend, *in the pursuit of love,* was probably getting naked with Wolverine—aka Kayla's ex-boyfriend, James, and the reason she and Shay were here—back at his place. The couple had disappeared a little while ago. Her friend had bailed on her. Again. Kayla had conveniently forgotten *that* section of the blasted handbook. Now Shay was stranded without her wallet, phone, or the keys to her trailer since she'd stashed them in her friend's bag.

Maybe her gran had given a spare key to Edna next door? The pair had been thick as thieves before her grandmother passed away and left the place to Shay.

Batman's heavy breathing cut through her thoughts. His fingers moved lower. "So tell me, are you a natural redhead?"

Ew! She gave his hand a slap-shove combo. "I don't think—"

"How about we go upstairs, and you let me find out?"

Oh, dear God. Shay ducked under his arm, but he still had hold of the leaf on her costume, and she felt it tear free as she made a dash for the door.

"Hey! Hold up. Wait for me," the idiot called after her.

Shay shoved open the door and burst out onto the street, the cool, LA midwinter breeze hitting her bare skin, seeping through the cheap fabric from all sides. She sucked in a startled breath. Her coat was also in Kayla's car. So not only did Shay have to walk home in the cold in a Poison Ivy costume with half her butt hanging out, she had to walk home in a *cheap*, crappily made Poison Ivy costume with missing leaves that, thanks to Batman, was now falling apart at the seams and losing more by the minute.

Speaking of The Caped Crusader, he stumbled out of the apartment building, spotted her and started in her direction. Fast... Faster than she would have thought possible with the sway he had going on.

She'd had her fill of creeps, enough to last her a lifetime. She didn't need this right now, dammit.

Okay, there'd only been one creep, in particular, but his creep factor had been abnormally high... So high, the guy easily equaled, like...a thousand creeps, at least. Not-so-old hurt and embarrassment reared up, hitting her in the face, heating her skin to excruciating levels.

Having a fling with your boss was stupid enough. Period. But having an affair with your boss then having to quit that job because you overheard him bragging and mocking you to his buddies around the water cooler, was a whole new level of mortification. Not to mention the hit to her bank account. Her two part-time jobs and the occasional graphic design gig she managed to pick up barely covered living costs, let alone the debt left by her grandmother. She'd been forced to take out a loan, using the trailer her gran had left her as collateral.

She slammed the door on those thoughts as quickly as they came. *Not now.*

Spinning on the heels of her boots, Shay speed walked down the street. There weren't many people around, but enough she was thankful for the thick green pantyhose she had on, which hid a goodly amount of cellulite and were tight enough to provide a small amount of wobble control. The idiot behind her kept coming, calling out for her to, "Wait up."

Like heck.

With her only thought to lose him and get home as fast as possible, she ducked down the next street.

Only it wasn't a street, it was more an alley-slash-parking lot. Cars surrounded her, filling the reserved parking spots for the expensive-looking restaurant beside it. *Crap.*

She spun around as the Dark Knight rounded the corner, blocking the exit. "Ivy, why are you running from me?"

She backed up until she bumped into the car behind her. The cold steel chilled her, lifting goose-bumps all over her skin. The guy wasn't overly tall, but he was heavily built and kind of intimidating. She expected the car alarm to start wailing instantly—the vehicles parked around her looked high end, like sports cars and, um…stuff like that—but no such luck. Screw it all. The damn thing stayed silent.

She held up her hands to ward him off and shook her head. "All right. The fun's over. Why don't you head back to the party?"

He kept coming, licking his over-abundant red lips until they shone like candy apples; only these were gross, icky candy apples she seriously did not want to taste. The fool kept up the Batman persona, clutching the ends of his cape, lifting it up and down like wings. "I've come for my kiss, Ivy."

"If you come any closer…"

He came closer.

"Back up. *Now.*"

"Just one kiss."

"No."

"Yes." He puckered up, crowding her.

"No!" She gave him a shove…

Gravel scraped behind her, loud enough that Batman heard it, too. He stopped his descent, lifting his head. She watched the guy's eyes go wide, jaw unhinging. The sound of boots moving closer came next and had her whipping around to see who it was. She gaped like a dying fish.

A huge mountain of a man rounded the trunk and walked right up to them. He stared down at the creep in front of her and growled, "You got ears?" *Yes, growled.* Like a lion, or a bear, or some other wild beast.

Batman stared up at the man, slammed his mouth shut, looked at her, then back at the mountain. "Um…y-yes?"

"So you heard the lady tell you 'no'," her rescuer said, his eyes going kind of wild and scary.

"Well…um…I…" Batman was suddenly at a loss for words. He also seemed to have sobered up rather quickly, the glazed look gone from his beady eyes.

The mountain crossed his muscled arms, heavy biceps straining the sleeves of his faded black tee, veins bulging along his corded forearms in a rather interesting way. Then, with his eyes still locked on his target, he said quietly, "Go."

His voice sounded soft and rough all at the same time, and set off some serious tingles—like, they were doing a high-energy gig up and down her spine. No, he hadn't shouted the word, but there was no mistaking the danger behind the order.

Batman finally snapped out of his stupor and started backing up, nodding rapidly. As soon as he hit the entrance of the parking lot, he spun on his boots and sprinted away, cape flying out behind him from the sheer velocity of his escape.

The mountain watched the creep go, then his head swiveled on his muscled neck, and he dipped his chin so he was looking at her. "All right?" he rumbled.

Holy Hell. Her belly flipped. The guy was kind of terrifying. He was also extremely handsome in a scary, rough, mountainous kind of way. His hair was a little shaggy, and he had a full beard, but it wasn't the Grizzly Adams, shaggy kind of beard; it was trimmed and neat and suited the heck out of him. He was also *tall.* So tall, she was a good couple of inches shorter than his shoulder.

His dark brown eyes, which were surprisingly warm and kind, and ringed with thick, black lashes, locked on hers. "You okay, babe? He hurt you? You look kinda freaked."

Babe? Eeek. Her nether regions did a highly inappropriate but extremely happy little quiver at that deep, gruff voice. Which was crazy, because not only was she usually shy around men—especially attractive ones—but this guy was so far from her type it wasn't funny. "Ah…yes, I mean, no. I mean, I'm fine…now. T-thanks to you. You know…for coming to my rescue." *Jeez, spit it out.* She sounded as if she had a serious speech impediment.

"No problem." He stared at her for a few seconds, as if he was waiting for something. When she didn't say or *do* anything, because she couldn't move, let alone make her mouth work, he added, "Think you're good to go. Guy's long gone."

"Um…" She stayed rooted to the spot, gaze fixed on the hulk in front of her. Bizarrely, it wasn't fear keeping her in place…it was that she was struggling to leave the big man's orbit; his gravitational pull was that strong.

What the heck is wrong with me?

His lips quirked up, just a little on one side, then those stunning eyes did a full-body sweep. The quirk turned into a grin. "What's with the outfit?"

Her face heated instantly. She'd almost forgotten she was wearing the stupid costume. She stared down at herself and cringed. Her wobbly bits were all on full display—butt, thighs, belly, boobs. *Perfect.* "I was at a…a costume party."

"What're you?"

Her face got hotter. "Poison Ivy."

He frowned, brow scrunching in obvious confusion.

"She's a villain. Batman's nemesis…in a comic book."

He kept his gaze locked on her, and his eyes started dancing. "Right."

He was more than likely laughing at her, but right then, she didn't care; that sparkle in his eyes just made him more appealing. Again, her reaction was completely insane. The men she usually found herself attracted to were business types—they wore suits, were clean shaven, were…*smaller*. Less imposing. But the scary, hard gaze he'd wielded like a weapon was long gone now. In fact, she felt safe standing there with him.

Without realizing what she was doing, she shuffled a little closer, drawn by that magnetic pull that seemed to surround him. He also looked warm and snuggly, and now the excitement had past, she was starting to feel the cold.

He watched her, something moving over his features, something that got those inappropriate tingles riled up all over again. Her hair rested over her shoulder, and he reached out, touching it with his index finger, as if he was testing her reaction.

"I like the hair."

"It's real," she blurted for some stupid reason, probably because of Batman's lewd suggestion that the carpet didn't match the drapes. Not that she wanted this guy to see her carpet. No, that would be wrong, wouldn't it? They'd only just met.

He continued to stare at her, eyes still dancing in that highly attractive way. He also didn't answer, so she babbled on in an attempt to explain herself.

"I mean, it's not part of the costume. Though, Ivy does have red hair…it's just…it's not a wig." Then, out of nowhere and just to make her humiliation ten times worse, she added, "I like your beard."

Okay. She had no idea why she gave in to the urge to share that. She dropped her gaze to his big black boots, to hide the fact that the temperature of her face had skyrocketed by at least a thousand degrees.

"You do, huh?" His voice was rougher now, and God, the sexiest thing she'd ever heard.

She glanced up. His grin was wider, a full-blown smile. *Wow.* He looked good smiling. Like, *really good.*

"You want a ride some place?"

She blinked up at him. "Um…" For some crazy reason, she wanted to say yes, she wanted to go with him, this complete stranger, this huge, bearded, mountain man. "I, ah, I can walk. It's not that far."

His brows drew together. "How far's not far?"

"Just a few blocks." *More like a million.*

His brown eyes did another sweep of her body, and she shivered.

"You're practically naked. It's cold"—his gaze went to her hands—"you got a phone?"

"My friend accidentally took my things when she left the party."

"She bailed on you?"

Why was she telling this total stranger she had no money and no phone…was essentially stranded? She had no idea. Still, she answered. "Yes."

"I'll give you a ride." There was no question in his voice this time.

"Oh, no. I couldn't…"

He moved to the next car along and opened the passenger door. "Yeah, you could."

Then he looked her in the eyes, and what she saw made her tummy…and lower…melt deliciously.

"Babe, you're in no danger from me. Just don't like seeing assholes fuck with innocent women. Brings out my grumpy side."

For some crazy reason, she trusted him. Heck, she wanted to get into the car with him. Maybe she was more her mother's daughter than she wanted to believe, because she said, "Okay," the word popping out of her mouth before she could think better of it.

His smile returned, wide and yummy, straight white teeth surrounded by sexy beard, and her heart did an erratic thump.

He motioned to the open car door. "Let's go."

Chapter Two

Hugh Colton glanced at the hot piece sitting beside him and wondered again what the fuck he thought he was doing. Jesus, he'd lost his goddamn mind.

Joe was gonna have a shit hemorrhage when Hugh pulled up with her—in the car he'd just *stolen*. She was an accessory to grand theft auto and didn't have a goddamn clue. She hadn't even questioned him when he'd hot-wired the thing in front of her, buying his lame excuse that he'd dropped his keys somewhere.

For some screwed-up reason, he hadn't been able to drive away, to just leave her standing there. Not after the way that guy had freaked her out, and not after the way she'd looked at him, as if she wanted to press those abundant curves against him and…

"Where are we?"

She licked her full, sexy-as-hell lower lip as he signaled the turn into the garage.

Jesus. His cock, which was already trying to punch through his zipper, pulsed harder. "My garage. Gotta drop off the car then I'll get you home."

He was hard as hell, desperate to get under that costume, no doubt. And not only because he'd gone without for a few weeks. The lust hammering him involved more than just a desperate need to get his rocks off. Yeah, her curves were fucking awesome, but they weren't the only thing he found attractive, although they had a fuck-of-a-lot to do with it. She was a combination of sweet and feisty. Sexy and innocent.

And he wanted a piece of that. Badly.

Jesus. Nope, he obviously wasn't thinking straight. But with the stress over his sister Lucy nearly getting booted from college... Making sure her and his mom both stayed out of the line of fire. And with Al's boys continually breathing down his and Joe's necks about the cars they were owed, he was running on empty. Only a couple more shipments and they were free and clear. His old man's debt would be paid off completely, and he could finally get on with his goddamn life. And at thirty-one, that was long overdue.

Al may be a criminal and a major asshole, willing to go to any lengths to make you bend to his will, but the guy also kept to his word. As long as Hugh and his brother Joe met the deadline for their deliveries, when the last shipment rolled out they'd be released from the debt.

Sleeping with a willing woman who could take it as hard as he could give it had always been his way to work off steam, de-stress from all the shit raining down on him. The lack of action lately was obviously messing with his head.

He pulled up out front, and the garage door slid up immediately. Adam, Hugh's best friend, was waiting on the other side, hands in the pockets of his faded jeans. The guy did not look happy when he saw Hugh had company. No surprises there. It was a dumb fucking thing to do, bringing her here. Giving her a ride in the first place.

He and Adam had boosted cars together when they were teenagers. Shit had been messed up at home, for both of them. Hugh had desperately needed money, and they'd taken the wrong path. A path they'd both gotten the hell off as soon as they could. A path they thought they'd left behind years ago, but thanks to his father, they'd been sucked back in.

Adam didn't need to be caught up in Hugh's mess, but when everything had fallen to shit, Adam had stuck his neck out. Now Adam was all in, which made bringing her here a dick move and one that could get them a long stretch in a prison cell.

Shutting off the car, Hugh climbed out. The passenger door opened and closed behind him, and Adam's blue gaze moved over Hugh's shoulder, locking onto Poison Ivy.

"Who's your friend?"

Yep, pissed.

She moved up, smiling brightly. "I'm Shay."

Shay. The name suited her.

"Well, hey there, Shay. Nice costume." Adam's disbelieving and very unhappy gaze slid back to Hugh.

He ignored the guy and glanced down at his new friend, who was now blushing. God, so pretty. "Wait here a sec, babe. Just need a word."

She gave him a little nod, turning that smile on him, big green eyes moving over his face then dropping to his mouth. His balls tightened. *Goddammit.* He gave Adam a shove in the other direction, and thankfully, he followed Hugh across the shop floor and waited until they were out of earshot before speaking up.

"What in the ever-loving fuck?"

Hugh rubbed the back of his neck. "I know I screwed up, so save it. Some guy was hassling her. I offered her a ride home. What else could I do?"

Yeah, judging by the way Adam's brows hit his hairline, a vein popping behind the feather tattoo on the side of his neck, Hugh's lame excuse sounded as stupid to his friend as it did to Hugh.

"I don't know, how about calling her a cab? You gave her a ride in a goddamn stolen car?" Adam gritted out between clenched teeth.

Hugh planted his hands on his hips, feeling his anger rise, not that he had any right to it. "I'm taking her home now. She doesn't know a damn thing." He glanced around the workshop. "Where's Joe? You're gonna have to do this one without me."

"He'll be here in a few." Adam shook his head, shoved a hand through his dark hair. "What in the hell were you thinking?"

He hadn't been. Not at all. "Don't have time for this conversation. You want her gone, right?"

Adam just stared at him. Hugh didn't blame him. He wasn't exactly acting like himself. He was the cautious one, the responsible one these days, weighing every option, every possible outcome. Every risk. He'd done none of that tonight.

"Go, by all means, have fun." Sarcasm dripped from Adam's voice, his eyes narrowed, pissed as hell. "You've already gone this far, may as well finish what you started."

I intend to. He didn't say that out loud, though; the situation was screwed enough without him starting a brawl with his best friend in the middle of their workshop.

He headed back to Shay, who was standing there in that barely there costume, showing off an abundance of soft, sexy curves and a sweet little smile that made his mouth go dry.

"Let's get out of here." Taking her hand, he led her out of the garage.

She followed him without hesitation, holding on as the roller door slid shut behind them with a loud rattle. He carried on around to the back of the building, where his truck was parked.

Adam would already be working on the car Hugh had brought in, switching out the VIN plates with ones cloned from other vehicles of the same make, model and year. They had it down to a fine art, were fast, too. One more car and they'd have enough to be picked up for export.

Couldn't happen too damn soon.

Two more shipments after that and they'd finally be free and clear.

Hugh pulled the key fob from his pocket and aimed it at his truck.

"So this is your business?" Shay said beside him. The breathy note to her voice did nothing to ease his rock-hard cock.

"Yeah."

"It's...it's very impressive."

He grinned at the way she said it. Jesus, the woman was sweet, the way her eyes widened, lips parting slightly. Would she look like that when he pushed inside her, when he thrust into her again and again? Shit. He needed to get a handle on it. But now he'd delivered the car and was alone with Shay, could relax, every one of his senses had zeroed in on the woman beside him.

He let his gaze roam over her. "Thanks."

"So you own this whole place?"

He shook his head. "Part owner."

"You must be good. The garage was filled with cars."

He shrugged. Moved closer. *Screw it.* You don't get if you don't ask, right? Then he got closer still, using the excuse of opening her door for her, testing the waters. She didn't step away, stayed where she was so her side brushed his front.

Instead of opening up, he stayed where he was but kept his hands to himself. He didn't want to freak her out if she wasn't on-board. She looked up at him. Damn, she really was pretty. He studied her for any sign of fear, any signal that she wasn't interested. Nothing. She was attracted to him. Shit, he'd bet everything he had that she was turned on—curiosity, heat, it was right there, written all over her face. Her color high, eyes shining, breath coming in little pants.

He rested his hip against the side of his truck, looked down at her. "I'm just going to lay this out for you, then the ball's in your court."

She blinked up at him. "Lay what out?"

"I'm really fucking attracted to you, Shay. I don't do dates. Don't like to waste time, either. You're not interested, I'll drop you home then I'm gone, no problem. But if you are, say the word, and I'll spend the night making you come so hard you'll forget your own name."

Her mouth opened then closed, opened again. "Um…" Color rose on her cheeks, and the pulse at the base of her creamy throat started to flutter rapidly. "You and me…? You're, ah…you want to…?" She cut herself off abruptly, her color getting darker.

His abs tightened, so much so, he was surprised he didn't get a goddamn cramp. "I want to spend the night with you, babe."

Her expression could only be described as stunned, and it wasn't changing. Shit. Had he called it wrong?

He pulled her forward gently and opened the passenger door. "What's your address?"

She did some more blinking, rapidly. Mouth clamped shut, biting her lips together.

"Shay?" He tucked a loose strand of red hair behind her ear, couldn't stop himself. It felt as soft as it looked. "I'm gonna need your address."

She gave a little start, snapping out of it. "Right, my address. Yes, you'll need that."

She rattled it off, and he scowled. A few blocks, my ass. She lived miles away from where he'd found her cornered by that asshole. Her place was over in Santa Monica, near the beach. A good twenty, thirty-minute drive. Hand to her lower back, because he couldn't stop touching her, he steered her toward the open door. She climbed up, and he closed it behind her.

The drive to her place was quiet. He wasn't great with small talk or conversation in general. Never had been much of a talker. Right then, with Shay sitting tensely beside him, he wished otherwise. He glanced over at her again. She was sitting frozen in her seat, like a damn statue, hands clasped tight in her lap.

He'd been wrong. She wasn't into him. And yeah, that more than sucked. He wanted in, badly. But going by her hands-off posture, he wasn't going to get what he wanted. Story of his fucking life.

A short time later, he was pulling up to a trailer park. The Happy Armadillo, read the faded sign out front. Not what he'd expected, not at all, but the grounds were taken care of, the trailers well kept. There were also colorful lights strung up outside each one, rows of flowers along their fronts. "Which is yours, sweetheart?"

She pointed through the windshield, and he noted the way her hand trembled.

"Over there."

Shit.

Shay's trailer was painted pink, the lights strung across the front the same color with some blue thrown in. It was cute. Like a freaking Barbie accessory. He had no goddamn business spending time with a woman like Shay. Not even for one night. He pulled to a stop in the space out front and turned off the engine. She remained quiet, didn't move to get out of his truck.

"Shay?"

She turned to him then, eyes wide, breathing unsteady. "Yes."

He'd freaked her out, seriously messed up, came on too strong. A big, stupid ox, clumsily making a pass at her. His size alone probably scared the shit out of her. That totally sucked. This was why he was usually so cautious, weighed his options, his words. He'd learned to control his true impulsive nature. Going with his gut never worked out well for him. This time, going with his gut had screwed up his chances with the woman beside him, and that was a damn shame. He didn't think he'd ever wanted a woman as much as he wanted this one.

He shoved a hand through his hair. "Look, I'm sorry for scaring you back there." He tilted his head toward her trailer. "You have a good night. Maybe I'll catch you around sometime."

The chances of that were minimal, at best, but still, a man could hope. He reached for the key and fired his truck back up.

"No," she blurted.

He dropped his hand, turned back to her. "No?" He was gripping the steering wheel so tight it creaked. He wanted to reach out and touch her, and she more than likely thought he was the scum of the earth. "You saying if I see you again, you want me to walk the other way?"

"No," she whispered.

"You don't want me to walk the other way?" What she was trying to say, he had no idea, since all the blood had evacuated his brain and taken up residence in his throbbing cock.

She shook her head, and her shiny red hair moved around her face and shoulders. He wanted to wrap it around his fist while he fucked her from behind.

"No." She bit her lip.

"I'm kind of confused here, babe." *And so hard, my balls are close to exploding.*

"What I meant to say is…thank you for the ride. It was really nice of you. And you…you didn't scare me. If I saw you again, I wouldn't want you to walk the other way." The light was muted, her face washed in a pink glow from the little lights on her trailer, but he didn't miss the way she blushed.

He needed her to get out of his truck so he could blast the air-con all the way home, cool his blood, because right now, he was *burning the hell up.* "You got keys?"

She seemed to snap out of it, whatever *it* was. The dazed expression washed from her face. "No…I. Crap." She turned to him. "I don't have my keys. Kayla took them when she bailed on me. Edna, my neighbor, might have a spare set." She glanced out the window toward the trailer next to hers. All the lights were out. Her brow scrunched.

He shoved open his door. "I got it."

Reaching into the bed of his truck, he got what he needed to pick the lock from his tool box then joined her at the door. He had it open in ten seconds.

"How did you do that?"

"Tools of the trade."

Her brow scrunched again. "I thought you were a mechanic?"

"People lock keys in their cars all the time. Every good mechanic has a set of lock picks." *So does every good car thief.*

"Oh. Right."

He turned the door handle and pushed it open. "Night, Shay."

She glanced up at him, teeth sinking into her bottom lip again, before her tongue darted out to slide across it. "Do you want…?"

"I better get going." Before he made things worse and kissed her, tasted her like he was desperate to.

"Okay," she rasped in a way that set tingles off at the base of his spine.

"Later, babe." Then he turned away, left her standing at her door, and got the hell out of there.

Knowing full well that later would never come.

* * *

Shay tugged at the front of her shirt. The uniform at Woody's came in two sizes—tight or tighter. Even wearing a minimizing bra, her boobs looked like two overblown cantaloupes trying to jiggle out the top of her shirt. And don't get her started on the required skinny jeans that hid

19

nothing. She was all wobbly belly, boobs and butt, and there was nothing she could do about it.

Her disaster of a relationship with Travis meant she'd been forced to leave her job at TBS Design. Desperate for money, she'd taken whatever she could get. She'd loved what she did at TBS, but so far, she'd found no other fulltime position. So, in the meantime, she worked at Woody's four nights a week. She also did three half days at Raggedy Janes, a pre-loved clothing shop, which was conveniently only a short walk from The Happy Armadillo Trailer Park. In between that, she did whatever graphic design work she could pick up from home.

Because of Travis—and her own naivety and lack of judgment— her career had taken a nosedive, not to mention her standard of living. As much as she loved the trailer park—it was home, after all, where she'd lived most of her life—she missed her old apartment. She missed the furniture she'd been forced to sell. She missed having space. The saying "couldn't swing a cat" came to mind, though in her case, it was more like "couldn't swing a gerbil."

Vinnie filled her drinks order, and she loaded up her tray.

He looked beyond her shoulder. "It's gonna be a busy night."

Woody's was always busy. The dive bar was a popular hangout for a large and varying crowd. College kids, business types, employees from the mall a short walk away, and most nights they had at least ten guys from the construction firm down the road.

This was also where some of her ex-coworkers frequented, including Travis, which was not ideal but how she'd gotten the job in the first place. She knew a couple of the waitresses pretty well, and when she needed a job, they'd set her up with an interview. Thankfully, she didn't work Fridays when the TBS staff came in for after-work drinks.

"I better deliver these before people start getting restless." Sliding her tray off the bar, she weaved her way through the crowd toward her section. All her tables were full. Once again, she wished her trailer was big enough for a full-sized tub. A shower just didn't cut it after a night on her feet.

She delivered the drinks and headed to the booth at the back to take their order. The corner was always dimly lit and after coming from the bar where the lights were a lot brighter, her eyes always needed a minute to adjust. Which was why she was standing, hip to table, leaning forward to hear her customer's order over the music, before she saw who was sitting there.

Oh, dear God.

Her mountain man.

She blinked, then blinked again.

Only she wasn't seeing things. He was sitting right there, big body lounged back, warm chocolate eyes locked on her.

Crap.

You're not interested, I'll drop you home then I'm gone, no problem. But if you are, say the word, and I'll spend the night making you come so hard you'll forget your own name.

His huskily spoken words had been stuck in a loop in her head since he said them three days ago. He'd shocked her with his frankness. He'd also turned her on beyond all reason. But he'd mistaken her warring emotions—the strong reaction she had to him, followed by her attempt at ignoring all commonsense, and her ever-present insecurities—for fear. She hadn't been afraid; she just hadn't known how to tell him what she wanted.

She'd actually convinced herself to go for it. Then he'd read her wrong, and she'd been too much of a coward to set him straight. She could almost see her grandmother jumping for joy when she climbed in the car with him—then shaking her head in disappointment when she let the opportunity pass, and he drove away.

His dark brown eyes were still locked on her, did not falter. She quivered. All over. A sizzle of electricity moved over her skin and just like that, she was sucked back into the big man's magnetic force field. She swallowed hard and fought the sudden urge to climb into his lap and wrap herself around him like a python.

"Shay?"

She jumped at the sound of her name coming from his lips, as if he'd snuck up on her and shouted, "Boo!"

He smiled.

The man really was ridiculously handsome. Things started tingling down below. She cleared her throat. "It's nice to see you again."

His gaze moved over her, before coming back to her face. "Glad to see you're not walking the other way."

No. She wasn't, she was leaning so far forward her boobs were almost resting on his chin. She straightened quickly, and his smile turned into a grin.

"Well, that might just get me fired." She was trying for easy confidence but didn't think she pulled it off. Not when he sat so completely at ease, those solid, muscled arms resting on the table, his thick fingers, rough and grease stained, held in loose fists in front of him. His shoulders relaxed and so wide, the sight of them made her heart whiz around in her chest like a stuck balloon deflating.

"Wouldn't want that, sweetheart," the guy with him said.

She hadn't even noticed him sitting there. He was a leaner version of her mountain man. He had tattoos on his forearms, extremely short hair, and instead of a full beard, he looked as if he hadn't shaved in several days. They had to be related.

He was grinning at her, as well.

She shook off her humiliating stupor. She was there to take their drink order, not stare like a nutcase. "So what'll it be, boys?"

What'll it be, boys?

She'd never uttered that phrase in all her twenty-five years of existence. She sounded like a gum chewing, cliché diner babe with an attitude problem.

The other man's eyes crinkled around the edges before he rubbed one tattooed hand across his cropped hair. "A couple beers should do it."

"Okeydokey." She inwardly winced.

"How long've you worked here?" her mountain man rumbled.

Yes, rumbled, pulling her attention back to him.

She had to clear her throat. *Again.* "Um, about two months."

His brow lifted, but he said no more, just stared at her in a way that made her want to squirm.

"I'll just"—she pointed to the bar—"get your drinks." Then she hustled in the opposite direction quick smart, before she fell on the floor and had a mini heart attack at his feet.

She'd never been more thankful that the bar was crazy busy. With her tables full she had an excuse to deliver their drinks and run. But as hard as she tried to ignore them—ignore *him*—she couldn't. Not when she felt his gaze on her the entire time, burning so hot her nipples tingled, and between her legs throbbed and ached to the point of distraction.

Her grandmother's voice echoed through her mind. *If opportunity doesn't knock, build a damn door, Cupcake.*

Did she want to build a door? And if she did, was she brave enough to walk though it?

Chapter Three

Hugh lifted his beer and took a deep pull. The bar was busy…busy enough no one would notice when it came time to do business. He seriously needed to be on his game for this, but all he could think about, all he could focus on was the lush redhead moving around the bar in painted-on jeans and a shirt that clung to her soft, round tits.

He'd thought he'd never see her again.

But here she was.

"That the redhead Adam popped an artery over?" Joe asked from across the table, forcing Hugh's attention away from her.

"That would be her."

His brother flicked at the label on his beer. "I see the appeal."

Hugh grunted. Joe, like Hugh, preferred his women on the curvier side.

"Going back for seconds?"

"Nothing happened." And he still cringed at the way he'd handled things that night, the way he'd screwed up.

Joe's brows lowered. "Why the hell not?"

"We're not talking about this."

His brother snorted. "You're the one staring at her as if you plan on knocking her on the head and carrying her home to your cave."

Yeah. That's exactly how he was looking at her. There was no point denying it, so Hugh just stared at his brother, not taking the bait.

Joe scowled, gaze sliding across the bar to Shay, then back, and Hugh knew the subject of the hot redhead he'd taken for a ride in a stolen car hadn't been dropped.

"Yanno, I don't really give a shit if you don't want to talk about it—this has to be said. What in the hell did you think you were doing, bringing some random to the garage? Yeah, she's hot, and I can't for the life of me work out why you didn't tap that, but shit, I had to talk Adam down."

Hugh scowled back. "He can talk." Their friend was no doubt off screwing his brains out right now. A different woman every night. But then who the hell was Hugh to judge? They all had their issues.

"Yeah, but he didn't take some babe for a joyride in a stolen car, numb nuts." Joe shook his head. "Look, I don't care what anyone says, you're not a giant freak to me...you're just...abnormally proportioned." Joe patted his hand. "Lucky for you, there are chicks out there with sasquatch fetishes. I get you gotta go for it when the offer's there..."

Hugh shoved his brother's hand off. "Dick."

"Buuut, we're *this* close to the finish line; why risk blowing everything to shit now?"

Guilt knifed through him. Joe was right. His younger brother was a clown, a joker, never took any-damn-thing seriously, but for once, Joe was spot on. Hugh had already failed his family enough. He'd let their old man screw up their lives repeatedly when he should have stepped up, when he should have kicked the fucker out. Not let him come crawling back again and again. They were in this mess because of Hugh. Because he'd been too damn blinded by the old man's bullshit, his promises of "never again", to see just how deep he'd sunk. Hugh had failed his mom, his brother and his sister. Put them in danger—turned his brother into a goddamn criminal.

He sipped his beer, ignoring the suffocating guilt tightening around his chest. "I have no answer for you."

"Jesus." Joe slumped back.

You'd think the guilt over what he'd done, what he'd risked, would have killed the hard-on he had for Shay. Nope. No chance. He hadn't been able to stop thinking about her, had stroked his cock to thoughts of her every night since he'd met her.

Joe dragged a hand over his buzz cut. "So what time's this cocksucker supposed to show?"

His baby bro never did have much patience, even as a kid. "He's got another ten minutes."

Joe fidgeted, shredding the cardboard coaster that had been under his drink. "I'm sick to fucking death of this. Seriously."

"You and me both."

They stayed quiet for a few minutes then Joe started tapping his fingers, jiggling his knee, making Hugh goddamn crazy. "I'm taking you to the park for a run before we do this next time. You're like an overexcited damn puppy."

Joe flicked a piece of torn coaster at Hugh's head. "You heard from Lucy lately?"

There were three kids in the Colton family. Joe was the middle child, big surprise there, three years younger than Hugh and had just celebrated his twenty-eighth birthday a couple weeks ago. And then there was Lucy. She was the baby of the family, a mistake, his old man had always called her. Asshole. She was twenty-two, nine years younger than he was, and as much as he loved her, would do anything for her, she was a constant pain in his ass.

"She's avoiding my calls."

Joe grunted. "After the way you lost your shit with her, I'm not surprised."

"She was screwing her psychology professor. What did you want me to do? Pat her on the head and increase her allowance? She nearly got her ass kicked out of school."

Joe winced. "First, let's not talk about what our baby sister was doing with that old fart. I'll either puke or murder the wrinkly fucker. And second, give her a break, okay? She's beating herself up enough."

"You want her back in LA? Because I don't. Not until we're free of Al. I want her out of the line of fire."

Lucy had no clue about his checkered past or how he'd supported the family when they were younger. She also didn't know what he and Joe had been doing the last few years to cover their father's debt. She just knew the old man had left them up shit creek without a paddle when he vanished...that her brothers had forked out a lot of cash when he had. Hugh intended to keep her in the dark, about all of it. Which meant making sure she stayed in school.

Joe's gaze moved to the door and his posture went from relaxed to high alert.

"Who?" Hugh asked.

"Don."

Hugh's gaze immediately moved to Shay, who was now at the bar, filling an order. Relief washed through him. For some reason, he felt protective of her, didn't want her anywhere near the asshole making his way over to their table.

Don was a special kind of snowflake. Young, stupid and a serious prick. The guy had a little power and had let it go to his overblown head. His boss, Al Ramirez, was rich, powerful and had connections to one of the biggest crime families in California. Al was also a major scumbag. How he'd gotten where he was, Hugh had no idea. He often wondered why someone hadn't ended his miserable life already.

Don strode toward them, a smarmy grin on his face, and slipped into the seat beside Joe. "Boys."

"Don't have time for your shit. Hand it over and leave," Joe growled.

Don's back went straight, face getting all squinty. "Who do you think you're talking to, boy?"

"A fucking moron. And if you call me boy one more fucking time…"

"Joe." Hugh cut him off before he said something he couldn't take back and made this shit even worse. The last thing they needed was to upset the idiot.

Joe slumped back in his seat and motioned for Hugh to take over. His brother might be a goddamn clown the majority of the time, but he also had a short fuse, and Don pushed all his buttons.

Hugh sat forward. "Let's get this over with. You have a message?"

Don scowled at Joe one last time then turned to Hugh. "Al wants to do a deal. Knows you're coming to the end of your father's debt but he's reluctant to end the partnership." He reached into his pocket, pulled out a piece of paper, sliding it across the table.

Hugh didn't even look at it. "Not interested."

"Aren't you even going to take a peek at his very generous offer? That's for each delivery."

"No." Hugh crossed his arms. "Tell Al, thanks, but no thanks. The minute the last car's delivered, we part ways. Free and clear. That's what we agreed."

Don grinned. "He won't be happy."

Hugh shrugged. He wasn't jumping for joy, either. He should have known this was coming. The asshole wanted to keep them under his thumb and on his payroll. Al Ramirez was ruthless. He'd sell his own mother if he could get a good price.

Don stood, leaving the piece of paper on the table in front of him. "Don't make any quick decisions. You have a week to decide."

"Then what?" Joe asked, the fury in his voice barely restrained.

The dick-wad smiled. "Then we go into negotiations."

Shit.

Joe watched him walk out then cursed repeatedly. "This is gonna to get ugly."

"Yeah." Al would stick to the deal they'd made, would never openly break it. If it got around that his word wasn't for shit, he'd lose business. But the guy would also do whatever it took to get his way. Which meant they had to be smarter, quicker. If they weren't, they were fucked, for good.

Joe's fists clenched and unclenched. "We need to make sure Mom and Lucy stay the hell out of LA."

"I'll talk to them."

Joe held his gaze, shook his head. "Leave it with me."

Great…now his irresponsible, flaky brother didn't even trust him to have a conversation with his own damn mother and not screw it up. "Fine."

Joe stood, grabbed his jacket. "Let's get the hell out of here."

A flash of red hair caught Hugh's eye from across the bar, and he couldn't make himself stand and follow. "I'm sticking around for a bit."

His brother shook his head. "Jesus." His gaze hardened. "Get her out of your damn system then, because after tonight, we need your head in the game, not on some piece of tail."

Hugh's fingers tightened around the bottle in his hand. "You finished?" His brother, Adam—the three of them—talked that way all the time about the women they'd been with, the women they wanted. Why his hackles rose when Joe called her *some piece of tail*, he had no clue.

"For now."

"First piece of good news I've heard all night."

Joe flipped Hugh off then strode out of the bar. Great, now not only did they have Al breathing down their necks, but his brother was pissed at him, and Adam wanted to tear him a new asshole.

Yet, here he sat anyway…

His gaze moved back to where he'd last seen her. He was better off staying the hell away from her, especially now. He got the feeling his brother was way wrong when it came to her, though. One night might not be enough to get her out of his system, and one night is all he'd ever allow himself to have. He turned away, tipped his head back, finished his beer then stood. Time to go. No point sitting there torturing himself.

31

Shay tried to concentrate on walking in a straight line, which wasn't easy while darting glances out the corner of her eye. *He* was back. He'd been back the last three nights.

But always on the other side of the bar. Besides that first night, he'd stayed away from her section. And with the way he affected her, she wasn't sure if she was pleased about that or not.

He'd sit there, on his own, nursing one beer for several hours, then leave. But the whole time he was there, she'd feel his melted-chocolate stare following her around the room, making it hard to breathe, to concentrate. So far tonight, she'd already screwed up three of her drinks orders.

"Ow!" Her shoulder glanced one of the big, floor-to-ceiling support beams positioned around the bar, and she stumbled back a step. Good lord, if he kept showing up like this, she'd likely cause herself a serious injury. Someone gabbed her hips to steady her as she reached up to rub her aching shoulder.

"Whoa, there." A young guy with a wide smile and scruffy blond hair stepped around her, one of his hands still on her hip. "Okay?"

"Yes, thanks." She rolled her eyes, giving him an I'm-such-a-klutz smirk. "I wasn't watching where I was going."

His gaze dropped to her chest, to the Woody's logo stretched across her boobs. "So you work here?"

Besides the uniform T-shirt, which all the staff members were wearing, and a rather obvious giveaway, she was carrying a drink tray, empty, thankfully, or she would have just made one hell of a mess all over the floor when she collided with the pole. "Sure do."

"When does your shift finish? Let me buy you a drink?"

"Oh." Crap, this kind of thing always made her feel so freaking awkward. Heat hit her cheeks. "Um…thanks…for the offer. But I'll, I'll have to pass." She offered a smile she wasn't feeling. All she could focus on right then was her mountain man, confused over his presence, wondering why he was coming to the bar every night—but hadn't yet to talk to her. "You have a good night though."

But he held on to her for a second longer. Preventing her from walking away. "You sure?"

She nodded, face getting hotter.

"If you change your mind, my table's just over there." He pointed to the opposite corner of the bar.

She pulled out of his hold, softening her rejection with another insincere smile, before turning away, then without conscious thought, darted another look over at *his* table. But the big man wasn't sitting there. He was on his feet, a fierce expression on his face, eyes locked on the guy she'd just turned down. As he disappeared into the crowd, her mountain man's shoulders visibly relaxed, then that fierce, hard stare slid to her. She felt rooted to the spot, pinned there by his dark gaze. Her breath spiraled out of her throat, pulse going nuts. He didn't look away as he slowly sat back down like a giant watch dog—danger over— and lifted his beer, taking a drink.

Heat burned her face—not from embarrassment this time but from the spike of her blood pressure, from the way need clawed at her, demanding she do something—anything—to stop him from walking out without her again.

But by the time she'd worked up the courage to approach him, it was too late.

He was gone.

* * *

Hugh was a goddamn glutton for punishment and a fool, to boot. He'd walked out of the bar the night before, frustrated as hell. Shay had been darting glances in his direction all evening, walked into a goddamn support beam because she was looking at him and not where she was going. But then after the incident, after he'd watched some guy rush to her, touch her, blatantly come onto her, she'd carried on delivering her drinks. Carried on pretending he wasn't sitting there, watching her every damn move.

Why the hell had he come back?

He'd sat in this goddamn bar, for four nights. Four fucking nights—waiting, hoping she'd come to him, give him the smallest indication she was interested in what he'd offered her that night behind the garage. No dice. She'd blatantly ignored him. Joe would say he was acting like a pathetic, desperate idiot. And he could admit, to himself, at least, that hypothetical Joe was right. Desperate was exactly how Hugh felt. He'd watched assholes pant over her, their eyes locked on her chest, her ass, barely keeping his seat.

And she'd given him nothing. Not a damn thing.

He didn't know if it was because she was insecure, shy, or if he'd been right the first time, and she had zero interest in him. She probably thought she had a giant ogre stalking her. Yeah, he could approach her, but he was afraid if he pushed, he'd scare her and blow it again.

Her silence was answer enough though, wasn't it?

"Shit." He shoved restless fingers though his hair. He shouldn't be

34

there.

Yeah, she blushed like crazy and stammered adorably, but no one was *that* shy or insecure. He had to face facts; she wasn't into him.

What was it about her that had him coming back night after night?

He lifted his beer, finishing it off, then glanced across the bar. No sign of her. Jesus, she'd left already, and he was still sitting there hard and restless like a moron.

Why the hell was he wasting his time on this chick? She was trouble with a capital T, the complete opposite of the women he usually went home with for a hot, no-strings night. He never went back for seconds. He sure as hell didn't chase or obsess. He fucked then he left. The end.

"Do you want another one?"

He jolted in his seat as Shay's husky voice ran over his skin like velvet, making his gut clench. He turned to her, gaze locking with her stunning bright green one. He tried to stay relaxed, but he was close to jumping out of his damn seat. Fuck, he wanted her.

He squashed down the budding anticipation making his balls throb. She was just doing her job, right? "Think I'm good, babe." He took in her features, soft and sweet. But those curves—pure sin. "I should probably head off?" It came out a question, full of pitiful hope.

Her hands were clasped in front of her, fingers twisting, then she glanced away, crossing her arms when she looked back at him—shoving her tits higher. "Your friend isn't joining you tonight?"

He shook his head, vocal cords suddenly tight.

"My shift just finished, actually. Would you...would you like some company?"

Her color was high, the pulse at the side of her slender throat fluttering like crazy. A throb started behind his zipper. "Sure." It came out a growl.

She slid in across from him, gaze still darting around, looking at anything but him, fingers tangling together. Then finally she turned those green eyes his way again. Stunning. "That guy? The one who was with you...um, when you first came in? Are you related?"

"He's my younger brother." If she was finally here, sitting at his table, just so she could ask for Joe's number, Hugh would have to kill him.

"I could see the resemblance, only you're"—she squirmed in her seat—"bigger." The blush increased, and she bit that full lower lip.

He grinned, couldn't help himself, whether she thought him being *bigger* was a good thing or not, though, remained to be seen. "Yeah, I guess I am."

Her gaze dropped to his neck then down to his chest and across his shoulder to his bicep. "Your, ah...muscles are bigger, too." Then more with the lip biting but now with an added wiggle and an awkward flip of her hair. "You must be so...um, strong."

Was she...

Christ.

He had to fight not to laugh and pounce on her, all at the same damn time. *Finally.* The woman was cute and sexy, but her pick-up lines totally sucked, which meant she didn't come on to guys often or at all. For some reason, probably because he was a goddamn Neanderthal, that pleased the hell out of him. "You flirting with me, sweetheart?"

Please, be flirting with me.

She blinked across the table at him. Then her blush turned thermonuclear. "No. No, I was just…I was making conversation."

"Really?"

She squirmed in her seat again, and he inwardly groaned. Was she already wet? Was she imagining what it would feel like when he pushed his cock inside her?

He sat back, watched her carefully as he spoke. "Cause it kind of sounds as if you're asking something else. Like you wanna know if I use my strength in bed? If I use it when I fuck a woman? Move her where I want, hold her where I want her?"

She sucked in a breath.

"The answer's yes."

Her gaze darted down, and she tucked a loose strand of hair behind her ear. "I wasn't…I didn't mean…"

Jesus. He couldn't control his dirty mouth around her. Something about her brought out the caveman in him, and he couldn't make himself shut the hell up. He also couldn't take much more of this, of her innocently sitting there, as if she didn't know what she did to him, driving him out of his mind. The need to get inside her hammered him with an incessant, heavy beat behind his ribs. "What do you want, Shay?"

His voice was rough with lust, so much so he sounded like a fucking animal. But he had no control over it, not after watching her night after night but not being able to touch.

He'd backed off, waited her out, going against his natural instincts. But this time she'd made the first move. She wouldn't be with him now if he'd freaked her out that night. That was a fact. "You're not sitting here with me just to shoot the shit."

She stared at him, and he watched different emotions move over her face. She was nervous, edgy, maybe even scared, but not of him—no, she was afraid of what she wanted, of what she needed to say to get it.

"No… I-I've thought about you and what you said, um asked. A lot." She fidgeted some more then looked down at her lap. "I don't usually do things like this…I've never…God, why is this so hard?"

"Say it." The words rumbled from his chest. Jesus, he'd scooted forward, ass literally on the edge of his seat.

She let out a shaky breath, and he held his.

"I-I want what you said, that night, at the garage."

She said it so quietly, he almost didn't hear her or maybe didn't hear her right?

"Look at me, Shay."

She lifted her gaze, and it was all there. Yeah, he'd heard her right, and he wanted to dive across the table, tear that clingy uniform off her curvy body, and fuck her right there in the bar. Instead, he reached out, slid his fingers under her chin when she tried to drop her gaze again and tilted up her face.

"You sure about that?" he asked.

"Yes."

"Nothing's changed. I don't do relationships. I want you, but I will walk away if we're not on the same page with this." The last thing he wanted to do was hurt her, and he had to be sure she knew what she was getting herself into. She said it herself; she didn't do this kind of thing. And as much as more time with her appealed, he couldn't offer her more than one night…for so many reasons.

She shook her head. "I understand. I-I don't want more than what you offered."

Hugh didn't need to be told twice. "Then let's get out of here."

He stood and took her hand when she just sat there staring up at him, tugging her gently to her feet.

"We'll go to your place," he told her.

She nodded, fingers flexing around his. "Okay."

Then he led her across the bar and out the door.

Chapter Four

Shay felt him move in behind her as she unlocked the door, big body towering over her, warm, hard. She shivered.

Was she really doing this? Was she going to sleep with this man?

It was crazy, insane, but the only answer she could consider right then was a resounding *yes!*

When he'd come into the bar again tonight, that steady gaze locked on her the whole time, she'd somehow pulled together the courage to approach him. The fear that he'd walk out the door and never come back—that it might be her last chance—had her moving in his direction.

The man had drawn her in with that magnetic pull that radiated from him; there was no other way to describe it.

Her grandmother's dying words had echoed through her head on repeat, boosting her courage. *Live life, Cupcake, don't let it pass you by.* She'd made Shay promise she would, trying one final time to get her only granddaughter to drop her guard.

She'd thought she was doing that with Travis, and look how that turned out.

Don't think about him.

Besides that…misstep…she'd always played it safe. The last thing she wanted to do was follow in her mother's unstable, irresponsible footsteps. That wasn't Shay. She wasn't made that way.

But no matter how many times she tried to tell herself that, she hadn't been able to stay away from Hugh, and the next thing she knew, she was saying ridiculous things about his muscles and doing a crappy job of getting his attention, of getting him to offer what he had the first night they met. Because she'd wanted it. Badly. She'd let nerves and insecurity stop her then. The last risk she'd taken had lost her her job *and* her self-respect.

But then this wasn't a risk. How could it be? This was about mutual lust, nothing more. The man wasn't even her type.

No, this was her taking life by the horns, taking what she wanted, on her terms. *Without* the risk. He wasn't the kind of guy she usually went for, which meant her heart was safe. She wasn't against having meaningless sex, but relationships were another thing entirely. Emotionally, she wasn't ready for something like that. Might never be. Travis had left her a little broken—and though she hated to admit it, even to herself—fragile.

Fate had dropped this man in front of her. A big, giant, yummy gift. Fate wanted her to have a one-night stand with her mountain man. Who was she to ignore fate?

Walking in, she flicked on the light then turned back to say something—she had no idea what—but talking seemed like something she should do at this point. As it turned out, conversation wasn't high on his *to do* list. *She was.*

He moved in, crowding her, until her back met the wall, cutting her off with his deep, rumbling voice. "Bedroom?"

She pointed to her room on the other side of the small living area, and though she wasn't looking, she knew her fingers were shaking embarrassingly. He didn't say a word, took her hand and led her across her grandmother's favorite pink floral rug. She followed blindly, clinging to his big, rough hand until he stopped at the foot of her bed.

Oh, my God! This is actually happening.

She'd never, ever done anything remotely like this in her life. She was not the kind of girl who slept with random strangers.

No, she was the kind of girl who dated creeps and uber jerks, who tried so hard to please but never quite measured up.

Which meant it was time to switch things up, right? And, *technically*, he wasn't a random stranger. They'd been in each other's company, or at least the same room, several times. She wasn't some serial…man eater. She'd been to his garage, had met his friend, *and* his brother at the bar.

Why was she overanalyzing this? Sure, she was probably making a huge mistake, but no way did she want to stop what they were about to do. Heck no. This was just a one-night stand. Her first. Probably her last. People did it all the time. And she wanted him. More than badly. Why deny herself?

No risk. She repeated the words over and over in her head. His only expectations of her tonight were simple—get naked and get it on, nothing more.

One night with her mountain man, then they'd go their separate ways. Perfect.

Insane!

Slamming the door on the voice of reason echoing in her head, she watched as he sat on the edge of her bed, tilted his head back and looked up at her.

"Come here, sweetheart."

That voice. It was pure sin, full of filthy, dirty delights that only he could give her, and she was helpless against it, wanted everything it promised.

She moved closer, and his hands went to her hips. *Oh God.* This beautiful, huge, delicious man was going to have sex *with her.* And yes, he was also going to see her naked. That thought kicked off a mini freak out, Travis's comments about the way she looked, bouncing around in her head.

"Fuck, woman," her mountain man growled. "You're so damn sexy."

His rough fingers slid up under her shirt, resting at her waist, scraping against her bare skin. And just the feel of his hands on her set her on fire, burning away any negative comments her memory had dredged up. *He thinks I'm sexy.*

He released her for a second, reached back and yanked his shirt off over his head and tossed it aside. She'd seen men take off their shirts like that in movies before. As if he was in a hurry and couldn't wait to get his hands back on her. It was an extremely sexy and utterly masculine way to take off a shirt. She made sure to memorize the entire thing.

Then she dropped her gaze.

Dear lord.

He was cut, ripped to perfection, all thick slabs of heavy, bulging muscle. He also had a tattoo, a simple cross on his ribs. It was the sexiest thing she'd ever seen. She wanted to touch him, but she couldn't make her hands move from her sides. While she was berating herself for being a coward, he solved her problem by grabbing her wrists and placing her quivering hands on his chest. She swallowed hard, nerves dancing low in her belly. *Don't just stand here like a dammed statue; do something!*

Letting out the breath she was holding, she flexed her fingers against his hard muscles. He was hot and perfect and so masculine. She'd never known another man like him. Courage growing, she lightly ran her hands over his chest, the hair there soft yet coarse tickling her palms. "You're so…just so…*big,*" she whispered, or more breathed on a shuddery exhale, unable to stop the thought from blurting past her lips.

He chuckled. "Think we established that."

Heat smacked her in the face, embarrassed over her awkwardness and her pathetic pick-up attempts all over again.

But then his hands came back to her shirt, and he yanked it up and over her head before she could process what was happening. Now the heat on her face was for a different reason.

"Jesus," he said, or rather groaned, then he tugged at the front of her jeans, popping the button and unzipping them.

Shay's breathing grew choppy as he shoved them down to pool at her feet, leaving her in her bra and panties.

He sat back, and what could only be described as hunger, blazed from his eyes as he took her in, all of her. His hands went to her hips, sliding up to her waist and back down. Exhaling roughly, he ran his gaze over her before it landed and locked on her chest. He reached around and undid her bra. She fought to control her breathing as he slid the straps down her arms, letting the bra fall to the floor.

Her breasts bounced free, and she instantly lifted her hands to cover herself, but he grabbed her wrists and pulled them down, holding them by her sides.

"Jesus *Christ*. You're perfect."

"No…I—"

He cut off her denial when he released her and reached up, cupping her breasts in his huge hands, growling, "More than a handful. Shit, so fucking soft."

She didn't know if he was talking to her or himself. "Um…"

Her words died again, because he leaned in, tongue flicking out, moaning as if he was tasting his favorite ice cream, causing pleasurable zings to shoot down to her core. Then he drew her nipple deep into his mouth, and she whimpered, hands going to his shoulders in an effort to hold herself upright and not melt into a puddle at his feet.

So good.

He sucked and licked until she was sensitive and squirming. Each tug of his lips felt as if it was connected in some way to the pulsing heat between her legs, causing her muscles to clench and flutter with need.

Cool air hit her damp nipples, making them tingle delightfully, then he dipped his head, face going to her belly, lips moving over her skin. His beard tickled, and she tried to squirm away, but one of his massive arms wrapped around her waist, hauling her back in, holding her where he wanted her. He kissed her just above the top of her underwear then caught the fabric between his teeth, tugging up so they put delicious pressure on her aching clit. Big hands moving lower, he smoothed them between her slightly parted thighs.

She shuddered at the different sensations all bombarding her at once. The way he tasted her skin just above the elastic of her thankfully reasonably sexy panties, the way those hands never stilled, always touching and caressing, squeezing. Her hands automatically went to his hair to hold herself steady.

He tilted his head back, eyes flashing. "You good?"

"I'm, ah…yes."

"Excellent." His thumbs slid down the sides of her underwear, and he dragged them down her legs. And when he *looked* at her, *there*, he did some more delicious growling. His hands slid around to her butt, and cupping her cheeks, he pulled her forward. "Gonna taste your pretty pussy first, baby. All I can fucking think about."

She slid her fingers through his hair, a moan of anticipation slipping past her lips. Then something occurred to her, and she tightened her grip on the thick strands and yanked his head back. "Wait!"

He stopped immediately, hungry yet concerned eyes moving back to her overheated face.

"I don't know your name!" *What a slut!* She was about to have sex with a man, and she didn't even *know his name.*

He grinned. "Hugh."

"Hugh," she repeated. "I like it."

"Glad you approve." Attractive lines crinkled the corners of his eyes. "Babe, you wanna ease up on the hair now?"

"Oh! Sorry." She loosened her fingers but kept her hands where they were. "You can…um, continue."

He laughed, the sound deep and sexy, and she felt it right there, right where he wanted to taste her.

"Tell me how you like it, beautiful." His brown eyes were hungry intense, offering to do whatever she wanted to make sure she got what needed.

No doubt, the women he usually spent time with would tell him; they wouldn't hesitate. She'd bet anything they could voice what they wanted. But that wasn't her. The heat that had been riding her hard, making her forget her insecurities, her doubts, started to cool as icy shards of reality began to hit home. This was a huge mistake. Her face was burning now. "I don't…I'm not…"

"Want you on my face." His voice was all heat, but there was a softness in his eyes that told her he knew she was out of her comfort zone.

Before she could respond—or die of mortification—he lifted her off her feet as if she weighed nothing, dropping to his back at the same time. Then he dragged her up until she was straddling his face, arm wrapped around her hips so he could hold her in place.

"I'm not sure if—"

The first swipe of his tongue had her crying out, her self-consciousness dying an immediate death, the restless heat firing back to life full force. He was strong enough to control her movements easily, keeping her where he wanted her as he worked her expertly with his tongue, his teeth, his lips.

The man hadn't been lying back at the bar; his muscles certainly came in handy. And *good God*, the sounds he made, as if he was a starving man and she was the meal he'd been craving. Nothing had ever felt this good. Nothing. Travis never went down on her while they were dating, and of course, she'd been too embarrassed to ask. She'd just assumed it wasn't something he liked. Hugh seemed to be enjoying what he was doing, though. A lot. In fact, judging by the energetic way he was going about it, he seemed to love it.

His fingers dug into her bottom, and she moaned helplessly, close to coming from just his mouth. But just when she thought it might happen, he stopped suddenly, holding her still, just above his lips. She was ashamed to say she whimpered, loudly, in protest.

He chuckled, the sound dark, sexy. "Not finished yet." He dragged his clever tongue over her, teasing, avoiding where she needed him. "Drop forward. Hands and knees. Spread wide. Want you to ride my mouth."

Shay did as he asked without question, too far gone to do anything else. She went to her hands and knees. *Oh.* He pushed a thick finger inside and encouraged her to move against him, to, "Ride his mouth." She did, grinding against him while his finger thrust in and out of her, his lips wrapped around her clit, sucking and licking. Her heavy breasts ached, and she dipped lower, nipples brushing the covers as she moved.

So good. Too good.

Then he added another finger, and when he pushed deep inside, sparks fired behind her eyelids. It wasn't gentle or just pleasant like the couple of times Travis managed to get her there. This was an explosion, an eruption, intense pleasure focused where Hugh's mouth and fingers were still working. She screamed, coming hard while he continued his exquisite torment, sucking on her as if he couldn't get enough.

She collapsed and had barely recovered when he flipped her onto her back, climbed off the bed and, standing at the end, yanked off his boots and jeans. *Wow*. He was commando, and he was big…*everywhere*. He took a condom from his wallet then rolled it down his long, thick length, eyes never leaving her. *Yum*.

Her inner muscles were still quivering from the orgasm he'd just given her when he came back down on top of her, covering her. His solid thighs between hers, he spread her legs wide, his heavy erection settling against her, hot and pulsing. Then he started pushing inside. *Oh, Jesus*. He was huge, stretching her to the limit. She squirmed beneath him in an effort to accommodate his size.

"Keep still," he rasped.

She did as he said instantly.

"You can take all of me, can't you, baby?" he said gruffly, then lifted up, sitting back on his heels.

"Yes," she whispered. She wanted all of him. Badly. Like, now.

His gaze dropped between her thighs, then lifting her butt in the air, he leaned forward a little, braced one hand against the mattress and started to ease in and out slowly. He kept his head down, watching the whole time, pushing in another inch with each slow thrust—until they were both shaking. Sweat glistened on his skin as he worked her. It felt amazing. Gentle and demanding, all at the same time. She moaned helplessly, biting down on her lip to keep from begging for more.

"That's it." He praised her. "You've nearly gotten all of me, beautiful. Just another inch." Then he slid in the rest, right to the root, big body shuddering. He dropped down on top of her again. "Hang on tight," he growled.

Shay wrapped her arms and legs around him.

Then he started moving.

"*Oh, God,*" she moaned.

He filled her so thoroughly, hit every nerve ending, went so deep, he grazed her G-spot every time he thrust that big cock inside her. Stretched her so wide, every grind of his hips put pressure on her sensitive clit.

She'd never experienced anything like it. His massive body covering her, filling her, surrounding her.

He watched her, gaze getting darker, more intense the longer he looked down at her. Then he started thrusting harder, and all she could do was whimper and writhe beneath him, take what he was giving her. He brought his mouth down on hers, swallowing her cries, kissing her for the first time, deep and intense, tongue sliding over hers. She could taste herself, taste him, overwhelming her with all that was Hugh. Her mountain man.

She pulled away and screamed his name as another orgasm slammed through her, clung tighter to him as he pounded her through it. His deep grunts grew more urgent, hips thrusting, harder, faster, then he ground in deep and stayed there, making the most erotic, animalistic sound she'd ever heard as he came, pulsing heavily inside her.

He grunted again and rolled to his side, taking her with him, warm breath ghosting across her cheek when he rasped, "Okay?"

It took her a second to find her voice. "Yes. I'm...I'm okay." Saying what had just happened between them was *okay* was like saying the Grand Canyon was insignificant and uninspiring.

His wide palm smoothed down her back. "Get some sleep."

"No, I'm—"

"Sleep."

Her face was up against his warm chest, those beefy arms locked around her. Damn, the man was like a furnace.

Then one of his thick thighs slid between hers, and she shivered. He chuckled softly, not missing how his touch affected her and obviously liking it. She clamped her eyes closed, because this felt weird, wrapped up with this man she barely knew. But good, weird. There was no other way to describe it. And that was more than a little disconcerting.

And no matter what he said, there was also no way she was going to fall asleep, not after that.

Not a chance…

* * *

Shay woke when she felt the bed move. Sprawled on her stomach, face to the side, hair in her eyes and so damn relaxed none of her muscles would work. A large, rough-skinned hand, radiating delicious heat, slid up the back of her thigh, coming to a stop on her butt cheek. He gave it a squeeze, callused thumb sliding back and forth. A shiver worked through her, turned on in an instant. How was it possible she still wanted him? Getting this hot, this fast should be impossible after last night.

He delivered what he'd promised—made her come so hard, she'd not only forgotten her name, she'd forgotten everything except what he was doing between her legs.

"Babe?"

"Hmm?" That was the best she could do.

Warm lips brushed her hip. "Gotta go. Got shit to do." Another butt squeeze.

She managed to move her arm enough to shove her hair off her face and smile sleepily in his direction. "'Kay. Bye."

The bed moved again, and she felt him lean over her, hand to the mattress beside her head. That warm hand slid back over her bottom, up to her waist, her side, then around to cup her breast, teasing her nipple. She sucked in a breath, still sensitive, and moaned helplessly.

"Lips," he rasped.

"Wha…?"

"Lips, babe. Give them to me."

That was nice. He wanted to give her a goodbye kiss. It wouldn't be polite to refuse, even if her limbs felt like overdone noodles. Not that she wanted to refuse. She wriggled, rolling to her back, blinking her eyes open.

He smiled down at her. "Shit." This was said under his breath.

"Shit, what?" she managed groggily.

"You're all sleepy and warm and fuckable."

She squirmed, suddenly not wanting him to go, either. "Oh."

He brushed back her hair, leaned in and kissed her. It was not a goodbye kiss; it was hot and hard and scrumptious. She wrapped her arms around his neck and kissed him back, loving the way his beard tickled her skin, trying to squirm closer. Her inhibitions had long since flown the coop, or she was still too sleepy to let them take over, and since this was a one-time thing, she forced her shyness, her insecurity aside and murmured, "Stay a little longer?"

His fingers dug into her hip. "Want to," he muttered against her lips. "But I gotta go." He gently pulled her hands from around his neck and stood.

She wanted to beg him to stay, which was ridiculous. This was for the best. Ending their night on a high note. Leaving her with a beautiful memory. Before her illusions of him could be shattered, and she found out he was just like the rest. Before she failed to live up to his expectations, before he realized she wasn't enough, and he walked away, as well.

He headed to the door but stopped and turned back, gaze raking over her. Finally, he said, "Later, beautiful."

Then he walked out.

The door banged shut behind him, and before she knew what she was doing, she was up and out of bed, racing to the bedroom window, watching him climb into his truck. It was all chrome and kick-ass paint job. Hugh didn't suit it. Not the way he looked, not her mountain man. It would suit him better if it wasn't quite so shiny, maybe had a few dents, not so perfect—and had mason jars full of moonshine loaded in the back, or maybe a pile of wicked-looking axes for chopping down forests singlehandedly.

He climbed in, started it up, and without a backward glance, drove away.

It was still dark out, early enough the sun hadn't fully risen, and she watched his tail lights until they turned onto the road and disappeared.

An uncomfortable, squirmy feeling settled in the pit of her stomach. She studiously ignored it. Thankfully, the big man wasn't her type, so she had nothing to worry about. He'd wanted one night, and so had she. Nothing more. Because she would never put her heart on the line again. Never again. Would never hand it over to someone, only to have them turn on her, ridicule her for the way she looked, or tell her she wasn't good enough. Pathetic.

It always happened, eventually. Everyone left or was taken from her. Her dad. Her grandmother. Both taken from her too soon.

And then there was her mom. Gah! She didn't want to think about her irresponsible, selfish, crazy mother right then. She hadn't heard from her in over a month; whether that was a good thing or not remained to be seen.

No, this was for the best.

Hugh would always be a beautiful memory. The best. One she knew she'd be calling on often.

She climbed back into bed and pulled up the covers. His scent surrounded her, still clinging to her sheets. And that's how she went back to sleep. Imagining she wasn't alone. That he'd stayed.

Chapter Five

The keys in Shay's pocket felt as if they were burning a hole with every passing minute. Was she really going to go to Hugh's garage and drop them off? It had been a whole week since she'd last seen him. She hadn't thought she'd ever see him again. But then she'd found his keys on the floor at the foot of the bed. They'd fallen just under, hidden enough that he'd easily missed them until she bumped them with her foot. Maybe she should just pop them into an envelope and post them? She cringed at her own cowardice.

She'd had the man in her bed, for God's sake.

That thought had her face heating.

She was being ridiculous. She was a strong, independent woman. Kind of. And anyway, though she knew the general area where the garage was located, she didn't know the address or the name of the place, so how could she look it up? Her only option was dropping them off, right?'

"Look what just came in," Jane called over the loud music.

Shay lifted her gaze to her boss, across racks of preloved clothing.

Raggedy Jane's had a bit of everything. Mainly clothes but other odds and sods, as well. Some small furnishings. There was also a rack with handmade jewelry, and a woman who lived a few blocks away made soaps in the most divine scents, rustic and gorgeous.

Jane was holding up a beautiful, royal-blue-and-white polka-dot dress, fifties style, halter top. Stunning. It still had the tag on it, never worn. "You gotta try this one, girl. It's so you."

It was. Shay wanted it instantly. "I couldn't." She'd gotten some pretty good tips the last couple of weeks, but that money was earmarked. She still had two more installments to pay on the loan she'd gotten to cover her grandmother's debts, as well as her funeral costs. Because Shay didn't qualify for a loan through the bank after losing her job, she'd been forced to go through a private lending company. The terms weren't great, and the only way they'd agreed to give her the money was if she offered up her trailer as collateral. With that payment looming, on top of all her other bills, she certainly didn't have enough, even from working three part-time jobs, to splurge on new dresses, preloved or not.

"Oh, come on. If you like it, you can pay it off." Jane walked over and waved it in front of her face. "You know you want to."

Shay bit her lip, mentally doing a tally of her finances. She *could* do it if she paid it off. "Fine. Let me try it on." She grabbed it and hustled to the changing rooms. A few minutes later, she pulled back the curtain.

Jane whistled. "*Hot.* You have to keep it on." She had something in her hands. "Here, I'll throw this in."

Shay caught the delicate fabric midair. It was a sweet bolero shrug. White, with elbow-length sleeves. Jane knew how self-conscious Shay was of her arms. She had been since high school, when, in front of everyone, one of the other girls told Shay they looked like overstuffed sausages. She'd been so mortified, so upset, she'd told her mother when she got home in tears. Her mother had told her to stop eating and lose weight.

She forced the memory away and slipped on the shrug.

"His mouth will hit the ground when he sees you in that."

"That isn't what this is about, and you know it." Shay had told Jane about the *encounter* she'd had with Hugh a week ago when she came in for work yesterday—well, she'd left out the details. But she'd had to tell someone, and since Kayla was still holed up with her ex, who was no longer her ex, and currently incommunicado, Jane was it. It also seemed too momentous not to share. Shay shook her head. "I don't want his mouth to hit the floor. I just want to drop off his keys and go. It was just a one-time thing, remember."

Jane shrugged. "No harm in reminding him what he's missing."

"He doesn't date. And I don't want or need a man in my life."

Jane's eyes narrowed. "Travis needs his balls kicked in."

She hadn't told Jane that her ex was still calling and leaving messages all the time, one lame excuse after the other. "This isn't about Travis. I'm fine, really. I'm happy on my own." Shay forced a smile. "Though I'm not averse to seeing someone kick Travis's balls in."

Her friend smiled, as well. "You and me both."

Forty-five minutes and four buses later, Shay was standing outside Colton Auto Repairs, hands gripping the strap of her bag like a life line, so tight she started to get a cramp in her pinky finger.

You can do this.

It was late afternoon, and the sun was starting to dip lower in the sky. She lifted her arm, shielding her eyes to get a better look at the large, steel building. Both of the big roller doors at the front were up, and she could see a couple of people moving around inside. She needed to get in there already, before they saw her hanging around out front like some scared, pathetic loser. Or worse, some insane stalker lady.

Taking a deep breath, she forced her feet to propel her forward. She'd always felt a little uncomfortable around men, blushing and stammering like a fool. Her father had died when she was only little, and for the longest time, it had just been her and her grandmother. She'd also gone to an all-girls private school, which she found out after her gran died had been paid for with her grandmother's life savings. Shay still struggled with that knowledge, with how much her gran had given up for her.

Anyway, a garage was her worst nightmare, any place overrun with men, for that matter. But being with Hugh, without the usual expectation that accompanied that type of encounter, the fear of what came next—and even though there had been some blushing and stammering on her part—she'd found their night together freeing. Not embarrassing.

She'd somehow gotten past her insecurities with him. Pretended she was someone else. And though he probably hadn't given her a second thought since he left that morning, she hated the idea that today he might see her as she truly was, that she'd somehow slip and reveal herself to him.

By the time she reached the first roller door, her heart was hammering and her legs were shaking.

She looked around the large space but didn't see Hugh. There was a man bent over one of the cars, and when she stepped farther into the workshop his head twisted toward her.

It was Hugh's brother. He gave her a head to toe before standing.

He was tall, probably the same height as Hugh, but he had less bulk, was leaner, and his forearms were covered in tattoos.

He grinned, and grabbing a rag from his back pocket, wiped his hands. "Hey there."

"Yes…hey."

He grinned wider. "What can I do for you?"

His dark hair was cut close to his skull. His eyes were brown, almost black, and his lip and eyebrow were pierced. She hadn't noticed the piercings in the dim lighting of the bar. He also had a good amount of whiskers covering his strong jaw. And somehow, he'd just made those simple words sound almost dirty, as if he'd asked her something highly inappropriate. She cleared her throat. "Sorry to disturb you, but I was looking for—"

"Shay?"

She spun around and spotted the man she'd met the night Hugh had saved her from Batman, when they'd dropped off his car here. The man with the feather tattoo on his neck. Adam?

"Oh." She gave him a little wave. "Hello." She felt her face flush, palms grow sweaty.

He smiled, all straight, white teeth and attractive dimples. What was it with this place? Were all the men this good looking, this ridiculously tall? Was it a job requirement?

"Nice to see you again, honey."

She forced a smile, her nerves now twice as bad with all this attention on her. "Yes, you too."

The other guy groaned. "Typical."

Shay had no idea what he meant, but Adam chuckled. It was rough and deep and kind of dark, but it sent a delightful tingle down her spine. "Unfortunately, in this instance, she's not mine."

Not mine?

Hugh's brother perked up and moved closer. "Well, move along then; I was just about to see to her needs." He winked. "So, what can I do for you?"

If her face was any hotter, her skin would start melting off. "Hugh? I mean…is he here?"

The hopeful look on his face dropped then his head tilted to the side, giving her another once over, and he cursed under his breath. "Shit. Sorry, babe, didn't recognize you out of your Woody's uniform." He motioned to her head. "It's your hair, right? It's different?"

She guessed she did look different out of that dreadful uniform, and she'd worn her hair in what she hoped was a cute, retro ponytail today instead of leaving it down.

Turning his head toward the back of the shop, he half growled, half yelled. "Hugh! Get your ass up here."

There was a scrape and a clatter, then a second later, she saw him, walking out from the back of the workshop. He was scowling at his brother, but then his gaze shifted to her, and as soon as he saw her, his expression went blank.

Oh, dear.

She locked her knees when they started to shake. His eyes stayed on her as he strode forward. Her gaze drifted over him as he moved. He was wearing pretty much the same clothing as he had the other night. Faded jeans and a T-shirt, this one black, as well, straining over his magnificent chest. There was grease streaked on his cheek and forehead, and when he lifted a hand, running his fingers through his sexily tousled hair, his thick biceps rolled and bunched, stretching the sleeve to the limit.

She swallowed, hard, fingers flexing around the strap of her bag, and forced another smile. "Hello, Hugh."

He stopped in front of her, crossing his heavily muscled arms. "Shay." His brow scrunched. "What're you doing here?"

His voice rumbled through her, lighting fires and setting off tremors in all her erogenous zones. Great, she was getting turned on when he was obviously not happy to see her. So much for his mouth hitting the floor when he saw her in this stupid dress. Not that she wanted that. Of course, she didn't. Why she'd listened to Jane in the first place, she had no idea. He probably thought she was going to turn all needy and clingy after one night together.

Desperate. Pathetic.

Travis's words echoed in her head.

She ignored them, forced them down and straightened her spine. Self-preservation kicked in, and a strength she didn't know she possessed rushed forward. She embraced it. Clung onto it with all she was worth. She knew herself well enough to know it wouldn't last long. She wasn't one of those feisty women, full of confidence and attitude, but she still carried enough residual anger from her disaster of a relationship with Travis, enough to get her through this encounter without looking as desperate and pathetic as he thought she was.

She smiled wider, doing her best to exude confidence, something she most certainly did not feel in that moment. Pulling one of the straps of her bag off her shoulder, she rummaged around until she found his keys. "You left these at my place the other night. I thought they might be important. I'm returning them."

His expression changed, softened a little as he took them from her. His grease-covered fingers brushed hers, rough and warm, and she shivered.

"Thanks, sweetheart. I've turned my place upside down looking for them. Forgot I had them with me the other night."

Gah! Why did he have to go and call her *sweetheart*? The way he'd said it all growly and sexy when he'd been inside her had been on replay in her traitorous mind since he'd walked out. Remembering the sound of his voice had also left her in a constant state of low-level arousal, just humming below the surface, waiting to be ignited. So it wasn't a surprise when that lust flared to life, just like that, as if he'd tossed another log on the fire in her loins. Damn him.

"Not a problem." She took a step back. "Anyway, I'll let you get back to work." Then she added, because her grandmother raised her to use her manners, "Nice to see you again." Though "nice" wasn't the correct word to describe how seeing him again had affected her.

She turned to leave, but Hugh grabbed her arm, halting her escape. Her belly flipped as she lifted her brows in question, in what she hoped was bored curiosity, when in reality she thought her heart might beat right out of her chest.

He tilted his head to the street. "Where you goin' now? You got plans?"

"Just home. No plans."

"You wanna get a drink? We were gonna close up in a few, anyway."

She wanted to say *yes*, badly. But this man, her mountain man, he was dangerous. She couldn't risk falling for someone like him, got the feeling if she did, the impact when she hit the ground would cause a heck of a lot more damage than what Travis had left behind. She couldn't risk it. Refused to put herself in a situation like that again. A beautiful memory, that's all Hugh could ever be.

She took a step back. "I can't; I'm sorry."

His hands went to his hips, gaze boring into her. "You said you didn't have plans."

"I don't." The words were out before she realized how they sounded. She inwardly winced. She sucked at lying, always had, and tended not to whenever possible.

Adam made a choking noise behind Hugh, and his brother barked out a startled laugh then proceeded to explode into hysterics. *Oops.*

Hugh's eyes narrowed on her, and he opened his mouth to say something, but she cut him off before he managed to change her mind.

"I better go."

"Shay…"

"Bye now!" Her voice was overly loud and kind of wobbly. Spinning on her heels, she hustled out of Hugh's magnetic force field…before she got sucked in and never got out.

His curse was loud enough she heard it as she walked away.

* * *

Hugh finished checking the transmission fluid in the Toyota and moved on to the radiator hose that needed replacing. He kept his head down, out of the way, because he sure as hell wasn't in the mood to talk. Shay had walked out of his workshop an hour ago, and he was still fighting himself, trying to stop from going after her. What the hell would he even say? It was a dumb idea. So he kept busy. If he was a different man, just a guy who owned a garage, who loved to work on cars—things could be different. But he wasn't that man.

Not anymore.

He'd wanted to be a mechanic for as long as he could remember. Ever since he was a kid. Had gotten a job in a garage as soon as he could. Had always known he wanted his own shop one day. He hated that Al had twisted it, turned it into something he could no longer be proud of.

"Yo!" Joe called. "I'm taking off."

Hugh stood, wiped his hands. "Where's Adam?"

"Office."

He gave his brother a chin lift and closed the hood. Joe walked out, and Hugh headed toward the front of the shop, as well. Adam was on the phone, so Hugh took advantage of the fact and left before his friend could stop him. Leaving Adam to close up on his own wasn't cool, but he would question Hugh about Shay, and he wasn't going there. There was nothing to talk about.

He climbed into his truck, fired it up and headed for home.

Twenty minutes later—and he still didn't know how the hell it happened—he found himself sitting in his pickup, staring across the road into The Happy Armadillo freaking Trailer Park. The name was messed up, no doubt, too damn cute, and by the looks of it, full of old people. But he'd never wanted to be anywhere more in his life.

What would Shay do if he rocked on up and knocked on the door? Would she welcome him in or turn him down again? Press those abundant curves against him and kiss him hello? His cock stirred. Shit, this wasn't like him. He didn't go back for seconds. He was a "hit it once and get the hell gone" kind of guy. He had to be. He didn't need the complications in his life; he had enough of those already.

Their deadbeat, asshole of a father had seen to that. Then he'd disappeared. Hugh had tried to track him down, but the bastard was smoke. Either that, or someone had fitted him with a set of concrete shoes and taken him for a swim. The guy had never been smart, had made a lot of enemies, and the longer he stayed away, the more Hugh was convinced it was the latter.

He should probably feel bad, have some remorse. He didn't feel shit. The debt the old man had dumped on Hugh and Joe had nearly sunk them both.

After the meet with Don, he should never have taken what Shay offered, not when he knew deep down staying away wouldn't be easy— he gripped the steering wheel—and not with Al coming after them. Shit.

He couldn't have her, but he couldn't regret it, either. Fuck no. Shay had been the sweetest piece he'd ever had. So much more than he'd imagined, and since the night he'd seen her in that costume, looking sweet and sexy as all hell, he'd imagined. A lot.

The woman was a mystery. Talked like class, dressed up like Poison Ivy, and lived in a goddammed pink trailer.

He straightened in his seat when Shay's door swung open, and the woman in question stepped out. Her hair was up in one of those messy buns, and she was wearing little pale-blue shorts and a tank that clung to her soft, round tits. *Jesus.* Was she wearing her PJs?

Christ, she was.

He wanted to go to her, pull her inside and peel those innocent-looking articles of clothing from her lush body and corrupt her every way he could think of.

She walked over to the trailer next to hers, calling something out before opening up without knocking. A few minutes later, she came out with a dog, one of those little rat-looking ones. She clipped on a lead and walked the rodent around a grassy area in the center of the park. The dog sniffed around, took a dump, then Shay picked it back up and went back to her neighbor's. The door opened, and a frail old woman stood there, arms out for the dog. Shay helped her back inside and shut the door behind them.

Shay was sweet.

The kind of woman who would help an elderly neighbor. The kind who lived in a cute pink trailer and proudly had on display in her living room an entire shelf of ceramic fucking cats. She was not for him. She was naive. Enough that she'd take home a total stranger and trust him with her body. He'd gotten the feeling that was a first for her. She'd been all in, but she'd also been a little hesitant, a little shy. The type of women he usually slept with had the moves, knew what they wanted as much as he did. Shay had lacked skill, but she'd more than made up for it with her enthusiasm. That subtle innocence had been as sexy as hell. Shit, she was the best he'd ever had.

For some reason, he couldn't drive away. Not until he'd seen her one more time. Thirty minutes passed before she came back out and headed to her own place.

Hugh watched her move, the way her tits and ass swayed as she walked, the way her soft red hair bounced.

"Shit." He needed to stay away, but he was starting to think that was easier said than done.

Before he changed his mind, he started his truck and pulled out onto the road, cursing himself for being the fool he was the whole way home.

Chapter Six

Shay turned her back on the crowded bar and drew in a steadying breath.

Birthday drinks! How could she have forgotten what today was? She'd walked in to start her shift and nearly turned around and ran back out again. But that wasn't something she could do, not when she needed the money so badly. Plus, it would put extra pressure on the other waitresses if she left, and that wouldn't be fair.

She had to deal with it, deal with the fact that right at this very moment, more than half of the TBS Designs staff, including Travis, were laughing and drinking at a table in her section.

Vinnie's brows lifted as he slid a tray full of drinks her way. "You okay, Shay?"

She wasn't. Not at all. "I'm...I don't think I can..."

Amanda dumped her tray on the bar. "That your ex, hon?" She jerked her chin toward TBS's table.

"Yes. Would you mind...?"

"I'm on it. Let me deal with king douche."

Some of the tension left Shay's shoulders when she released a relieved breath. "I owe you."

Throwing Shay a wink, Amanda headed across the bar to the crowded table and started taking orders. Not everyone who worked at

TBS was like their horrid boss, and Shay felt bad for not going over and at least saying hello.

As it turned out, she had an excuse for avoiding them—the place filled fast, and she was nonstop just keeping up with her tables. She was heading back to the bar after delivering a round of drinks when someone grabbed her elbow, pulling her to a stop. Shay spun around and came face to face with Travis. *Wonderful.*

"Shay?"

She didn't bother answering. It was obviously her. And how much of a surprise could it be seeing her here, when he knew damn well this is where she worked. She raised a brow in question, mustering up the same fake attitude she'd used on Hugh the day before, pretending this didn't affect her, didn't upset her.

He shoved his hands into his pockets. "I've missed you around work…I've missed *you*."

Seriously? "I doubt that very much. Now, if you'll excuse me, I have drinks to deliver."

He grabbed her arm again. "Please, will you talk to me, let me explain? You won't answer my calls…"

He called her several times a week, not to mention the continuous texts. He needed to take the hint, already. "There's nothing to explain. I heard what you said, the way you truly felt…"

"You overreacted, were oversensitive. I was just kidding around, Shay. You know how it is, right?"

No, she didn't. If you cared about someone, had *real* feelings for that person, you did not ridicule them. You certainly didn't put them down because you were embarrassed people found out you were seeing them.

"I have to go." She pulled her arm free and rushed to the bar. He'd seen her, talked to her face to face, heard her tell him she wasn't interested; maybe now he'd leave her alone. Maybe now he'd stop calling.

The rest of the night was thankfully uneventful. A couple of her old friends from TBS came over to talk to her when she was collecting drinks. Most knew why she'd left her job, and more than a few had heard his hurtful comments and let her know what they thought of him. But he was their boss—that was all the support she could expect, and she appreciated it. But now, she just wanted to put it behind her, all of it.

Three hours later, the place had thinned out, and her feet felt like they had their own heartbeat. She was ready for a hot mug of cocoa followed by bed. Unfortunately, she was still a bus ride away, which sucked, since she needed to be up early to let Edna's dog Rocky out, followed by a shift at Raggedy Jane's, then a website design to finish for a client. Thankfully, Jane's was walking distance and didn't require public transport.

Shay handed in her tips to be split between the waitresses. The manager divided them up and handed over her share. They'd done well. But she'd need a few more nights like this to cover everything for the month.

She grabbed her jacket from behind the bar, slung her bag over her shoulder and waved goodbye. "Night, Amanda, thanks again for covering my table."

"Anytime, hon. See you Monday."

She sucked in the cool night air as soon as she walked through the door. She usually enjoyed her shifts at Woody's, but tonight, she felt deflated and exhausted. Keeping it together had been harder than she thought. She hadn't talked to Travis face to face since she walked into his office, told him she'd heard what he'd said, and walked out without giving notice. At the time, she'd believed she'd loved him...that he'd loved her. Idiot.

"Shay, wait."

She stiffened then turned around. Her ex-boyfriend stood by the door, leaning against the wall.

"What are you still doing here?" she asked.

"I was waiting for you."

"I don't know why..."

"You do."

Travis walked up until she had nowhere to go, the chain-link fence surrounding the parking lot at her back.

"You need to let me explain," he said.

"I don't need to do anything."

"Please, Shay."

"Why are you doing this?" she whispered.

He blew out a breath. "I made a mistake. I thought..."

"You thought what?" She straightened her spine.

"Look." He lifted a hand, fingers curling around the fence beside her head. "Don't take this the wrong way...but you're just *you*, and I'm the manager of a highly successful business. My family is wealthy, have connections, expect certain things. The woman on my arm needs to *behave* a certain way."

He dropped his hand to the side of her neck, and she flinched at his touch, the way it made her skin crawl.

"Shay, that woman needs to *look* a certain way."

"Travis…"

"I mean I love the curves. I do. You know that."

His gaze did a sweep of her body, and she inwardly cringed at the bulge at the front of his trousers. *Gross.*

"I've missed the curves a lot, darling. All I'm asking is that you lose a few pounds. I don't know. Maybe get a makeover? Get your hair and make-up done by a professional. Get someone to help you out with your clothes? What we had was special. I want it back." He smiled down at her, eyes softening, as if his words would have her jumping for joy. "It's not much to ask to get us back, don't you think? I want you back, Shay."

Stunned, she stood there for several seconds, trying to get her thoughts together, her feelings over his messed-up, highly arrogant declaration. In the end, all she could come up with was, "Wow."

His smile grew wider. "I know. I've surprised you. I mean, we'll have to keep our relationship quiet until we have you looking your best, but I think—"

"Travis…"

"You'll be more than acceptable after you've dropped a little weight, done something with that hair, maybe dye it? Lose the red; it's kind of, well, it's red…"

"Travis."

She said his name with more force, and he finally shut up.

"No."

His brow scrunched. "No?"

She shook her head. "No. I won't be going on some crash diet, and I sure as hell won't be dying my hair. My hair is the same color as my grandmother's was. I like my hair, and I like my life."

"Darling…"

She shoved his hand away from the side of her neck. "Why you think I'd be jumping for joy over your offer, I have no idea; maybe you're delusional? Even if you wanted me back the way I am, I would tell you to take a flying leap. You want me but only if I'm someone else. You mocked me to your friends, to cover your embarrassment when they found out you were seeing me. Like I was some charity case. Like I was some pity fuck."

He flinched. "Shay." This time his voice was sharp, reprimanding. Travis didn't like it when she cursed, which was why she'd done it.

"Look, Travis, don't take this the wrong way," she said, firing his words back at him. "But I could do better. In fact, I have done better."

His mouth tightened, lips thinning. "Don't play games with me. I know you haven't been with anyone else."

She just smiled.

Travis grabbed her arm. "You haven't."

"Walk away, Travis," she said, yanking her arm free.

He stared at her for several seconds, face red with anger, then finally he spun on his dress shoes and stormed off across the parking lot. She slumped against the fence, getting her emotions, her heart-rate back under control, then pushed off and started toward the street before she missed her bus. He wasn't worth the slice of pain his words had caused. He wasn't. He never had been.

"Shay?"

She jumped at the deep, rumbling voice coming through the darkness. Then he stepped forward, big body moving out of the shadows.

Hugh.

"Who was that? You okay?"

Her gaze moved over him, ate him up. "What are you doing here?"

"I was working late; thought I'd stop by."

She swallowed the lump forming in her throat. "But your garage is twenty minutes away."

He shrugged. "You gonna tell me who that guy was talking to you?"

"My old boss."

His brows lowered. "Was he giving you a hard time?"

She hugged herself. "Yeah, but I don't think he'll be bothering me anymore."

His wide shoulders seemed to grow wider, expression going from easy to hard in a split second. "He's been bothering you?"

"I'm fine, really."

"Your car here?"

"No, I…"

Closing the gap between them, he planted a hand on her lower back and directed her to his truck. "I'll drive you home." He pulled open the passenger door.

"No, I couldn't…"

"You could."

It was late. She didn't want to walk to the bus stop, even though it was only half a block away—and Hugh made her feel…good. Just being around him made her feel good, and she needed that right then. *A solid reason to stay away from him*. Still, when she opened her mouth, instead of declining, she said, "Thank you. That's really very nice of you."

For some reason, her statement made him grin. It was highly attractive, but then she lost sight of it because she climbed up, and he shut her in. His smile was gone by the time he got in with her.

A few minutes later, they were on the road, Hugh's formidable presence filling the cab.

"What was that back there?"

She blew out a breath. Telling him about the most humiliating moment in her life was not something she relished, but she got the feeling he wasn't in the mood to drop the subject. The determined look in his eyes, not to mention the way the muscle in his jaw jumped every so often, spoke volumes. Why he cared, she had no clue. They'd shared a night, and yes, he'd shown up at her work and offered her a ride for some unknown reason. And okay, she was a little confused about that, since he'd made it clear he didn't want anything more than casual. They both had. Still, she found herself confiding in him. "That was my ex-boyfriend."

"You were fucking that guy?"

She ignored the slight growl to his voice and carried on. "We were dating. Well, that's what I thought, but in reality, I was his dirty little secret."

She watched his fingers tighten on the steering wheel. "He screwed you over?"

"I, ah…I heard him talking about me, making excuses for seeing me. He said a bunch of things, hurtful things… He was…embarrassed of me." She glanced over at him. "I was forced to quit my job. I'm a graphic designer, and finding another job doing what I was at TBS is proving difficult." She motioned to her Woody's shirt. "Which is why I work three jobs."

"What did he want just now?"

She swallowed the lump in her throat. "He told me he'd take me back."

"What?" Okay, now his voice was all growl.

She wrapped her arms around her waist, trying to stop the nausea caused by just thinking about Travis's words. "Yes, and all I have to do for the pleasure is lose weight, change my clothes, my make-up, and dye my hair a different color."

Hugh was silent, so she kept talking. "But there's another condition on top of all of that…we have to keep our relationship a secret until I look…" She lifted her hands, doing air quotes. "Acceptable."

"Motherfucker," he finally said, quiet fury radiating from his deep voice.

A sudden rush of emotion rose up from nowhere. Hearing it out loud, that she wasn't good enough, hit hard. Why, she didn't know. She'd heard the words before, many times, and not just from Travis. Her mother had said the same on numerous occasions. She turned away as hot tears suddenly filled her eyes, ran down her cheeks.

"Babe?" Hugh reached out, took her chin between his thumb and finger and made her look at him. "That asshole still mean something to you?"

She shook her head. "What? No. God, no. When he touched me

my skin crawled. Ignore me, I'm just…"

"Don't let that fucker get to you. He sure as hell isn't worth your tears."

She smiled through them. "I know you're right. It just doesn't feel good to have all the reasons you weren't good enough, all your faults, listed and thrown back in your face."

"Faults?" He was growling again. "Not faults, Shay. You do not need to lose fucking weight. You got curves, and those curves are sexy as hell. As for make-up, clothes? I don't know shit about that stuff. But I like the way you wear what you have, it's you, it's hot, it works in a seriously good way. But your hair, your hair is fucking gorgeous. I'd be pissed if you dyed it."

Everything he said, God, the way he said it…she couldn't doubt he meant every word. Hugh was real. He didn't play games. She'd learned that the first night she met him. Her face crumpled again, a fresh round of tears sliding down her face. "That was a really nice thing for you to say."

"I meant every word," he said, voice gruff, then he surprised her by reaching out and brushing some of her tears away with the pad of his thumb. "Shit. Was trying to make you feel better, not make it worse."

"You did make me feel better." It was almost alarming how much better she felt hearing that from him, how important it was that he felt that way, saw her that way. "But unfortunately, you've caught me at a weak moment. I used up all my fake attitude yesterday on you at the garage."

He was quiet several seconds. "You what?"

"When you asked me for drinks." She sniffed and rummaged in her

77

bag for a tissue.

"I'm not following."

She wiped her eyes and blew her nose. "I'm not feisty or…or one of those strong, independent types. I try to tell myself I am, but I'm just…" She glanced out the window. "I'm just not. I faked it."

"Bullshit."

His voice was extra low, and she turned to look at him across the cab. He glanced at her then back at the road.

"But I'm still not following, sweetheart."

"I turned you down for drinks."

"I'm aware." He gave her a small grin, but it didn't reach his eyes. "Why would turning me down use up all your attitude?"

After repeating her words back to her, the grin did reach his eyes. The effect was devastating.

She ignored how ruggedly handsome he was, or tried to, and carried on. "*Fake* attitude," she corrected. "And, well, it's because I…I didn't fully, one hundred percent want to say no."

Everything seemed to grind to a standstill, the air in the truck changed and though she wasn't looking at him, she felt his gaze move back to her.

"Look at me, Shay."

She sucked in a shuddery breath, but did as he said, was powerless to do otherwise.

"You wanted to have a drink with me?"

Her mouth felt dry all of a sudden. "Ah, maybe."

His gaze moved between her and the road ahead. "You gonna tell me why you said no?"

Why had she opened her big fat mouth? "No."

"I'm gonna need a different answer."

She played with the edge of her bag. "Well, I'm sorry to disappoint you, but that's the only one you're going to get."

He shook his head, eyes aimed forward. "And she says she's not feisty."

His words made her belly do a loop-de-loop.

"You're full of shit, babe. Know that for a fact. If I hadn't been there when that fucker in the Batman costume cornered you, I get the feeling that guy would still be walking funny. Your fuck-wit ex? I saw him get into his car. Guy looked as if he'd just eaten shit. I don't doubt you tore the little prick a new asshole before he stormed off." His voice dropped. "And, babe, that isn't the only way you're feisty. I've had the pleasure of you unleashing it on me when I was in your bed, in a way that's had my dick hard for a fucking week. So, yeah, I call bullshit."

She was speechless. No one had ever said anything like that to her before. Ever. "Hugh…"

His thick fingers flexed around the steering wheel again. "Now, you gonna tell me why you turned me down?"

He'd been sweet and kind, in his gruff, blunt way, and he deserved the truth. She cleared her throat and blurted, "Because I wanted to say yes." Then for reasons unknown, she added, "Badly."

Chapter Seven

Because I wanted to say yes.

She licked her lips, and Hugh's dick jerked behind his zipper as if she'd just swiped her tongue across the head of his cock.

Shit.

He'd pushed for her to tell him, and now she had—he was screwed. Totally and royally.

When he'd gotten into his truck and driven to Woody's, he'd known why he was going, he'd wanted—no, needed—to see Shay. It was messed up, out of character, but he'd banked on her telling him to get lost.

He'd *needed* her to tell him to get lost.

When she brought his keys to the garage, she'd turned him down flat. It was for the best; he was no good for her, no good for anyone. But he'd seen the heat in her gaze, he'd felt sure of it. It had fucking niggled at him the last few days, to the point he'd had no choice but to get into his damn truck and drive over here—just so she could tell him he was wrong.

The plan had blown up in his face.

"It's not just a drink you want from me, though, is it, Shay?" he asked, voice shot to shit. Pushing when he should be keeping his mouth firmly shut.

She shifted in her seat, and he glanced over. Her lids lifted, and her green eyes locked on his.

"No."

Shit. His cock pulsed, trying to fucking punch through his jeans. "You remember what I said to you that first night? I'm not looking for a relationship. I don't have room for that in my life right now."

She shook her head, gorgeous red hair sliding over her shoulder. He still couldn't believe her asshole ex wanted her to dye it. Fucking twat.

"I'm attracted to you, and I…I want you, but I don't want anything more. Me and relationships…" She shook her head again. "Well, let's just say I don't have room for one in my life, either."

His heart started to pound. "So, what're you saying here, sweetheart?"

"I'd like to…"

She blushed. Even in the dark cab of his truck, he could see her cheeks darken. Made his cock even harder.

"*Us*…to have an affair," she finished.

Even the prim way she said it, calling it an affair, just turned him on more. Made him want to corrupt her, do dirty things to her, taste every damn inch of her sweet body and not stop until she was screaming his name. "I'm in your bed, or you're in mine. Nothing more?"

"Yes. That's what I'm proposing."

He was insane for considering this, with the way things were right now, but he didn't think he could walk away from her offer, either, not until they'd had a few more wild nights. Not until he'd well and truly gotten his fill. The entrance to her trailer park loomed ahead. She shifted beside him again, but he kept his eyes on the road as he turned in, pulled up outside her trailer and shut off his truck.

The cab was engulfed in silence.

She stayed put, quiet at his side, waiting. *Goddammit.*

Undoing his seatbelt, he reached out and undid hers. "Look at me."

She lifted her head, beautiful eyes meeting his.

"You sure this is what you want?"

"Yes," she whispered.

He cupped the side of her face, smoothing his thumb over her cheek. Her eyes were still a little puffy from crying. "You want me in your bed tonight, sweetheart?"

She licked her lips, gaze never leaving his. "Yes."

She'd taken the keys to her place from her purse already, and he slipped them from her fingers. "Let's go."

"Pardon?"

"Inside, beautiful."

He shoved open his door, and she met him at the front of his truck. His gut tightened when her small, warm hand slid into his. Shit, just the feel of her skin against his set him on fire.

He opened the door, and she followed him inside. Dumping her keys on the counter, he watched Shay do the same with her bag then move to the middle of her tiny trailer. She was standing three feet away, looking cute and sexy and nervous as hell.

He wanted her under him badly, but first, he wanted that lush mouth on his. "Come here, Shay."

The uniform she wore hugged her curves. The woman was a perfect hourglass. All tits and ass, and lots of both. She came toward him, hips moving in a way that made his balls ache. But it wasn't an act or a come on; this wasn't Shay trying to be sexy, it was just her. And he got the feeling she didn't have the first clue how damn hot she was.

"Woman, you are goddamn gorgeous."

She was right in front of him now, and at his words, she stilled, blinked up at him, eyes wide.

"You don't have to say things like that. I know I'm not…"

"Not what?" He slid a hand up the side of her neck, tugging her closer.

"Well, I'm—I'm not slim, I'm…"

Jesus. "Babe, I don't know what kind of guys you've been hanging with…no, scratch that, I fucking do."

She shifted, as if she was going to take a step back, but he grabbed her hip with his other hand and kept her close.

"Let me make one thing clear. I like curves. I like soft, and I like round. I like a woman who, when I fuck her hard, her hips, ass, they're cushioning mine while I'm doing it."

"Oh."

Her lips parted, not much, but enough he could see the tip of her little pink tongue. He wanted a taste.

"Yeah, beautiful, I think you're getting it. What you got going on fucking turns me on. Makes my cock hard as goddamn steel. Don't ever think otherwise."

"Okay." Her eyes crinkled at the corners and even though her lips only lifted a little, her entire face lit up.

Jesus, she was gorgeous.

Cupping the side of her face, he threaded his fingers in her hair. The soft, smooth strands were warm and silky against the back of his hand. Tightening his grip on her hip with the other, he pulled her even closer, so her tits were flush against his abs, and leaning in, brought his mouth close to hers. "Can't wait to get inside that body. But first, I want a taste of this mouth." Then he closed the gap.

Her lips were soft and pliant under his, and he nipped her lower one so she'd open for him. She did, moaning softly as he slid his tongue inside. Finally getting the taste he was starving for. She tilted her head back farther, and he kissed her hard and deep. Her hands came up to his chest, gripping his shirt, holding him to her as he took her mouth the way he'd wanted to since he found her in the parking lot earlier. She clung to him, kissed him back, as hot for him as he was for her.

They did that for a while, until he couldn't wait any longer. Bunching up her shirt, he dragged it up, breaking their kiss to pull it over her head. He stared down at her. Shit, her tits were perfect. So pale, so full her bra was struggling to hold all she had. He wanted to bury his face between them, use them as a pillow after he'd fucked her. Feel the heat of her skin against his cheek, his lips. Sleep like that all night. "Take off the bra."

A blush brightened her cheeks, turning them a lovely shade of pink. Then traveled down, doing the same to the tops of her tits as she reached back and unhooked the thing. She slid the straps off her shoulders and let it drop to the floor. Shay stood in front of him, naked from the waist up, breathing rapidly, nipples pebbled and hard. A goddess. He dropped to his knees, because he had every intention of worshiping her magnificent breasts before he did anything else.

Panting, because she had his heart going a million miles an hour, he shuffled forward. Shay wasn't tall, and even with her standing, he was mouth level with her pert, rosy nipples. Cupping her with both hands, he groaned at the weight, the warmth filling his palms. Her hands went to his hair, threading through, nails raking his scalp in a way that sent tinkles down his spine. He looked up at her.

"Tell me you want me to suck these sweet, pink nipples, that you want me to tongue and nibble them until your pussy is drenched and your thighs are slick."

Her eyes were glazed, lips parted, panting softly. "Yes. I want that. Please, do that."

She tightened her fingers in his hair, and he nearly came in his pants. Leaning forward, he dragged the tip of his tongue around one of the stiffened peaks, moaning when she moved closer, pressing all that soft flesh against his face. He loved the way his whiskers abraded her flesh, darkening her pale skin, marking her.

He teased her until she was breathing rapidly, until her thighs were quivering. Moving from one then back to the other, never sucking hard or deep, waiting until she couldn't take anymore and asked for it. He needed to hear her ask for it. She needed to know she didn't need to be shy with him, like she had their first night, that he'd give her anything she wanted. He'd almost given up when her fingers flexed in his hair again, and she breathed the words, so quietly he almost missed them.

"Can't hear you, beautiful."

"Please. Suck harder."

His cock jumped in his jeans, balls drawing up tight. *Shit*. He did what she said immediately, sucking her in deep and hard, rewarding her for her bravery. She cried out, holding him tighter until his face was surrounded by smooth, creamy flesh, her taste, her smell making him goddamn dizzy.

Dropping his other hand to her jeans, he got to work on the button then dragged down the zipper. "You wet for me?"

"Yes."

Her hands went to his shoulders as he helped her step free. Then he cupped the heat between her thighs, over her panties, and groaned. Soaked. She was ready, more than ready for his cock.

He dragged down her underwear, and she came down to the floor with him, grabbing at the front of his shirt and yanking it up and off. He hadn't planned on fucking her on the floor, but when her shaking hands reached for the front of his jeans and she yanked them open, he knew that's exactly what was going to happen. Her hand went inside, and she grabbed his dick, freeing him, moaning softly when she felt how hard he was for her. Wrapping her fingers around him, she started working him.

He dropped back on his ass, against the couch, and hissed through his teeth. Grabbing her hips, he lifted her onto his lap. She straddled his thighs, hands going to his shoulders, rubbing her pussy up and down the length of his shaft.

"Please," she whimpered.

He shoved his hand into his pocket, grabbing his wallet, and quickly found a condom. After suiting up, he tightened his grip on her hips, and lifted her. "Sit on my cock, beautiful. Show me how you like it."

She shook under his hands as she lowered herself onto his dick, easing down his length inch by painstaking inch. Her little gasps and moans made him crazy, until he was close to snapping, to yanking her down hard to the hilt or thrusting up inside her.

"You can take all of me, Shay. I know you can. Fuck, baby, you're nearly there."

Finally, she sank down the last couple of inches, taking him fully. *Holy shit.* Her hips did a slow, little roll, and her head dropped back on a hot moan.

He dug his fingers into her ass, squeezing more soft, warm flesh. Jesus, she was perfect. Spectacular. "That's it, beautiful. Work it the way you like it."

She started to move against him, taking her time, slowly sliding all the way up, until he thought he might slip out, then dropping back down 'til he was filling her, stretching her. Then she'd do that sexy little roll again but now with an added grind. Her tits were smashed up against him, her hard nipples grazing his chest. His head was spinning, close to coming, close to shoving her to her back and slamming into her hard and fast.

But he didn't, he was enjoying the show far too much, watching her take what she wanted. Shit, every time she sank down, she got wetter, hotter. Her skin was flushed, all inhibitions gone. Hottest thing he'd ever seen. He gritted his teeth as she went up and slid back down, rocking against him.

"Shit, baby, you're killing me, way you're grinding that pretty pussy down on me." He hissed out another breath. "So good...so fucking *tight.*"

At his words, he felt her clamp down even harder, and he was goddamn seeing stars, then she started to move faster, bouncing on his dick, deep and hard and so fucking hot. He dug his fingers into her ass, egging her on. Her forehead dropped to his shoulder as she moved, grinding and pounding.

Then he felt it, her orgasm, the way her muscles clutched at him repeatedly. She cried out and a second later, he felt her teeth on his skin, her nails scoring his back, and she blew up. He held her down and took over, slamming up inside her. His balls exploded, and he shot hard enough to make his vision blink out for several seconds.

Shay lay limp against him, her breath rushing from between her lips, tickling his sweat-dampened skin.

Jesus Christ. He knew that first time between them had been good. The best. But this? What they'd just done…

Shit.

When his legs didn't feel as weak as a newborn foal's, he carefully slid his arm below her ass, the other at her back, and stood. She was warm and soft, curling into him as he carried her to bed.

After reluctantly putting her down, he tucked her under the covers and went to the bathroom to get rid of the condom. Washing his hands, he stared at himself in the mirror. At the rough beard, the overlong hair. "A big, clumsy, waste of space," his old man had called him. Then he thought of Shay, all soft, smooth skin and lush curves and that gorgeous red hair. He was a fucking giant ogre, and she was a fairy princess. He had no business with her, tainting her with the filth that clung to him now. Not even if their affair, as she'd put it, had a use-by date.

He should get in his truck and leave, never come back, but he couldn't make himself go. Instead, he walked back to her bed and climbed in beside her, dragging her in close. He wanted more of her cries, more of her soft body, just more—of everything. She snuggled in, made noises in her sleep that were equally sexy and cute as hell.

He stared up at the ceiling while he smoothed his hand over her waist, down over her ass and back. Getting hard all over again and not trying to stop it. Fuck that…while he had her, he intended to enjoy the hell out of her.

Chapter Eight

Shay wrapped her fingers around the thick wrist resting on her hip. The coarse hairs tickled her palm, making her shiver at the sheer masculinity of the man in her bed. On a sigh, she lifted the hand splayed across her belly and scooted out from under him.

She didn't want to leave the warm cocoon Hugh had created when he'd wrapped himself around her. The whole night, she'd felt small and delicate, safe—but Edna would be up and waiting for her to take Rocky out for his walkies. The dog's bladder seemed to have a built in timer, and 7:00 a.m. on the dot was taking care of business time. Edna's arthritis was worse in the morning and evenings, so whenever Shay wasn't working, she made sure she was around to help out her neighbor. Between Shay and a couple of the other park residents, they had Edna covered.

Scooping up her PJs—that had been knocked to the floor after Hugh had carried her to bed last night and then proceeded to prove his recovery time was as impressive as…well, everything else about the man—she dragged on the shorts then tugged the tank over her head. Looking back at the bed, she felt an achy heat course through her, remembering the things he'd done, the way he'd handled her—the things he'd said.

His big body dwarfed her double bed, feet hanging over the end.

Right then, he looked like a huge, hibernating grizzly bear. But sexy...and human. Despite the man's stature, he wasn't rough or clumsy; he had full control over his size and strength. Boy, did he have control. Another wave of heat rolled through her. Goodness, he overwhelmed her, turned her on. So much so, the last thing she'd thought about when they were together was the way she looked. A first for her. All she could do when they were together was feel.

She had no idea what had come over her last night. But whatever it was—temporary insanity, maybe—the outcome had been the beginning of a casual affair. For a short time, Hugh Colton was hers.

She wanted him. There was no point denying it. He didn't want a long-term relationship, and neither did she. She'd sat beside him in the cab of his truck, body throbbing and hot, and she'd reminded herself that Hugh was safe. The men she'd fallen for in the past were his complete opposite, which meant no messy emotions would be getting involved. He was also exciting, enthralling and the most masculine, sexy man she'd ever encountered.

No risk.

She did another sweep of his body just as he rolled onto his back. He threw one arm over his head, the other coming to rest on his abs. The sheet had dropped low, giving her an unrestricted view of his impressive abdominal muscles...and lower. *Oh, my.* He had his knee bent, one solid thigh exposed, and resting across his lower belly was his thick, very erect penis.

Without thinking, she took a small step toward the bed. She wanted to trace that sexy cross tattoo on his ribs with her tongue, lick him all over, then slide down and take him into her mouth. The sudden urge to climb on top of him, to soak in more of the delicious heat that seemed to radiate off him and have her wicked way, was almost too hard to resist. But then she remembered Edna and Rocky.

Dammit.

Tearing her eyes away, she slid on her flip-flops and tip-toed from the room. Her overheated skin felt tight and tingly, and she was thankful for the hit of cool morning air when she stepped outside.

Edna's door banged opened before Shay reached it.

"There you are, girl. I didn't think you were coming." Edna shuffled forward. "It would've been a crying shame if Rocky crapped all over my good rug. I love that rug."

Edna may have looked like a sweet, little old lady, but she had a mouth like a sailor and a tendency to blurt everything she was thinking.

"Sorry, Edna, I had a late shift last night and slept in."

Edna cackled and clamped her morning cigarette between her lips. "More like all the hanky-panky goin' on in your trailer after you got home. At one point, I thought a freight-train was gonna burst through my living room wall."

Shay felt her face go up in flames. "No, I…"

The sound of her front door opening had her freezing on the spot.

Edna's gaze moved beyond Shay's shoulder, eyes going big, mouth dropping open, cigarette dangling perilously from her bottom lip. "Jumping Jehoshaphat," she whispered.

Shay's sentiments exactly. She'd had a similar reaction when she'd seen Hugh for the first time. She took Rocky from Edna before she forgot she was holding the dog and dropped him.

"Babe, what're you doin' out here?" Hugh asked, his sleep-roughened voice sliding through her, setting off happy tingles all over again.

Tucking the dog under her arm, she turned and stifled a lust-filled moan. His chest was still bare—her gaze dropped—but he'd thankfully pulled on jeans, except he'd left the top button undone, and she couldn't drag her eyes away from the thick hair peaking from the top.

"Babe?" There was amusement to his voice now.

Forcing herself to lift her gaze, she met his smiling brown eyes. "Yes?"

"Come back to bed."

Edna thrust her hands forward. "Give me Rocky, girl. I'll manage his walkies this morning."

Shay choked out a startled laugh. "Don't be silly, Edna, and no, you won't. If you fall down these stairs and break your hip, I'll never forgive myself. And anyway, I can't go back to bed; I have to get ready for work."

Edna took a drag of her smoke. "You're looking a little flush to me." She waggled her eyebrows. "Maybe a day in bed would do you good."

Good lord. Ignoring them both, Shay strode to the middle of the grassy patch in the center of the trailer park. Setting Rocky down, she held the lead Edna had already attached and waited. The dog did his business quickly. The poor thing had obviously been close to bursting. Picking him back up, she walked back to Edna, who was still standing in her doorway staring at Hugh. Hugh hadn't moved, either—only his eyes weren't on Edna, they were on Shay.

She handed over the dog. "I'll see you after work."

Edna nodded so enthusiastically, the lose skin hanging from her neck swung back and forth like an empty hammock in the breeze. "You get a better offer, I'll be fine." She tilted her head toward Harold's trailer. "That old coot can help me with Rocky." Then, with another cackle, she slammed her door shut.

Hugh stepped back so Shay could get inside.

"You gotta work?"

"Yes." And didn't that just totally suck. "I need to be there in an hour, so I better get moving."

"An hour's plenty of time." He grabbed her hand when she tried to walk to the bathroom. "Give me fifteen minutes, and I'll have you screaming my name before your PJs"—he tugged on the silky blue ribbon hanging from the front of her shorts—"hit the floor."

She didn't doubt it, and she wanted that…badly. The man had proven he could do it, too, several times. "I can't." Her voice came out breathless, needy. "I have to get ready, that's at least thirty minutes, right there. The walk to work, that's another thirty. I'm already late."

His brows dropped. "You're walking?"

"Yes."

"Why?"

"I don't have a car."

He straightened. "How do you get home from Woody's?"

"The bus."

She'd had to sell her car after she lost her job. She hadn't had much in the way of savings to start with, and when her grandmother died, she'd used what she did have to go toward her funeral costs. Funerals were expensive. She still had two installments left to pay on her loan.

Her grandmother was a generous lady, had been her whole life, would give the sweater off her back, and had done so. Shay had seen it with her own eyes. But this also meant her grandmother had left behind some debt, because if someone was in need, Gran gave, even if she didn't have it to spare.

Her grandmother had also been sweet and funny, and at times a little flighty. That meant she often didn't plan ahead. Sylvie Freestone had lived life to the fullest, for each day. She didn't like to think about the future, not for herself, at least. She'd also loved with everything she had. And Shay had loved her right back for it. Finding out her grandmother had somehow scrimped and saved to make sure Shay had gotten the best education possible had been a shock. She couldn't repay her gran for everything she'd done, but Shay could give her grandmother the best funeral she could afford. And that's what she'd done. Which meant she had to rely on public transport or walk for the foreseeable future. Considering her grandmother had lived in a trailer her entire life so Shay could go to a private girls' school and college, it was a small price to pay.

Hugh's brown eyes bored into hers. "You're telling me you take the fucking bus at one o'clock in the fucking morning?"

Well, that seemed an excessive and unnecessary amount of cursing over her use of public transport. Also, she sometimes finished at two or three but decided to keep that to herself. "Yes."

"On your own?"

"Well, yes."

He bit out another curse. "Only people on buses at one in the morning are crazies and drunks after a night out getting wasted."

He wasn't wrong. She'd encountered more than her fair share of both. "It's fine." And why he cared or was getting so hot under the collar about it, she had no idea. "I only do it four times a week. I've never had any trouble."

"You working tomorrow?"

"No."

He stared at her for several seconds, then his posture changed, and he seemed to let go of whatever was getting him so riled up. "I'll give you a ride to wherever you need to go this morning."

"You don't have to do that."

He fisted the front of her tank at her belly and tugged her forward. "I do if I wanna watch you come. You wanna come, princess?"

Princess.

She felt her face get hot but refused to care. "Yes."

A grin lifted the corners of his mouth. "Good."

It was sexy and wicked and had her squeezing her thighs together to relieve the ache.

"We can save time by multi-tasking."

Then he took her hand and led her to the bathroom.

He was wrong, though, it didn't take fifteen minutes—it barely took five.

* * *

Shay ran the steamer over a dress to remove the wrinkles then slid it along the rack. She'd spent most of the day in the back of the store. They'd had several deliveries of clothing arrive the day before, and Jane wanted to get them out front as soon as possible, so Shay had spent all morning unpacking, hanging, steaming and pricing to get them ready.

She was kind of glad for the solitude. It meant she had uninterrupted time to relive her night *and* morning before Hugh had dropped her off at work with a deep, hot kiss and a rumbled, "Later, babe".

God, the man made her weak at the knees and totally destroyed her ability to think clearly whenever he touched her. She'd never felt anything like it. The energy between them felt almost electric.

She'd watched him drive away and only realized when he was out of sight that they hadn't made any plans. Usually, that type of thing would have had her stressing out. Worried that she'd messed up, put off her date, somehow. But she didn't have to worry about that with Hugh. That wasn't what they were about. She knew he was attracted to her, and that was all that mattered. It was freeing. He didn't owe her anything, any explanations, and she didn't owe him a thing, either. She was fine with that, too. They were free to do as they pleased, and if they decided to get together again, that was more than fine with her, as well.

It was exciting. Exhilarating.

Fun.

Her grandmother's voice echoed through her head. *Carpe-that-fucking-Diem, Cupcake.* One of her gran's favorite sayings. One that never failed to make Shay laugh whenever she said it. And in this instance, Shay couldn't agree more.

A spark of pleasure shot through her lower belly as she remembered their shower that morning. His big, naked body all wet, muscles rippling as he moved closer, backing her into the corner. The way he'd looked when he dropped to his knees in front of her then lifted her thigh over his shoulder as if she weighed nothing. The way he buried his face between her legs…

Her phone started ringing, startling her from her daydream.

Flicking off the steamer, she grabbed her bag from the small table where they ate their lunch and rummaged around until she found her phone. She checked the screen, and her stomach dropped to the floor.

Mom.

Alice Freestone was the kind of woman who followed the party, regardless of her responsibilities—and Shay had found out at a very young age, that included her daughter—going wherever it took her. She only had one prerequisite—that someone else was paying. In between parties, or guys willing to pay her way, she liked to play the doting mother. It was all an act, of course, and Shay's mother had never been a great actress.

She stared at the screen until the phone finally stopped ringing. Guilt niggled, stirring up that edgy feeling she got whenever her mother surfaced.

Dammit.

She went to shove her phone back into her bag when it started up again. She'd keep calling until Shay answered. Her mother was persistent, which was how she'd secured so many men with bulging bank accounts over the years. Unfortunately, or fortunately, depending on who she'd been seeing at the time, her mother got bored easily and would move on to her next conquest quickly, and if not, they eventually saw through her and ended the relationship.

In-between men, she came to Shay.

As much as she wanted to turn off her phone and pretend her mother hadn't called, this *was* her mother, and no matter how many times she hurt Shay and let her down, she couldn't just ignore the woman.

Shay put the phone to her ear. "Hi, Mom."

"Sugar Angel! It's so good to hear your voice."

Her heart squeezed. When Shay was young, she'd craved the sound of her mother's voice, had prayed every night for a call, a letter, anything. "It's good to hear yours, as well. It's been a while."

Her mother was quiet a second then cleared her throat. "Don't be like that, Shay Shay. You know I lead a busy life."

Shay could hear her mother taking a drag of her cigarette. A habit she'd had as long as Shay could remember.

"That's why I'm calling, actually. I'm planning on paying you a visit. Thought you might put your mom up for a few nights. What do you say, honey?"

She wanted to say *no*. She wanted to hang up the phone and convince herself the conversation never happened. Guilt shot though her again. "When are you coming?"

"Oh, baby, you won't regret it. We'll have so much fun!" Another deep drag of her smoke. "I'll be there tomorrow evening. Cook something nice, and we'll eat together."

Shay slumped back onto a chair. "Sounds good." *Sounds terrible.*

"Okay, I gotta go. See you tomorrow, honey."

Then the phone went dead.

Wonderful. A few nights could mean anything. Once she'd said she was coming for a *few nights* and had stayed two months. She'd also cleaned out Shay's wallet before she left. Neither of them had ever mentioned it. It was easier to lose the money than confront her mother and listen to the woman's vitriol. Shay hated it when they fought. The guilt always ate at her during the months of silence in between visits.

Not that it bothered her mother. She'd had years of practice at pretending Shay didn't exist.

"Mommy, I don't feel so good."

"Now you hush. I don't want to hear any of your complaining. Mommy's gonna be busy with her new friend for a while." Gripping Shay's arm, she dragged her to her room at the end of the hall. *"You stay in here 'til I say you can come out."* She shoved Shay inside. *"Not a sound out of you, you hear me?"*

Shay's tummy rumbled. "I think I need my dinner."

"It won't hurt you to miss a meal or two, not going by the looks of you. Now remember…not a sound."

Shay bit her lip, holding back her tears. Mommy didn't like it when she cried.

Then the door was slammed shut and Shay was all alone…

Shay sucked in a breath, a shudder moving through her.

Don't go there.

She tried her best not to think about that time in her life, but the memories dogged her harder when her mother called or showed up.

Then another thought occurred to her, one that had her belly sinking like a stone. This new development would pretty much end things with Hugh. He wouldn't be able to come to her place, and even if she wanted to go to his, she'd have to take a million busses to get there, since he lived so far away.

Dragging herself out of the chair, she got back to work and tried not to think about it—her mom coming or the end of her short affair with Hugh.

* * *

The rest of the day passed without any more drama. She usually worked 'til two, but Jane had a dentist appointment, so Shay stayed until six and closed up, then headed home. Which meant she'd be pushing it to get the website design she was working on for her client finished in time.

The lights were on at the trailer park when she got there, all colorful and cheerful. The opposite of how she was currently feeling. She waved to Harold, who was sitting outside his army-green double wide when she walked past. He flicked up his fingers in return. Her grandmother had never said, but Shay knew they'd had a secret relationship for years. The pair had been thick as thieves, and of course, there was the fact she'd heard her gran sneak in and out of the trailer at all hours on a regular basis. And on several occasions, Shay had actually gotten up and watched her tap on his door in the middle of the night.

Why they chose to keep it a secret, she had no idea. She'd tried to broach the subject once, and her gran had shut her down instantly, laughing it off and mumbling something about Harold and their weekly poker games...

Oh, God, she hadn't meant...

Ew!

But then maybe Shay wasn't so different from her free-spirited grandmother, after all. Her gran had wanted excitement and exhilaration without the commitment. She'd definitely lived life to the fullest. Shay had never met her grandfather—he'd left before Shay had been born— but she knew her gran had loved him like crazy, that when he'd walked out on her, it broke her heart. Maybe her gran had been hurt one time too many, as well, had given up on unconditional love and commitment, as Shay had?

Harold wasn't her grandmother's great love, she'd already had that and had lost it—but Gran and Harold had each given the other something they'd both needed. Though it was kind of hard to imagine surly old Harold Harper stirring those kinds of feelings in anyone, let alone Shay's sweet, fun-loving grandmother.

She tapped on Edna's door, and a second later, it opened and Rocky was thrust out, then Edna shuffled back to her armchair in front of the TV. *The Price is Right* was blaring in the background. Edna hated being disturbed during her programs. Shay took out the dog, waited for him to do his business then carried him back inside, putting him on his doggy bed. Then, after filling Rocky's bowl with fresh water, she grabbed one of the meals she'd made Edna the week before out of the freezer and put it in the microwave to heat while Shay tidied the bench and did the few dishes that were there. After plating up Edna's dinner, Shay filled a glass with iced tea and served it up on her dinner tray.

Edna didn't take her eyes off the TV all through this, but she did pat Shay's hand when she slid the tray close.

Shay left her to it and headed to her own trailer. After a quick shower, she pulled on a pair of yoga pants and her faded Hello Kitty tank, and got her own dinner underway. Usually, she loved to cook, but tonight, her heart wasn't in it. She threw on some pasta and warmed up half a jar of store-bought sauce. She'd just tipped the noodles in the colander to drain when her phone rang.

She smiled to herself when she saw who it was. "You've finally come up for air."

"Har-har," Kayla grumbled down the line.

"What's up?"

Her best friend was quiet a few seconds then sniffed loudly. "It's over."

Shay sat on the couch. "Oh, honey. What happened?"

"The usual. He says jump, and I'm supposed to say 'how high'." She blew her nose loudly. "Well, screw that. I'm done with James. In fact, I'm done with all men, forever." She went quiet again. "I'm sorry I've been MIA this last week. I've been a shitty friend."

"Don't be silly. You're not a shitty friend. You were just temporarily diverted by the promise of frequent, non-self-induced orgasms." She knew the feeling all too well. "Let's have dinner. We can tear the jerk to shreds. I'm working tomorrow, but I can do Sunday night?"

Her friend sniffed again, followed with a watery chuckle. "Can we go to my favorite Italian place?"

As bad as she felt for her friend, Shay was glad to have her back. And certainly Kayla deserved better than James. "Where else would we go?"

"Excellent," she whispered.

They talked for a little longer, until Kayla's takeout arrived, then after promising to text her over the weekend, Shay ended the call. She was just about to put the phone down when it beeped. A text. She quickly checked it, butterflies kicking up a little dance in her belly. Hugh had grabbed her phone before he'd left and had added his number to her list of contacts, doing the same to his. No, they couldn't carry on with their affair with her mother coming, but one more night would be nice. She checked who it was, and the butterflies dive-bombed to their deaths in a screaming heap.

Travis: *Call me, Shay. Please?*

She didn't know what else she could say to him. She'd told him every way she knew how to leave her alone, that it was over. Why was he still pursuing this?

Throwing her phone on the couch beside her, she fired up her laptop so she could work on the website while she ate.

She planned to enjoy her last night of peace and quiet, even if she was spending it alone. Her mother would arrive tomorrow, like the tornado she was, doing what she usually did—blowing in then blowing out, leaving wreckage in her wake.

Chapter Nine

Joe kept watch while Hugh picked the lock on the Mercedes. Adam was waiting at the garage, ready to make quick work of the VIN plates, switching them out with fresh ones. Hell of a way to spend a Saturday night. Yeah, he could think of something else he'd rather be doing, someone else he'd rather be spending it with.

It'd been two nights since he'd seen Shay. Two nights that he'd gone without the taste of her on his tongue, and he was fucking ravenous.

He shut those thoughts down fast and returned his focus to what it should be on, cracking this damn lock...

Joe slammed into him, shoving him down beside the car. Lifting two fingers, his brother motioned to the opposite side of the parking lot. It was badly lit, and the car was parked in the far corner. Joe had spent the last couple weeks scoping it out, making sure their mark would be here in his usual spot. From years of doing this shit, they knew how to find security camera blind spots, made sure they had guard rotation schedules down. But they couldn't be one hundred percent sure, either. Hugh tugged the hood of his black sweatshirt lower, making sure his face was still completely covered, then lifted his head and peered through the side windows. A security guard stood in front of the building. He was on his phone, looked edgy, scanning the lot while he talked. When he finally disconnected, he pulled out his flashlight and started doing a sweep of the lot.

"Shit," Joe murmured beside him.

They both hunkered down, which wasn't easy or comfortable, considering the size of both of them. All they could do now was sit tight and hope like hell the guard going for a midnight stroll didn't find them, or the owner of the car didn't come back before they got the hell out of there.

The guard's boots scraped against the asphalt. He was close. The guy stopped, the beam of the flashlight lit up their corner for several seconds, then it was gone, and he was heading back to the building's entrance. Too damn close. Beside Hugh, Joe released a shuddery breath…

Hugh's phone suddenly made a series of loud beeps. A text message.

Fuck. He had the volume set at its highest, so he could hear it over the noise in the garage, which meant the guard had to have heard it ring out loud and clear. He grabbed for it in his pocket to turn it off. Joe tensed at his side, cursing under his breath.

"On three," Hugh whispered.

There was another scrape against the asphalt; the guard was heading back in their direction.

"Two…three."

They both shot to their feet and propelled themselves at the chain-link fence, were up and over in a heartbeat. The guard yelled behind them as they took off down the street. Hugh took the first alley they came to and dragged off his sweatshirt, shoving it into a dumpster. Joe did the same, and they jogged through to the next street, slowing their pace to a stroll as soon as they were back in the open.

"You left your motherfucking phone on?" Joe panted beside him.

Shit. He had. He'd never done that before. But when he'd texted Shay earlier to see if she wanted to hook up later…

Fuck. He couldn't believe he hadn't switched his phone off, that he'd made such a stupid mistake.

They made their way back to Hugh's truck in silence. He shoved his hand through his hair. Goddammit. No way they could take the Merc now. The guard was probably on the phone to the cops already.

When they reached his truck, Joe shoved him. "What the hell is wrong with you?"

Hugh kept his mouth shut. He was in the wrong, and they both knew it.

His brother planted his hands on his hips and stared at Hugh in disbelief. "It was her, wasn't it? You were waiting to hear from that redhead!"

When Hugh didn't answer right away, Joe's face went from disbelief to stone cold.

"We could have been caught. This could have blown up in our faces because you've got a hard-on over some random pussy?"

Hugh clenched his jaw, hard enough his teeth ached, to stop himself from saying something he couldn't take back. Kept his arms crossed firmly over his chest, so he didn't reach out and clock the bastard for speaking about her like that. Which was screwed up, since that's exactly what she was supposed to be. Only she wasn't. "I made a mistake," he gritted out.

"Yeah, seems you're making a few of those lately." Joe yanked open the door and climbed into the truck, slamming it shut after him.

Shit.

The drive to the garage was quiet. His brother was pissed. When that happened, he let you know all about it then stewed in silence—but never very long. Joe could never keep his trap shut for long periods of time. Hugh pulled up in front of the garage, and the door slid open. Adam stood there, expecting one of them to be following, driving the Merc, and when they both climbed out, no fucking car, both brows shot up.

Joe strode in, pointing a finger in Hugh's direction. "Ask this dickhead why we don't have a car."

His brother was obviously not in the silent mood anymore.

Adam leaned against the wall. "Shit, what now?"

"He didn't turn off his fucking phone," Joe yelled.

Adam frowned. "You were nearly caught?"

Hugh stared his brother down. "There was a guard."

Adam rubbed his palms against his eyes. "How the hell could you forget?"

"Car Thievery 101: Never leave your goddamn phone on," Joe barked. "It's a no-brainer. Though, I can see why you'd forget, since your thinking with the little head these days."

"No one got caught." Hugh kept his temper on lockdown, which was not easy right then.

"He was waiting for a call from the redhead," Joe added, un-fucking-helpfully.

Adam shoved a hand in his dark hair. "Jesus Christ. You've got to be kidding me. Tail? You were thinking about a woman while you were boosting a car?"

Hugh clenched and unclenched his fists. "Won't happen again."

"You sure about that?" Joe asked.

Hugh's temper slipped its reins. "I've boosted more cars than the pair of you put together, and you're questioning me? Don't need this shit. Wasn't for me, little brother, Al would own your ass, and you'd still be scraping together nickels and dimes to pay off that asshole. Wasn't for me, we wouldn't be only eight cars away from getting free of the fucking prick." *Wasn't for me, we wouldn't be in this mess in the first place.*

And yeah, it was still up in the air with Al going back on his word, but the rest? The rest was true, and Joe knew it. As for Adam, he helped them because he was a good friend, and because he wanted to. Enjoyed the rush or some shit. *Highly appreciated* but totally fucked up.

The pair of them stared at him tight jawed.

"Nothing to say all of a sudden?" he fired at them. "Yeah, didn't think so." Then he walked out, got in his truck and got the hell out of there. He was being an asshole. He knew it. What he'd done was stupid, total amateur hour. But right then, he didn't give a damn. He was so sick of this shit, fucking exhausted.

When he stopped at a set of streetlights, he pulled out his phone and checked his message.

Shay: *Sorry. Can't tonight.*

His fingers tightened around the phone. Not the answer he was hoping for, not the way he was feeling right then. He fired off a quick answer: *U sure?*

Her answer was almost instantaneous: *My mom's staying with me. First night.*

Her mom? Christ.

Hugh: *Tomorrow?*

Shay: *Going out with a friend.*

Hugh: *After?*

He sounded desperate, but that was because he damn well was. A car horn blared loudly behind him. He hadn't even noticed the lights had changed. Planting his foot, he headed for home. Her return message came through as he was pulling up outside his place.

Shay: *Um…maybe? Logistics might be kinda hard though.*

He stared at the screen. Something was hard, all right, painfully so, and it had nothing to do with goddamn logistics.

Hugh: *Two nights too long babe.*

Shay: *For me too.*

His cock started to ache in his jeans.

Hugh: *I'll sort something.*

The first thing that needed sorting was her lack of wheels. It'd make this thing a hell of a lot easier if she could come to his place, as well, especially with her mother there for however long.

Shay: *K. Night, Hugh.*

Hugh: *Night, princess.*

He shoved open the truck door and made his way inside. After what happened tonight, he should be losing her number, should be back in his truck, off to some bar to work off the lust thrumming through his veins with some faceless, nameless woman. A woman he could easily forget the next day. A woman who wouldn't bury herself under his skin and have him making stupid mistakes. But he couldn't do it. The idea of sleeping with someone else didn't do a damn thing for him. The only way he was getting off tonight was in his own fist, thinking about Shay. All sweet and curvy and warm, curled up in bed in her cute PJs, in her cute fucking trailer.

Jesus.

* * *

Hugh closed the hood on the Honda, wiped his hands and shoved the rag in his back pocket. It wasn't much, one of their old loaners. It'd been parked up a few months, but it hadn't taken much to get it back on the road. A new set of tires and a good service and she was good to go.

Now he just had to get Shay to agree to take it. He didn't know her that well, but from what he'd seen, and despite what she said about herself, she was independent and self-sufficient. She was working three jobs with her graphic design stuff thrown in the mix, and he doubted she'd just happily take the car from him without a fight. He'd have to get creative to get her to agree.

He locked the car and shoved the keys into his pocket. As much as he wanted to stay tucked away back here behind the garage, he was shit out of luck. He'd been there since 5:00 a.m., after tossing and turning all damn night. Joe either hadn't heard him arrive from his apartment above the garage or was ignoring him, because he hadn't seen his brother. Either way worked for Hugh. But his reprieve was over. Adam had arrived a short time ago and had opened the front doors.

Hugh headed around the side of the building and in through the front. His friend gave him a chin lift when he walked in then turned back to the car he was working on. Adam didn't ask about the Honda or why Hugh was working on it. Thank Christ. No way did he want to answer those questions, not after last night. He doubted they'd even know it was missing once he took it. He scanned the room; his brother was nowhere to be seen.

"Where's Joe?"

Adam shrugged. "No idea. Wasn't here when I opened up." His friend rubbed his whiskered jaw, stared at Hugh for several seconds. "Look…" He threw up his hands. "I *may* have overreacted a teeny bit last night. I know you, more than anyone, have busted your balls to get outta this shit. I just don't want any of us to be sitting behind bars before we finally are."

They'd been friends since high school. Were boosting cars together when they were teenagers, low on cash—and in Hugh's case, with a family to feed and mortgage payments to make. The guy didn't need to be caught up in this. He could have walked away, but the crazy son-of-a-bitch had signed up to help without batting an eyelid. They were like brothers, and he hadn't hesitated to help his brother out of a bind.

Hugh often wondered how many times Adam regretted that decision, especially after the stupid shit Hugh had pulled last night. "You and me both." He rubbed the back of his neck. "And you weren't overreacting."

Adam grinned. "Tell me you at least got laid after all that."

Hugh gave him a flat stare.

His friend clapped him on the shoulder and chuckled. "Struck out, huh? And here I was last night with one to spare."

Shaking his head, Hugh punched Adam in the shoulder. "Dick."

"It certainly got a workout with the two I had in my bed."

"Jesus, you're an asshole."

"Got some of that action, too."

"How the hell do you get all these women to trail around after you? Can't be your winning personality." Women flocked to the guy. Hugh doubted Adam spent many nights alone. Though, Hugh knew that was the point, what drove him out to the clubs and bars every night in the first place. The guy had his own demons to deal with. Now, thanks to Hugh's old man and Hugh's failure to protect his family from the waste of space, Adam had taken on theirs, as well.

"And that, my friend, is why you spent your night alone, while I had a couple honeys in my bed, begging to fulfill all my dirty fantasies." He shrugged. "It's a gift."

"You must be running low by now. How many dirty fantasies can one man have?"

Adam chuckled. "There are infinite possibilities."

Hugh opened his mouth to answer when a car drove in. Al's car. "Shit."

A week had come and gone since Don gave them Al's ultimatum. It had only been a matter of time before the old bastard decided to pay them a visit. Don jumped out and opened the back door. Al climbed out, looking skinny, pale and kinda frail. Hugh glanced at Adam, seeing the same thought running through his friend's head.

The rumors were true.

Al was sick. Really sick.

But even sick, an air of authority radiated from the guy. He still had that arrogant expression on his smug face, and despite his frail appearance, carried himself like the cocksure bastard he was.

"Boys," he said as he approached. "I can see how excited you are to see me." Don took position beside his boss, a smirk on his stupid-looking face.

"We weren't expecting you," Adam said.

"Of course you were." Al grinned. "Let's cut to the chase, shall we? I think we make great business partners, and I'd hate to see that partnership dissolve when there's a lot more money to be made. Once you've paid off your debt, you'll be getting a cut. A very generous one."

Hugh crossed his arms. "Not interested."

The old bastard's gaze sharpened, locking onto Hugh. Hugh stared back. He wasn't backing down on this. Being a professional car thief wasn't something he aspired to be, despite his past and the stupid mistakes he'd made as a kid. Mistakes that had brought him to this very point. He wanted out, but if Al had his way, this is where they'd all stay.

Screw that.

"You're making the wrong decision," Al said, expression cold, blank.

"We disagree," Adam answered.

Al stared at them. "I see." His fingers curled into fists. "Well, thank you for your time. I have to be going. We'll talk again soon, though." Then he turned, got back in his car and left.

Adam watched the car roll out. "I'd say negotiations are about to start."

They'd learned first-hand the way Al conducted negotiations.

They were fucked.

Chapter Ten

Kayla stumbled, and Shay reached out to steady her friend before she fell on her butt. Things were getting messy. They'd both had too much to drink. Well, she hadn't had as much as Kayla, but then, it didn't take as much for Shay to get tipsy. She'd always been a lightweight when it came to alcohol.

The night had started off great, gone really well until the fourth round of Tequila Sunrises, then things had taken a turn for the worse. She'd had to wrestle the phone out of Kayla's hand several times. In her intoxicated state, her friend had decided she needed to call James. He apparently *needed* to know how much she loved him…was positive the reason they broke up for the third time was because she hadn't expressed her feelings for him enough.

The real reason they kept breaking up was that James was an A-1 jerk. End of story.

Shay opened the door of the taxi and ushered her friend in. "Let's get you home, honey."

Kayla crawled inside, collapsing on her belly, butt in the air.

"You have to sit up. Come on." Shay grabbed her friend under the armpits, stumbling a little when she leaned in to drag Kayla into a sitting position.

Climbing in after her, Shay secured her friends seatbelt before

Kayla did another face-plant then glanced at the driver, who was now scowling at them, and gave him Kayla's address.

"If she pukes in my cab, the fees double."

"She won't." *She better not.* Shay could barely afford the ride as it was.

Kayla reached out and poked Shay in the side of the face to get her attention. "He doesn't know, Shay. I need to tell him I love him. I *neeeed* to."

"I know, honey."

After taking the phone off Kayla for the third time, Shay had stolen the battery out of it while Kayla wasn't looking. She would thank Shay in the morning. Kayla rested her head on Shay's shoulder, and a second later, she was passed out. Wonderful.

Shay managed to rouse her long enough to get her into her place. Kayla's roommate was thankfully home, and the two of them got her into bed. Shay handed over Kayla's phone and battery with strict instructions not to let her have it until the morning and then headed for home.

The trailer was dark when they pulled up outside. Her mom must be in bed. Something about the intense darkness beyond the windows made Shay freeze...had her weak, alcohol-addled mind filling with a memory she never allowed herself to revisit.

Mom forgot to pay the electricity again. Shay huddled under her blanket on their old couch. She hated the dark, especially when she was home alone. She gripped the flashlight tighter, whimpering when it started to flicker, knowing the batteries were about to run out. This was the second night her mommy had stayed away. Shay's tummy rumbled, and she hugged herself to stop the ache. A shadow moved

116

outside the window. It was just the trees, she knew it was, but it still scared her. Clutching her teddy tight, she prayed her mommy would hurry up and come home, and that morning would come fast…

"You all right?" the driver asked impatiently.

"Oh…! Yes. I'm fine. Sorry." She paid him then climbed out, letting the memory fade, locking it away with the rest.

She headed to the trailer, glad her mother was asleep. She couldn't deal with another one of her tirades tonight. Her mom was unhappy, *extremely* unhappy, which was common on these visits. When she was like this, she wasn't satisfied until everyone around her was just as miserable as she was. She accomplished this by being nasty, and, at times, cruel. She put Shay down constantly, whenever the opportunity presented itself.

Another reason to end things with Hugh—she'd be humiliated if her mother spoke to her that way in front of him. The idea of the two of them in the same room was enough to give Shay hives.

Thankfully, she didn't have to worry about that happening. Hugh said he'd work something out so they could get together after she'd been out, but she hadn't heard from him all evening. His text message: *Two nights, too long*, though short, was to the point and had triggered some serious happy tingles. Now she felt disappointed. Disappointed, tipsy and because she was thinking of Hugh, aroused.

Dammit.

She unlocked the door as quietly as she could and tiptoed inside. The smell of cigarette smoke hit her first, which annoyed the crap out of her. She'd told her mom she couldn't smoke inside. But then her mother did what she wanted when she wanted. That's how it had always been. Loaded with bags, she'd arrived the day before as she'd promised. And after she'd found and opened the cheap wine Shay had bought for cooking, she'd plonked her butt on the couch and proceeded to drink the whole thing until she passed out. So much for their dinner together.

Since her mother had taken the bedroom, Shay flicked on the light and stared at the couch. She'd slept on the foldout for years while she'd lived with her grandmother, before she'd gone to college. Right then, she missed her gran more than she ever had.

Dumping her bag on the counter, she grabbed a bottle of water from the fridge, which was when she spotted a note stuck to the front of the refrigerator door. It was held on by one of the hula girl magnets her gran had bought on her honeymoon to Hawaii. They were faded and cracked. She'd loved them.

Staying with a friend. See you tomorrow.

Mom.

A friend?

She checked the bedroom, and sure enough, it was empty. She'd never heard of a friend, let alone met any of them. Still, it didn't come as a surprise; her mom had trouble sitting still. She'd probably met some random guy while Shay was at work. Wouldn't be the first time. She'd be after her next meal ticket. But Shay refused to lay awake all night worrying. She'd spent far too many nights doing that to last her a lifetime.

The sound of a car pulling up outside her trailer was loud in the silence, and she stiffened. God, had her mother come home after all? Did she have someone with her? Shay headed to the door and pulled back the faded floral curtain covering the small window, squinting into the darkness to get a better look. She didn't recognize car.

But then the door was shoved open, and Hugh's huge frame unfolded from the driver's side.

Her heart kicked into gear as she gripped the door handle and pulled it open. She took the first step and gave him a little wave. The urge to run at him and jump into his arms was almost too hard to contain. He was just such a welcome sight after the last couple of days.

"It's you," she said stupidly.

He grinned. "Looks like it." His gaze moved over her, lingering on key areas before lifting to meet her eyes. "You look hot, princess."

She had on dark jeans, platform heels and a fifties-style baby-doll top with a sweetheart neckline. She'd say it was more a cutesy look than hot, but hey, she'd take it. "What are you doing here?"

His eyebrows lifted, gaze dropping to her lips.

Oh. She felt her face heat. "I wasn't expecting you."

"Said I'd sort something. Came to pick you up…"

She shook her head. "My mom…well, she's not actually here tonight." Her heart started doing some serious fluttering. "Not back 'til tomorrow."

He grinned. "Perfect." Shutting the car door, he headed her way, but before he reached her he tossed the keys in his hand toward her.

Her hand lifted automatically, catching them.

"Yours," he said when he stopped in front of her.

"What?"

"The car. It's yours."

She blinked up at him, trying to clear her fuzzy brain. *What?* He couldn't be serious. She couldn't afford a car. "What do you mean, *mine?* I don't have money for a new car."

"Don't want your money, princess." His hands went to her hips, and he gave her a squeeze. "Car's yours," he said again, as if he'd given her a frickin' donut and not a *whole car.* "You gonna let me in?"

She stepped back, and he kept coming, until they moved inside and her back met the kitchen counter.

"Um, Hugh. I can't accept a car from you."

He stared down at her. "Why not?"

"Why not?" she sputtered.

"Yeah."

"Because it's a car."

"Think we've established that."

She tilted her head back, lifting her hands to his chest. The firm muscle flexed under her palms, and she sighed. The man truly was scrumptious. He grinned. Oh wow…

His brows lifted a little. "So you'll take it?"

"What?"

He grinned wider. Crap. *Focus!* She shook her head, forcing her brain back to the conversation at hand.

"You can't just give me a car. That's…it's…well, it's nuts."

"You need one?"

"That's…that's not the point."

He chuckled. Gave her another squeeze. "It's not a big deal. It's our old loaner. We were gonna junk it cause none of us could be bothered fixin' it. I fixed it today. It'll run sweet until you're ready to upgrade."

It was a nice thing to do, a really nice thing to do, but she couldn't accept it. That wasn't what they were about. She flexed her fingers against his pecs and tried to suppress the shiver that moved through her. "It's really sweet of you, and I appreciate it. I do. But I can't accept it. It's just too much." She ran her hands over his pecs, down to his abs and back up, watching her hands as they moved over him. "God, you're big."

He chuckled. "You drunk?"

She shook her head. "Just tipsy."

"You get horny when you're tipsy?"

She stared up at him, mouth dropping open. Dear lord, the things he said. "What…? No. I'm not…" She couldn't make herself say it.

His soft brown eyes transformed, gaze sharpening, a determined expression coming over his face. Then he rubbed his hips against hers, and she nearly moaned out loud when she felt his erection against her belly.

"No?"

Yes! But horny didn't quite cover how she was feeling in that moment. Still, she couldn't *say it.* "No."

His nostrils flared, and he licked his lower lip before a sexy, extremely dirty grin lifted the corners of his mouth.

Eeek!

Hugh grinned down at Shay. She was a sweet, soft, little armful, and he'd thought about nothing else but the woman currently pressed up against him—lying through her teeth.

She was as hot for him as he was for her.

After last night, nearly getting caught, he knew he shouldn't be there—letting her get in his head like this was stupid, reckless. He had so much shit raining down on him, he was close to suffocating. But for some messed-up reason, he couldn't stay away. And the thought of her walking to the bus stop in the middle of the goddamn night, unprotected, had been driving him bat-shit crazy since she told him how she made it to work and back. She could refuse to take the car all she liked, but it was going to happen. By the time he walked out of here, Shay would have agreed, happily, to take the damn thing off his hands.

She licked her lips and blinked up at him several times in a way that made him want to savage that innocent-looking mouth, made him want to push her to her knees and watch those pretty eyes go wide when he slid his hard cock into her mouth.

His thoughts scattered when she took his hand in hers—until she placed the keys back in his palm.

"It's too much, Hugh."

Yeah, he liked it when she said his name. A lot. He also noticed she'd changed the subject back to the car, away from the way she was clenching her thighs together. "That the answer you're gonna stick with?"

Her lips were slightly parted, breath coming faster, sexy little pants forcing her tits against his abs. "Yes."

"Stubborn," he muttered.

Her spine straightened, which just pushed her closer. "I am not."

"Yeah, you are." He tucked her hair behind her ear. "But I like it, makes changing your mind a fuck of a lot more fun."

Her jaw tightened. *Cute* as *fuck*.

"I'm not changing my mind."

Yeah, she was, she just didn't know it yet. He stepped away, and she watched, eyes wary, throwing off a shit ton of attitude. So much for having to fake it. That was cute, as well, kind of like a pissed-off kitten. He went to the couch in the small living space and sat down. "So you wanna watch some TV?"

The attitude drained away, and she frowned. He wanted to laugh at the confused look on her face. The woman couldn't maintain even a little bit of anger; it wasn't in her nature. Yeah, she got pissed when she needed to, but it wasn't her. Shay Freestone was sweetness—inside and out. She was also turned-way-the-hell-on and denying it.

She crossed her arms over her chest, pushing up all that soft, round flesh. "TV?"

His mouth went dry. "Yeah." He patted the couch beside him.

"Um…okay. Sure." She walked to the television, a slight wobble in her step, and bent over to turn it on. That full, round ass was now aimed at him, and the denim coving it hugged those sexy cheeks to perfection.

He reached down and adjusted his hard-on because it fucking ached. "Awesome."

She went back to the kitchen and opened the fridge. "Are you hungry? Would you like a drink? I'm going to have a sandwich."

"Yeah, I could eat. Beer if you have one?"

He watched her move around the small space. He liked watching her, the way she moved, the little noises she made while she worked. Everything about her drew him in a seriously big way.

She brought him a beer, handed him a cheese and ham then took a seat beside him. They ate in silence. It wasn't uncomfortable, but he could feel the tension between them, feel it building. Her face was flushed, and every now and then, she'd sneak a glance his way. She was waiting for him to make the first move. He grinned to himself. Shit, she was irresistible. Sexy and so sweet she gave him toothache. He got a kick out of just watching her eat, listening to more of her noises. The little moans she made with each mouthful.

When they finished, she took their plates to the kitchen and headed back to the couch, coming to a stop in front of him. "So, um…do you want to watch this?" The Discovery Channel was playing. "Or…?"

He lifted a foot, resting his boot on the coffee table, blocking the path to her seat. "I'm done watching TV, princess."

She looked down at him, brows raised in question. "You are?"

"I'm in the mood for something else."

Her eyes glazed over, and her hands fluttered around at her sides.

"Stand right there," he told her.

She sucked in a breath.

He took his time looking at her, letting his gaze travel over every soft curve. "Shirt off."

"My shirt…"

"Now, beautiful."

Her throat worked for a second, then she lifted her trembling hands and gripped the bottom of her shirt.

"That's it."

Slowly, she lifted it, revealing her breasts, beautifully encased in bright-pink lace. Then she pulled it up the rest of the way and off, letting it fall to the floor.

His cock surged behind his jeans painfully. "Bra," he murmured. "Take it off, let me see 'em, sweetheart."

She reached back and did as he asked, freeing her luscious tits, all creamy and smooth and full. Her nipples were stiff and pink, and he wanted that soft flesh in his hands, wanted to take it in his mouth now. But that wasn't happening, not yet. Her face was flushed, and her eyes were bright. So damn gorgeous. She was getting off on him telling her what to do bigtime, loving every damn minute.

"Turn around. Show me that ass." His voice was getting rougher every time he opened his mouth, with every pulse of his hard cock.

She gave him her back, and he wanted to grab her waist, yank her back and press his lips to that pretty spot at the small of her back, trail his tongue along the top of her ass, dip it down the crease. "Take off the pants…panties, too."

She took in a deep breath, kicked off her shoes then, sliding her thumbs in the sides of her underwear, pushed them down. Bending forward, she stepped out of them and gave him a spectacular view of her swollen, pink, juicy little pussy. *Jesus fucking Christ.*

Tugging open the button of his jeans, he dragged down the zipper, shoved the pants down his hips a little to free his cock. Grabbing a condom from his wallet, he quickly rolled it on.

"You turned on now, Shay?"

She shivered, a full-body shiver. "Y-yes."

Keeping his legs spread, he reached forward, grabbed her by the hips and got her to back up, nice and close. "Sit on my lap, slowly."

Her hands went to his knees, nails digging into the denim as she lowered herself. He fisted his cock with one hand, guiding her down with the other. When the head of his cock met her hot, slick flesh, she moaned in a way that made his balls draw up tight. How the hell was he going to hold out?

"That's it, sit down on my hard cock, take all of me inside that hot, little pussy."

When the head breached her tight opening, she gasped. He controlled her descent, keeping it painfully slow, torturing them both. Her head was tilted to the side, and he watched her face flush darker as she took each inch.

Nothing was hotter than the way she stretched around him, swallowing him in that tight grasp. When he was all the way in, he reached around and lifted each of her thighs over his, so she was wide open, feet dangling off the floor—fully under his control.

He wrapped an arm around her waist and held her down tight. He wasn't letting her move, no matter how much his balls ached, not until he got the answer he wanted. Sweat started to break out across his skin, the urge to lift her and slam her down on his cock damn near impossible to ignore, especially when she wriggled her lush ass.

"Hugh...please. I need...I need to move."

He slid a hand over her soft belly, her ribs, up to cup one full breast and squeezed, working and tugging her nipple. "No moving, not until I say so." He was goddamn thrilled when his voice came out more than a rough growl.

"But I..." She wriggled again. "I need you to...ahhh."

She moaned helplessly when he tugged harder on her nipple, his arm tightening around her hips to keep her immobile.

"Please, Hugh," she gasped.

He nearly gave in when she said his name in that needy voice. "You gonna take the car?"

"What? I-I…no."

She was flat-out panting now, every second he was inside her, she got hotter, tighter—shit, wetter.

"Then, no, I'm not moving. And neither are you."

"Y-you can't be serious."

"I get what I want, and what I want is for you to take the car."

She shook her head, red hair sliding over her bare back, making him want to fist it and pound into her until they both blew up.

"Stubborn."

Her hand moved down between her legs, and he felt her pussy tighten, which should be impossible. Jesus, it felt so good, his goddamn eyes rolled back in his head. He grabbed her wrist, pulling her fingers away from her slick, stiff, little clit.

"No you don't. You don't come 'til I say you can."

He felt her spasm around him, and he groaned. He gripped both her wrists in one of his hands, the other still massaging her breast. If she didn't give in soon, he was gonna blow; no way could he hold out much longer. He kissed and sucked lightly on her shoulder.

"You gonna take the car?"

"I…I…ahh, oh, *God*." She moaned then jerked in his arms.

And fuck him, she started coming, pussy gripping his cock, milking him without either one of them moving, clamping down on him so damn hard he struggled to drag in his next breath.

"Yes!" she cried out, rocking against him as best she could with the way he held her.

Jesus Christ.

"That's it, that's my girl." He hissed out a breath. "Pussy so greedy I don't even have to move, and you come for me." Then he snapped. Moving his hold to her hips, he yanked her down hard, slammed up into her, once, twice, a third time, and he came with a shout. So hard his fucking ears were ringing, and his limbs felt like Jell-O.

Shay slumped back, his cock still buried deep, all soft and sweet and sexy as hell.

"That's my girl," he rasped again, the words out of his mouth before he knew what he was saying. Words he shouldn't be saying but that felt right, more than right.

But she wasn't his girl; that option wasn't open to him, not until they found a way to get free and clear of the shit hanging around their necks. The way things were going, that might never happen. And even if they did? He was kidding himself if he thought he was good enough for Shay. He'd only let her down like he had his whole damn family.

"You're a sadist," she murmured.

He buried his nose in her hair, breathed her in, shut down his thoughts. He didn't want to think about any of that, not now. "You said yes."

She stilled. "No, I didn't."

"Yeah, you did. Shit, you screamed it, babe. If you don't use it now, you'll hurt my feelings." He'd also be royally pissed. He wanted her safe. "I'm doing it for purely selfish reasons," he said. "If I can't get to you, you've got a way to come to me when we wanna hook up."

She turned to him, skin pink, eyes glowing and gorgeous. "I don't know...it doesn't feel right..."

"It's really just a time-efficiency thing."

"You're very pushy."

"I am when I know I'm right."

"Hmm. Arrogant, too."

"Bend to my will already, woman. You can't win." He grinned. "Tell me you'll use it."

"Well." She screwed up her face, looking fucking adorable. "I suppose you make some sense."

"Of course I do."

"With my mom here, I thought we'd have to end this…what we're doing, but if I borrow your car…"

He gave her a squeeze. Like hell this was ending, not yet. No way. "Use the car."

She smiled. Bright. Beautiful. "Okay, just until we…until…" She stopped mid-sentence.

Until this is over. Jesus, he couldn't think about that, not now. "Good." He gave her ass a pat. "Now we've got that sorted, let me get rid of this rubber." He lifted her to her feet.

She turned to him, and her smile slipped slightly. "Are you going?"

He should, he should keep this thing sex only—sleepovers shouldn't come into it—but he'd enjoyed sleeping in her bed, having her pressed against him all night. "Climb into bed. I'll be there in a minute."

Then he strode to the bathroom before he pulled her in close, before he kissed her just for the hell of it, because he wanted to taste her. For no other reason than he couldn't think of doing anything else.

Shit.

Chapter Eleven

Shay woke to the sound of voices coming from the tiny living room beyond her bedroom door.

She grabbed her phone, checking the time. *8:30 a.m.*

Crap.

Shoving back the covers, she jolted into a sitting positon then scrambled out of bed. She groggily pulled on her robe, stumbled to the door, and yanked it open…

And ground to a screeching halt. All remnants of sleep vanished in an instant.

Hugh stood by the door. It was open, so he was either coming back inside the trailer or going out. Her guess? Making a hasty retreat if the expression on his face was any indication. He was staring at her mother, who was back and lounging on the couch, a cigarette in one hand and a cup of coffee in the other. He did not look happy.

Her mother looked rough, hair out to *there*, mascara smudged, still wearing her outfit from the night before. The ragged-edged, cutoff denim skirt she wore was heading into micro-mini territory, and the bright-pink tank she had on had the words *Daddy's Girl* stretched across her enhanced breasts. One of her boyfriends had paid for her boobs a few years ago, and not a day passed that she didn't have those things out on display.

Shay stepped farther into the room, dread swirling in her belly. "Mom, I ah…I wasn't expecting you home so early."

Her mom took a drag of her smoke and stubbed it out in one of the antique saucers left to Shay by her gran. It was from a tea set that had once belonged to her great grandmother. Her mom knew this, knew how precious it was to Shay.

"So I see." Her mother's gaze narrowed, slid back to Hugh. "She doesn't have any money; you know that, right?" She climbed to her feet, planting a hand on her hip.

Oh, God.

Pain shot through Shay's chest.

Hugh gave her body a sweep, but it wasn't in appreciation. Her mother was an attractive woman, and though her face showed signs of the hard life she'd chosen for herself, there was nothing wrong with her body, and she knew it. But the way Hugh was looking at her, you'd think she'd sprouted a third arm…from her forehead. "What the fuck did you just say?"

His voice was low, rough, and Shay shivered. He sounded angry. No, he sounded *pissed off.*

"Um…Hugh, maybe…"

"You're here, with her." Her mother cut her off, pointing a pink tipped finger at her only daughter, and Shay braced for what was coming. "You want something, why else would you be here? She doesn't have any money, she doesn't have jack shit if you want to know the truth. I love her to bits, but she's no supermodel. So why are you here?"

Oh, my God.

Her mom was a mean drunk, but hungover she hit a whole new level of ugly. Usually, though, she waited until company left before throwing the insults at Shay. "Mom…"

"No, Shay, someone's got to look out for you."

Since when? "Mom, please…"

"Guy like that has no reason to be with the likes of you. Jesus, look at yourself, girl." She shook her head. "He's after something."

"Are you fucking serious?" Hugh growled.

Shay quickly moved to him, put a hand to Hugh's stomach and pushed, trying to get him to take a step outside. The muscles clenched under her palm, but he didn't move, didn't budge. It was like trying to move a…mountain. A mountain man.

His hard gaze was fixed on her mother. She gave him another shove. Again, he didn't budge.

"Please," she whispered.

His brown-eyed gaze dropped to her, searching her features. A second later, jaw tight, he gave her a subtle nod and stepped back.

"Thank you," she whispered and pulled the door shut behind her. "I-I'm sorry about that, she's…she's…" She had no words to describe what her mother was.

"A bitch?" Hugh finished for her.

Obviously, he didn't have the same trouble. "She's hungover. She's not herself when she's been drinking."

He just stared at her, not commenting, which said it all, really. She wasn't fooling anyone, least of all Hugh.

"Look, I gotta go." He didn't look overly happy, but then he lifted a hand and tucked a strand of hair behind her ear.

She probably had serious bed-head going on.

"Okay." That feeling, the one that hit whenever he was leaving, bunched tight in her belly. She ignored it and forced a smile.

He shoved a hand into his pocket and pulled out the car keys he'd tried to give her last night and held them out. "Come to my place tonight. I'll text you the address."

The happiness that lit her up inside just because he asked her to go to his house was way off the charts. Enough that it freaked her the heck out. Made her pause before jumping. Made her want to take a step back. "I don't know." She bit her lip. "Maybe we should slow things down."

"Why?"

"I don't know…"

He tilted his chin toward the trailer. "Don't let her get in your head."

But her mother's words had gotten to her. No, she didn't think he had some nefarious plan to steal her minimal possessions out from under her, but her mother was right about one thing. Hugh could have anyone he chose. Why he chose to spend time with her, she had no clue. What they were doing would come to an end, and soon. It was what she wanted. What they both wanted. She had to remember that.

"It's not about my mother," she lied. "I just thought…"

"Don't think. I want you. You want me. It's as simple and as complicated as that."

Was it? He obviously wasn't concerned about messy emotions. Of course he wasn't. That's not the way he saw her. She wasn't a threat to his heart. She just had to make sure Hugh didn't become a threat to hers. "Okay."

His hands slid into her hair either side of her face. "Don't overanalyze this, Shay. Don't over think it. You like what we do together?"

"Yes," she rasped, throat suddenly dry.

"Me, too. Let's enjoy it while it lasts, yeah?"

While it lasts. The knot in her stomach became impossibly tight. *This is what you want. No strings. No commitment.* "Yes," she forced out.

What on earth is wrong with me?

"Good." His voice dropped lower. "Now press those curves up against me, and give me a goodbye kiss."

She did what he asked, and he kissed her in a way he never had before, slow and sweet. It was intoxicating. He touched his mouth against hers one last time then ran his nose along hers before lifting his head. She felt a little wobbly on her feet when he finally pulled away.

"We good?" he asked.

She smiled. "Yes."

Edna's door squeaked open behind her, and Shay jumped.

"Rocky! *Shoot.* I completely forgot."

Hugh gave her a squeeze. "I took care of it."

Shay's mouth dropped open. "You what?"

"I turned off your alarm. Looked like you needed the sleep."

"You took Rocky for his walkies?"

Lines crinkled the corners of his eyes. "Yeah."

Wow. That was a really nice thing to do. Really nice. "You didn't need to do that."

He shrugged.

"Catch ya on the flipside, Hugh," Edna called from her door.

Hugh's smile got bigger. "Bye, Edna." Then he leaned in and kissed her one last time. "Later."

She watched him walk away. So caught up ogling him, the way that large body moved, the way his jeans hugged his butt just right, that she only remembered he didn't have his truck when a taxi pulled up outside the trailer park, and Hugh climbed inside.

He'd given her a car to use. So they could spend more time together…

She turned away quickly before she stood there and watched him go like some pining idiot.

Her mother coughed from Shay's now-open trailer door, the kind of smoker's cough that cracked like a whip, making her wince.

"You're playing with fire, girl. He's using you."

She didn't know why she let her mother's words get to her, why they stung so damn much. She wasn't sure if it was because her mom thought so little of her, or if it was because she was kind of right. Shay was playing with fire. And she couldn't help but wonder…if Hugh was the type of guy who had committed relationships, would she be the girl he would have chosen?

Shay turned to her mother, who was watching Shay closely, expression hard.

"I'm not talking about this with you," Shay said.

Her mom eyed Shay over the rim of her coffee cup, taking her in from head to toe, and Shay knew nothing would stop her from spewing her poison. "No man's going to stick with a chunky girl. I've told you that a hundred times. Men want a woman who looks good on their arm.

He doesn't give a rat's ass about the fancy education your grandmother shelled out for. Or the stuck-up way you talk because of it. You've got a pretty face, baby, but you're never going to find the right kind of guy unless you take care of yourself. No man's going to keep you around, let alone show you off when you look like a slob. Remember that."

Shay stood there, rooted to the spot, her mother's words hitting with agonizing accuracy, one after the other. Until they twisted, began to merge with what Travis had said to her the other night outside Woody's. They were different words than the ones her mother had just cruelly flung at her, but they amounted to the same thing.

"No man's going to stick around if she's a raging bitch, either," Edna said from her doorway, eyes locked on her mother. "I take it you're still single, Alice?"

Her mother's eyes narrowed, but she wisely kept her mouth shut and disappeared back inside the trailer, slamming the door shut behind her. Great. Now mean would become out-and-out nasty. Her mother was the queen of backhanded compliments, but when she was like this, she didn't even try to veil them, she just let the insults fly.

"Don't listen to her, girl. I know she's your mother, but she's got a cruel streak a mile wide. That young man thinks a lot of you. Why else would he come over here and help an old woman out? He didn't need to do that." She pointed to the Honda parked outside her place. "Or bring that for you." She patted Rocky. "Your mother's just pissed off her life didn't go the way she wanted. Angry as hell that the men she digs her claw into get sick of her skinny ass as soon as she opens her big mouth. She's just taking her unhappiness out on you; you remember that."

God, she loved Edna. A wobbly smile curved Shay's lips. "What would I do without you?"

Edna waved a hand. "Bah. Don't go getting all mushy on me." Then she shuffled back and shut herself inside her trailer.

Shay turned back to her door. Dammit. She wished she'd gotten dressed before she came out. Now a walk to give her mother a chance to cool down was out. There was nothing else for it. She braced and opened the door to her trailer.

Time to face the music.

* * *

Hugh drove the Mercedes like his grandmother would. Making sure not to draw attention to himself as he passed a cop heading in the opposite direction. It didn't slow or turn to follow him, which meant the car hadn't been reported missing yet. The owner was probably still holed up in that cheap hotel with his bit on the side. Hugh had spent the last couple of days looking for another Merc to replace the one he'd cost them.

He'd found this one outside a nice residential property, had watched as the guy kissed his wife goodbye then met up with someone else. He deserved to have his car stolen. Served the bastard right. That was what he told himself, anyway. Anything to stop from feeling like the piece of shit he was. He wasn't a stupid, punk kid anymore; he understood the ramifications of his actions, how they affected the people he took from. He ignored the way his gut knotted.

He was doing this for his family. His mom and his sister. They were all he could allow himself to worry about. Thinking about any of that other stuff was just added guilt he didn't need. He carried around enough already.

He couldn't let them down again.

This time, he would protect them. This time, he wouldn't fail.

His mind drifted to Shay, where it always went lately. Since he'd met her, he'd taken some stupid risks. Risks that could have cost the people he cared about most in this world. He had to keep a lid on it, on what they were doing. The way she made him feel.

He shook his head. How the hell was he going to do that?

He couldn't keep his hands off her, no matter how hard he tried. That's how strongly she affected him. But it wasn't only that…he admired her. She worked her ass off. Had three jobs to keep on top of things, as well as helping out Edna, and fuck knew what else.

This morning, Shay had looked so damn peaceful beside him but also exhausted, dark circles under her eyes even in sleep. That was partly his fault for keeping her up most of the night. So he'd turned off her alarm and had gone to let out Edna's dog. Her mom had arrived while he was waiting for the dog to take a dump.

She hadn't introduced herself, but he'd known who she was instantly. Shay had taken nothing from her mother…except her eyes. They were the same shade of green. That's where the similarities started and ended.

She'd asked him a ton of questions, all, he'd noted, geared toward finding out how much money he had. He'd worked out her angle from the second she opened her mouth, so he'd held his tongue. Then Shay had woken up, and the woman had lashed out at her daughter, putting her down and talking to her like she was nothing. He'd held his tongue then, as well, though it had cost him to do it.

Meeting her mother had only amped up his protective instincts where Shay was concerned. How did someone so sweet and lovely come from such a poisonous bitch?

Until he knew the deal with the pair of them, how Shay felt about the woman, he'd keep his opinions to himself. He didn't want to upset her.

Jesus. What the hell was he thinking?

He shoved a hand in his hair and signaled the turn into the garage. No, he'd keep his opinions to himself because it was none of his damn business. Getting involved with that part of her life wasn't part of the deal. They were sleeping together. That's it. Nothing more.

Shaking his head, he banged a fist against the steering wheel. If that were true, why was his stomach in knots? Why did he crave her every damn minute of every damn day, and not just because he wanted her in his bed?

It was dangerous thinking. Stupid and goddamn reckless.

He shut the thoughts down as the garage door jolted open. He'd called ahead, told Joe and Adam he was bringing in a car. They were there, waiting to switch out the VIN plates.

The last thing he wanted was to involve Shay in any of this mess. He was a thief, a criminal, and if he couldn't find a way to shake Al, he would stay that way…or worse, wind up in prison.

He needed to end it. Tonight.

But as an image of Shay, naked and flushed, standing in front of him last night, filled his head—followed by the pain he'd seen in her beautiful eyes this morning after her mother's cruel insults—he knew it wasn't going to be that easy.

Not yet.

He just needed a little bit longer.

Chapter Twelve

Shay parked the Honda outside Hugh's house, or at least she thought it was his house. She checked her phone again to make sure she had the correct address. This was it.

It was late evening, the place lit up by streetlights. She couldn't see much, but what she *could* see was—nice. Not what she was expecting at all. She hadn't expected a family home. She'd thought maybe an apartment or a warehouse. Not a house you'd see Mom and Dad and their two-point-five kids stroll out of on their way to baseball practice.

She climbed out, slung her overnight bag across her shoulder and headed to the front door.

The nerves fluttering in her belly made her heart pound a little faster. Which was silly. They'd slept together several times now. What on earth was there to be nervous about?

She should be jumping up and down with excitement. A guaranteed night of hot sex and an evening away from her mother. She'd worked her butt off all day to get the website finished for her client, just so she'd have the whole night free for Hugh. Why she was close to freaking out, she had no clue.

Her palms were growing clammy, so she quickly wiped them on the sides of her dress and clutched the strap of her bag tighter. Reaching out, she knocked on the front door. The sound of footsteps hitting what had to be a hardwood floor was followed by the click and scrape of a lock being disengaged. Then the door swung open.

And there he was. In all his huge-masculine-sexy-growly glory.

Her mouth went dry.

His gaze did a sweep of her body as soon as he saw her, and her lower belly clenched, that heavy gaze setting off exquisite little zaps of electricity even lower. He had on a flannel shirt that was faded and soft looking, his sleeves rolled back to reveal those muscular, corded forearms. The jeans he wore were faded, too, and a nice, snug fit. Her gaze lowered. To his bare feet. God, even his feet were sexy. He reached out and grabbed her overnight bag off her shoulder, hefting its weight.

His brows lifted. "What's this?"

"I have work in the morning. I thought I'd save time and get ready here." Plus, that way, she wouldn't have to see her mother until she got home later that afternoon to change for her shift at Woody's.

His forehead creased. "Right."

Was that the wrong thing to do? She'd just assumed since he always stayed the night at her place, she'd do the same at his. But what the hell did she know? She'd never had a casual affair before. "Um... I can... I don't need to..."

"Inside, Shay."

He held the door open for her, so she stepped over the threshold and watched him disappear upstairs with her bag.

She took in his place. The living room was fairly large and looked like it'd been recently decorated. Dove-gray walls, big leather couch and chairs. There was a solid-looking dresser against the wall, but there was nothing on it, and a coffee table that matched in front of the couch with a couple of car magazines and the TV remote sitting on top. She could see the kitchen at the end of the hall but not much from where she stood. The appliances looked new.

He came back down the stairs, and she turned to him.

"Are you redecorating?"

His dipped his chin. "Haven't done much lately, though."

He was watching her closely, but she couldn't work out what he was thinking, which just made her nerves ten times worse.

"It's a great house."

"Thanks. You want a beer or something?"

What was going on here? He was behaving strangely. Standoffish. "Well, I thought maybe we could go grab something to eat? Maybe you'd like to head out…"

He shook his head. "Not in the mood to go out, babe. I got food here, or we can order in if you want?"

Did he even want her here? He wasn't exactly making her feel welcome…or wanted. He'd moved closer but made no attempt to touch her. She swallowed the lump forming in her throat.

"Um…if you'd rather I not be here tonight, it's fine, really. I'll go."

His hand shot out, and he grabbed the front of her dress, fisting the fabric, and dragged her up against him. "Had a shit day. You being here has improved the hell out of it." He frowned, the grip on her dress tightening. "I don't want you to go."

"Okay," she whispered. "If you're sure?"

He sucked in a breath, and it came out a little shaky. "I'm sure."

"So you haven't eaten?"

"No."

"Are you hungry?"

His eyes grew heavy and hot, tongue swiping over his lower lip. "Princess, I'm fucking starving."

Eeek! She wanted what that hungry gaze promised, badly. But she also wanted to do something nice for him, something she'd go out on a limb and assume he didn't get very often.

"How about I make you dinner? Let me try to improve your bad day. I've been told I don't suck in the kitchen."

He shook his head. "You don't have to do that. Let me order in."

She stepped back, and his hand dropped.

"When was the last time someone cooked for you?"

He rubbed the back of his neck, his lack of an answer, answer enough.

"That's what I thought. Let me check the state of your supplies, and we'll decide from there."

She felt him trail behind her as she walked into his kitchen. There was a big island in the middle. Dark countertops and white cabinets. More hardwood floors. It was lovely. The kind of kitchen she'd dreamed of but knew she'd never have. She'd probably be in her little trailer the rest of her life. Just like her grandmother. At least she could pick it up and move on if she wanted to.

"This is gorgeous. Did you do it yourself?"

He dipped his chin, watching her move around the room.

"Wow. It's amazing. When I was a little girl, living in crappy places with Mom then later, in the trailer with Gran, I used to imagine having a home like this." She trailed her fingers along the countertop. "Having a beautiful kitchen like this one. A mother who'd teach me to bake…" She cut herself off abruptly. She didn't want to think about her mother, not here, not tonight. She shut down the memories creeping in and turned back to him, plastering a smile on her face.

Hugh wasn't smiling, though; his brown eyes were locked on hers, expression back to unreadable. Intense.

"Anyway, it's great. Have you redone the whole house all on your own?"

He continued to stare at her, unwavering, in a way that made her want to squirm.

"Yeah, still got the bedrooms to do and the upstairs bathroom."

The way that dark gaze had locked on her, the thoughts she had no chance of deciphering moving behind his eyes, made her feel strange, not quite unsettled but…bewildered. They sent pleasurable tingles down her spine and at the same time made her want to head for the front door and run like hell.

Instead, she went to the fridge and opened it. "Oh, I can definitely whip up something easily from what you have here."

She took out what she needed and started cooking. Hugh stayed where he was, leaning on the island, and watched her work. She found it hard to concentrate with his intense gaze on her. She sipped at the beer he'd given her and tried to stay focused, making small talk, trying to lighten the mood, random stuff, and definitely avoiding the subject of her mother. But the whole time, she felt that weighty stare on her. Following every movement. She didn't need to look at him to know he was watching her; she felt the heat of his gaze licking across her skin, a tingle following in its wake.

When she finally handed him his plate, he stared down at it as if he'd never seen steak, potatoes and salad before. He lifted his gaze to hers, and she watched the way his Adam's apple slid up and down his thick neck before he spoke.

"Thanks."

His voice was rough, low, and her knees went weak. She forced a carefree smile when she was feeling anything but carefree. "No problem. Eat up."

"Let's eat in the living room." He grabbed both of their plates and led the way, putting them on the coffee table then flicking on the TV.

They ate in charged silence. Only she didn't know what it was charged with. Oh, there was lust. There was always lust. But there was something else, as well, something that confused her, made her feel fidgety, made her belly feel weird and squirmy.

Shay had only dished herself up a small portion, but she could have had less. The vibes Hugh was throwing off made her too nervous to eat. They finished up, and he stood, taking their plates to the kitchen.

When he walked back to the couch, he reached down, grabbed the remote, turned off the TV, and stared down at her. "Bedroom's upstairs."

Her breath seized, pulse starting to race. She took him in. His fingers were curled into fists, clenching and unclenching at his sides. He looked tense. He also didn't reach for her, still not even attempting to touch her.

"Okay."

She got to her feet, and he headed for the stairs, leading her up to his bedroom. His shoulders were stiff, forearms bunched tight. What the hell was going on? He said he wanted her here, that having her here improved his shitty day, but he was acting as if—she didn't know what this was.

He pushed the door open, and she spotted her pretty polka-dot bag sitting on his bed. A huge California king. The bed looked wrong—too masculine with its navy-blue comforter and chunky, dark wood bedside tables—against the faded, peeling, floral wallpaper. The floor was hardwood but in need of sanding and finishing. He'd obviously gotten as far as pulling up the old carpet.

"I'm gonna go lock up."

The butterflies in her belly erupted at the sound of his retreating steps. What did she do now? *Calm down, for starters.* Grabbing her toiletry bag, she went in search of the bathroom. It was just down the hall. She washed her face and brushed her teeth then went back to his room. He still wasn't back. It felt weird just stripping off and getting into his bed. But she hadn't brought her PJs. She hadn't thought she'd need them. Now she wasn't quite so sure.

She went to his dresser and grabbed the first T-shirt she could find. It was gray, faded and soft and smelled like Hugh. She quickly stripped off and pulled the shirt over her head then climbed under the covers and waited.

He seemed to take forever. Then she heard him moving around downstairs, and when he did finally come up, he went straight to the bathroom. He wasn't in there long, though, and she couldn't help but shrink under the blankets when his massive body filled the doorway.

His eyes said it all.

Oh, yes. He definitely wanted her there.

Things heated up down below—they'd been at a low-level, delicious hum since she'd walked in the front door, but now, with that look... She was on fire.

He didn't say a thing, just stared at her as he reached back and yanked off his shirt. She stifled a moan at the sight of his bare chest, all that thick muscle, the dark hair dusting his pecs—that enticing trail that stopped at the top of his jeans. She dropped her gaze as his fingers went to work on the zipper, and this time, she did moan. His erection was heavy and thick through the soft denim, and she unconsciously licked her lips as he slid down his jeans, freeing that beautiful cock.

He shoved off his jeans, kicking them aside, and before she knew what she was doing, she'd shoved back the covers and climbed to her knees. The soft fabric of his shirt swamped her, felt delicious against her hard nipples, making her squirm.

He started toward her but stopped in his tracks suddenly. "What are you wearing?"

His voice was nothing but grit and the sexiest thing she'd ever heard. She looked down at herself. "I didn't think you'd mind?"

He made a rough sound. "I don't." He came closer, so he was standing at the edge of the bed. "Come here."

She moved toward him on her knees until she was in front of him.

He gripped the bottom of his shirt, eyes locked on her the whole time, and dragged it up and over her head. "You can wear it whenever you want, but right now, I want you naked." He cupped her breasts in his huge hands. "Wanna watch these bounce while I'm buried inside you, when I fuck you nice and hard."

Her nipples puckered tighter. Hugh was intense—she'd learned

148

that much in their short association—but tonight, he was even more so. She shivered.

He dragged his thumb over a tightened peak, and she shivered again.

"You like that? You want me to fuck you hard, use my size, my strength to get you off? Work this lush body any way I want?"

She squeezed her legs together and licked her suddenly dry lips again.

"Answer me."

"Y-yes." She didn't know what was going on here, why he was acting this way, but she loved it.

"Good girl." His hand slid up to the side of her neck, and he gave her a little squeeze, thumb sliding over her jaw. "Now, get on your hands and knees for me. Before I let you bounce on my cock, you're gonna let me fuck your mouth."

Oh, God. She scrambled to do as he said. She wanted to take him in her mouth, badly. He was so tall that even on her hands and knees, him standing beside the bed, she was perfectly lined up with his massive erection. He was so hard, his penis stood straight up against his stomach, the head fat and purple. She tilted back her head and looked up at him. His nostrils flared as he brushed back her hair then fisted it and moved closer. Grabbing his cock with his free hand, he angled it down, so the head brushed her lips.

"Let me see that little pink tongue. Lick it," he rasped.

She did, darting out her tongue to taste him, moaning at his decadent taste, so dark and erotic. She lifted a hand and slid it up his thick length. Pre-come leaked onto her lips on an upward stroke, and she lapped it up on a needy groan. If she didn't need a hand to hold herself up, she'd reach down between her legs and work her clit; that's how turned on she was.

"Fuck." His grip tightened. "So fucking greedy, aren't you, princess?"

She was. She wanted more, but he held her back with his unrelenting grip, controlling how much of him she could have.

"You want more?"

She nodded, moaning helplessly.

"Open your mouth for me then, open those sweet lips," he growled. "You've never sucked a cock like mine, have you, beautiful? Those soft, fucking innocent lips weren't made to suck a man like me. A man like me shouldn't come anywhere near someone like you. But I'm a bastard like that; I'll take it anyway, and I'll enjoy every damn minute of it."

A man like him? She didn't know what he was talking about. And he wasn't taking a damn thing. She'd never wanted anything more in her life. She opened her mouth, and he pushed past her lips, farther still, 'til he reached the back of her throat. She hollowed her cheeks as best she could and sucked his length, rubbing her tongue against the thick, pulsing vein on the underside.

He growled and finally let her move, using his grip on her hair to set the pace. "That's it, let me corrupt that sweet, innocent mouth."

She worked him as best as she could, sucking and licking, feeling frustrated that he wouldn't let her move faster. She wanted to devour him. She cupped his testicles, squeezing them gently, massaging, and he cursed a blue streak. They drew up, and, God, she felt him grow thicker in her mouth. He held her still and started moving his hips faster. Knowing she caused that reaction, that she was making him this out of control, made her hot in ways she'd never imagined possible.

He loosened his grip. "Gonna come. You don't want it down your throat, pull away now."

She didn't pull away; she slid her free hand up to his butt and dug her fingernails in, sucking harder. His grip immediately tightened again, and he pumped that big cock into her mouth, shouting as he came. It hit the back of her throat, and she swallowed him down, everything he had.

When he pulled his cock from her mouth, her eyes widened. He was still hard. She lifted up, rose to her knees, watching as he walked to the other side of the bed and climbed in. Back against the headboard, he reached over, shoved open a drawer, and pulling out a condom, rolled it on. His gaze lifted to her.

"Come here, Shay. Not finished with you yet."

Everything tightened—her nipples, her belly, her pulsing sex. She crawled closer, so turned on she could barely see straight.

His gaze moved over her face, down to her lips. "Like that, the way your lips are swollen, the color of cherries from sucking my cock."

"I love it, too," she whispered.

His nostrils flared. "Get on. Get your reward."

She lifted her hands to his shoulders and straddled his hips, groaning when the head of his cock slid against her slick opening. She reached between her spread thighs, held him in place, mouth opening on a cry as she sat down, taking him as deep as he could go.

"Ahhh." Her head tipped back. "Feels so good."

"Fuck yeah, it does."

Then his hands came down on her hips, slid around to her ass, and he used his strength to lift her and slam her back down. She screamed. *So good.* Her inner walls struggled to take all of him but took all of him, anyway. With how wet she was, she had no choice. She'd never experienced anything like it. *So incredibly good.*

She ground against him, but Hugh took over, lifting her then bringing her down hard enough to make her teeth rattle. He fucked her hard, harder than she knew was possible. In a way she knew she'd be feeling for the rest of the week. She loved it.

"Your ex fuck you like this, princess?" he growled.

Shay shook her head and cried out when he went impossibly deep.

"No?"

"No," she half yelled, half screamed.

"I'm not a nice guy. Don't fuck like a *nice guy*," he bit out.

She couldn't process what he was saying. She couldn't think. Could only feel.

"Touch your clit," he growled. "Make yourself come."

She dug her fingernails into his shoulder with one hand to hold on and slid her other hand down between them and started circling her aching, swollen clit. Her inner muscles clamped down hard, and her head dropped back. "Ahh, yes."

"Jesus, I can feel your tight little cunt squeezing my cock. Come for me, princess. Let me see it."

One of his arms slid around her waist, holding her upright as he pumped up into her hard and fast. The pressure built until it was unbearable. She screamed his name, begging, pleading, a second before her orgasm tore through her. Hugh's grip tightened then he flipped her onto her back, and while she was still coming, he rammed back in, pounding into her, hard, jarring thrusts, using her body the way he wanted to get himself off. It was the hottest thing she'd ever experienced.

Then his cock started pulsing inside her, he shoved his face against her throat and growled through it. She clung to him, running her hands over the wide expanse of his back, little moans escaping with every slow glide as he wound them both down.

Finally, he collapsed to his side and rolled onto his back. Pulling off the condom, he dumped it in the trash by the bed then rolled back. Sliding his arm around her waist, he dragged her in close, tucking her into his side, and held her there, as if he thought she might get up and go. As if that were even possible. Her legs were like spaghetti.

He was quiet for the longest time. She struggled to think of something to say. What did you say after an experience as mind blowing as that?

Finally, he gave her a squeeze and whispered. "Sleep, princess."

After what they'd done, she didn't really have any choice. She slept.

Chapter Thirteen

Shit, her ass felt good pressed against his dick. Perfect.

He held one soft breast in his hand, hard little nipple against his palm. Yeah, shit, that felt pretty fucking good, as well. Shay was still asleep; he could tell by the way she was breathing, the crazy-cute mewing sounds she made every now and again. He'd spent enough nights in her bed to know the difference. He liked that he knew the difference. Too damn much.

This was the first time a woman had spent the whole night at his place. He'd never had a woman in his kitchen, cooking him food—and he sure as hell never had a woman show up at his door with an overnight bag. Even now, her toothbrush was sitting on his bathroom cabinet. He liked that, too.

She wriggled her ass, and he groaned.

He liked all of it. Liked her in his house, his kitchen, his bed. Seeing her clothes in his room. When he'd opened the door and saw her standing there on his doorstep with her bag, that open, beautiful smile aimed at him—it had messed with him. Fucking unhinged him. Seeing her there, in his house, had changed things for him. He'd tried to fight the feeling, the feeling that this was where Shay belonged. That he wanted her there with him every day. In his bed every night.

And when he'd walked into his room and had seen her in his bed, in his shirt, he'd known in that moment he didn't want to let her go. That knowledge scared him. He'd tried to fight it, had fucked her in a way he'd wanted to since the first time he'd laid eyes on her, in a way he'd decided he never would because Shay didn't need to see that side of him. The part of him he was sure would scare her away. That pissed-off, dirty-mouthed asshole with a self-destructive streak a mile wide.

But last night, he'd wanted that side of him to scare her away.

Needed it to.

Because he knew now he couldn't end this thing between them. He'd thought hammering it home to her, *to himself*, that what they were doing was only sex, showing her that side of himself, might force her hand. That this sweet, sometimes shy, gorgeous woman would be so disgusted by his base behavior that she'd walk.

She hadn't.

She'd fucking matched him stroke for stroke. Loved every minute of his brutal thrusts, begging for more, for him to fuck her harder.

He didn't know what that meant.

He just knew he wasn't ready to walk away from her yet. But he also had to keep what they were doing quiet. Until he could find a way to get free of Al, his hands were tied.

He felt it the minute she woke. She stilled, then her hand slid up over his, the one covering her soft, smooth breast, and squeezed his grip tighter around her. She twisted so she could see him, her silky red hair sliding against his chest. Sleepy, sexy as hell green eyes blinked up at him, puffy suckable lips parting on a sweet moan.

"Hey," she whispered.

His cock, which was already hard, surged against her ass. He had to press closer to stop the ache. "Hey."

A small smile played at the corners of her mouth. "Are you going to do something with that?" She wriggled her ass again. "Or are you trying to torture me?"

He let his free hand drift down between her thighs and growled when he felt how wet she was. "I'm torturing us both at the moment, princess."

She rolled over fully, so her front was pressed to his, and stared up at him. Jesus, that felt good.

"I'm not really into all that kinky stuff. Torture isn't my thing."

He lifted her bent knee over his hip and tugged her closer. "Me, either." Then he surged up, sliding inside her, filling her with one quick, hard thrust.

She cried out, eyes slamming shut, mouth dropping open. Fucking hot.

"Feel good, beautiful?"

She whimpered. "So good."

He pushed her to her back, keeping one knee lifted to keep her spread wide, and slid back in nice and deep. *Jesus.* So damn hot and tight and wet. So good he lost control completely and started thrusting with all the finesse of a rutting bull. He couldn't keep his eyes off the woman beneath him. The way her beautiful breasts bounced with every jolting thrust of his hips, the way she watched him through half-lidded eyes, biting into her lower lip. Shit, he couldn't get enough of the small gasps and cries that filled his ears every time he pounded inside her.

Then her head tipped back, neck arching, and she came hard. Her fingers dug into his ass, pussy clutching him so tight, he had no choice but to blow up with her. Shay moaned helplessly as he pumped her full of everything he had, clutched him tighter, grinding up against him, body trembling beneath him.

He collapsed on top of her, struggling to catch his breath.

He'd fucked around, had his fair share of women, but nothing had ever topped this. Nothing felt as good as him and Shay when they were together.

"Hugh?"

"Shit, baby." He kissed the side of her neck, her shoulder.

"Um…Hugh?"

"Love it when you say my name when my cock's still inside you."

She squirmed beneath him, pushed at his shoulders. He lifted up so he could see her face.

"We didn't…" Her eyes were round, huge. "No condom."

What? *Shit.* How could he have forgotten? "You on the pill?"

She shoved her hair back from her face. "Yes."

Thank fuck.

"I've never gone bareback with anyone else. Ever." He couldn't believe he had now. Not once had he been so caught up he'd forgotten to wear a rubber. "Think we're good."

She let out a relieved breath. "Okay. You're right. It's fine. And I haven't…you know, never not used a condom, either."

He should be more freaked out, but he just…wasn't, which was messed up for a lot of reasons. He was just about to kiss the worry from her cherry-red lips when someone knocked at the door.

He waited. Maybe they'd go away? He hoped like hell they'd go away. But the knocking came again, harder this time.

"Jesus Christ." Shoving back the sheet, he grabbed his shirt from the night before, cleaned up with it and tugged on his jeans. "Back in a sec."

Jogging down the stairs to the front door, he checked who it was through the peep hole.

Joe.

Thankfully, he'd moved Shay's car last night. He'd hidden it in his garage before he'd come up to bed. Just in case. He yanked open the door. "What is it?"

"Nice way to greet your baby brother."

This was all he needed. Joe and Adam already thought he was playing with fire by spending time with Shay. The less people who knew they were seeing each other, the better, as far as Hugh was concerned.

* * *

Shay could hear voices coming from down stairs. Hugh had been gone a while, and she felt weird just lying up there.

Pulling back the covers, she wrapped the sheet around herself, opened the door and tiptoed to the bathroom to clean up. When she got back to the room, she pulled on some clothes and after tearing her brush though her tangled hair, walked to the top of the stairs. She could see Hugh. He was standing in the living room facing her. Joe stood in front of him, T-shirt pulled tight over his wide shoulders and back.

"So what the hell are you doing here so damn early, anyway?" Hugh asked, sounding impatient, which made her smile.

Joe patted him on the stomach. "Thought you might wanna go for a run with me. Do something about that gut you're getting."

Hugh gave his brother a playful shove, and Joe chuckled. Nope.

158

She had to disagree. He definitely didn't have a gut. He was all hard, ripped muscle. And lots of it.

"I'll pass," Hugh said, planting his hands on his hips.

"Fine. Let the middle-age spread grow." Joe headed for the kitchen. "I'm gonna grab a bottle of water."

"Sure. Help yourself. Take the whole damn fridge while you're at it."

Okay. Enough skulking up here. Shay took the first two steps. Hugh, obviously sensing her movement, looked up at her, and when he saw her coming down the stairs, he shook his head and tilted it in the direction she'd come. Silently telling her to *get back up*.

She quickly reversed a step—and stumbled, tripping over her own feet and falling ungraciously onto her butt. Thank God Joe was singing, or rather wailing some song with lots of curse words from the kitchen and didn't hear her crashing around. She made it back to the room without being seen, but she'd bumped her elbow, and it hurt like hell.

An uneasy feeling settled in her belly and stayed there. It tightened and twisted until it physically hurt—a heck of a lot more than her arm. Was he embarrassed of her? Was that why he had her hiding in his bedroom? Yes, she understood what they were doing was casual, but still... His brother didn't look like the kind of guy who'd worry about such things. Why would Hugh?

She bit her lip. But then last night...this morning, what they'd done. It had felt like more. It felt like...

She threw up a wall, blocking those thoughts before they could fully form. She didn't mean anything to him. She didn't want to. They had off-the-charts sexual chemistry. That's all it was between them.

That's all she wanted from him.

She told herself that as she shoved her things back into her bag, as pain and anger welled up inside her. She thought Hugh was different. That he didn't care what others thought. He and Travis were like day and night. Chalk and cheese. That's what she'd believed, anyway. Perhaps not so much.

With nothing else to do, she sat on the end of his bed and waited, her humiliation increasing with every passing minute she was forced to hide up there.

A little while later, she heard the front door shut and Hugh climbing the stairs. She stood when he pushed open the door.

"Sorry about that. Joe thinks he can come and go as he pleases. This was our family home. He sometimes forgets it's mine now." His gaze moved over her, to the bag in her hand. "What's going on? You leaving?"

"I need to get to work." She was proud of herself when her voice came out strong.

He stared at her. "It's seven thirty in the morning."

She shrugged. "I have stocktaking to do for Jane today. I want an early start."

He planted his hands on his hips, frowned. "You're pissed?"

"No. Not at all. I just need to get going."

He frowned. "It's just easier… Joe not knowing about us…"

"Of course. There's no reason for him to know." Though there was no reason to keep it a secret, either. Unless he was ashamed to be seen with her.

"Stay for a bit longer. I'll make you breakfast."

She shook her head. "No, I really need to go." Breakfast wasn't included in their deal. This was an affair. Sex. She'd do well to remember that. She lifted her bag to sling over her shoulder and winced.

"You're hurt?"

She tried to move past him, but his hand snaked out and wrapped around her upper arm, tugging her closer. "What happened to your arm?"

She stood straighter. "I bumped my elbow hurrying to get back up the stairs."

"Let me see." He took her arm in his large, warm hand, gently rubbing it. "Okay?"

It felt nice. Too nice. She didn't want his sympathy right then. "Yes."

Her voice sounded sharper than she'd intended. She tried to pull away, but he wouldn't let her go and tugged her closer.

"What are you...?"

He bent down, and the next thing she knew, his mouth was on hers, kissing her hard. He cupped the side of her face with one hand, the other sliding around the side of her neck, and he deepened the kiss, refusing to let her retreat. Before long, she was kissing him back just as enthusiastically. By the time he gave her a gentle squeeze and pulled back, she was tingling all over.

She blinked up at him, feeling dazed and highly aroused. "What was that?"

"I'm sorry you hurt your arm, princess." He ran his nose along hers. "And that was the kiss I wanted to give you before we were interrupted."

"Oh." She swallowed. "It was very…nice."

His eyes narrowed. "Nice?"

She nodded. "Mmm-hmm."

He made a rough sound and backed her up against the wall. "I think I can do better than nice."

"You could try," she said against his lips, then gave a start when her phone started ringing.

Hugh let out a frustrated breath. "Ignore it."

"I can't. It could be my mom or Edna." And if it was her mother, and she was up this early, the chances were high she hadn't made it to bed in the first place, or at least her own bed, which could mean all kinds of bad things. "I have to get it."

She stepped away from him and quickly rummaged around in her bag. "Mom promised to let Rocky out this morning. If she's let me down…" She trailed off. "God knows why I believed her in the first place."

She put the phone to her ear without checking. "Hello."

"Good morning, Shay."

She froze, the familiar voice raising her hackles in an instant. "What do you want, Travis?"

She saw Hugh stand up straighter, move closer, but was too pissed that Travis was bugging her again to pay much attention.

"Honey, please, hear me out."

"I'm not your honey. And I've already heard what you have to say."

"Jesus." He huffed out a breath. "At least tell me you've thought

162

about it, about us."

"I can honestly say I haven't thought about you at all. I've been too busy working three jobs to give you a second thought."

He was quiet for several long seconds, then, "You chose to leave. You didn't have to."

"You humiliated me, you broke…" She stopped herself. He didn't deserve any more of her time and energy. "I have to go."

"I messed up, Shay. I know that. Come back to me, please. Meet me somewhere for lunch?"

Gah! Had he lost his mind? "That's not a good idea. Look, I have to go." Then she disconnected.

She was so damn weak. One kiss from Hugh and she'd forgotten all about what happened when Joe showed up. How Hugh kept her hidden, kept her his dirty little secret, just like Travis had done. But at least Hugh was honest about it. He hadn't made her believe they had a future or that he wanted more from her than sex.

But she'd thought he at least liked her, respected her.

God, she was so confused.

If she'd harbored a shred of hope that her and Hugh might mean more to each other one day—it was certainly gone now.

She grabbed her bag. "I have to go."

Chapter Fourteen

Hugh watched Shay shove her phone back in her bag as something swirled inside him like a goddamn hurricane. Rage and—jealousy. The emotions mixed together, making his voice sound rough as hell.

"What the fuck did he want?"

She was walking toward the door but stopped in her tracks at his tone.

"The same thing he wanted the other night."

His knuckles cracked when he squeezed his hand into a fist. "He's still trying to get you back?"

She hitched her bag higher, fingers gripping the strap. "Yes." She turned away, stared out the window, slender throat working. "All of a sudden, he can't live without me."

Hugh's heart started to pound. Shit, he wanted to kill the asshole with his bare hands. "That what you want?"

She shook her head, looked back at him. "I used to. I used to want the white picket fence, the kids, all of that stuff. For a while there, I thought I might have that…with Travis. But no. To answer your question, I don't want to get back with him. I don't want those things anymore. Not with Travis." Her gaze darted away again. "Not with anyone."

Her words felt like a kick in the guts. Which was messed up. He'd never thought about kids, about something permanent—not until this minute. Not until Shay. To hear that she didn't want that, it kind of stung in a way he struggled to process. "So you don't want to settle down someday, raise a family?" *Shut the hell up.* Why was he pushing this?

She crossed her arms over her stomach. "That's not for me." She smiled, but it looked forced. "I guess there's no need to ask you the same question." She lifted her hands and waved them around. "This will make a great family home one day."

He took a step toward her, words he had no damn right to say on the tip of his tongue. "Shay…I…"

"I like my life the way it is." Her green gaze dropped to his chest, stayed there. "I like my trailer. I love that if I get a wild hair one day and decide to move, I can just hitch it up and take my home with me. I like my freedom too much now to tie myself down."

Hugh took her in, her posture, her body language. She was uncomfortable as hell.

And because she sucked at it, he knew the woman was lying through her teeth.

She was also scared shitless of letting anyone in. His girl had been hurt and not just by that asshole who used her and treated her like shit. And he got that. He understood that fear. Only his came in the form of feeling like a failure, from letting down his whole family.

Because he'd been so damn blind they were in danger. The only difference between him and Shay? He was what he believed himself to be. Shay had done nothing but be the open, sweet, beautiful woman she was, and for her troubles, the people she trusted, cared about most, had stomped all over her.

Travis had lost her, and it had taken that loss to finally make him see what he'd thrown away. The guy had screwed up in a big way. In a way he could never repair, could never take back. He'd lost his chance with her. If Hugh was a different man, a better man, and Shay had given that to him, what others had abused… Fuck, he would have protected it with his life.

But he wasn't a different man.

Jesus. He wanted to punch something.

She cleared her throat. "Well, I better go."

He stepped back because as much as he wanted to keep her there, he couldn't. If nothing else, it was too damn dangerous. She brushed past, out into the hall, and he followed her down the stairs to the front door. He wanted to take her hand and drag her back up to his bed, keep her there all day.

She walked into his living room, and his gut tightened. He liked seeing her there. In his space. Moving around his house. Shit.

Scooping up her keys from the coffee table, she held them up. "Can't go without these."

She walked to the door, and they stood there, staring at each other. The woman had a great mouth. A mouth he wanted to spend days kissing. Wanted to see stretched around his cock again. He cupped her jaw, pressed his thumb to her full lower lip, slid it across the plump flesh, couldn't stop himself.

"Can I see you tonight?"

"I'll need to check with Harold, make sure Edna's covered."

"So that's a maybe?" He wanted to demand she come over. Tell her he wanted her in his bed every night. That he was getting used to sleeping beside her. Jesus. He couldn't think like that.

"It's a maybe," she said in that husky way he was starting to like a whole hell of a lot.

"I have to work late." They had two more cars to get for this next shipment. Cars they had to find tonight. "I'll text you when I'm home. Could be late, though."

"Okay." She still wouldn't look at him, gaze darting around the room.

"We good, Shay?"

"Of course."

He slid his fingers into the hair at her temple but kept his other hand at his side. If he touched her, felt the warmth of her skin through her clothes, the softness of her body now, he *would* drag her back upstairs. "Look at me, princess."

She did, but something wasn't right. He just didn't know what.

"We good, Shay?" he repeated.

"Yes," she whispered.

He held her gaze, hoping she'd say more, reveal more, but she gave him nothing. He needed to know they were okay, that this wasn't ending between them, not yet. So he leaned in, going after a response from her the only way he could, the only way he had a right to ask for one. He touched his lips to hers.

She was still for a heartbeat, then her little tongue darted out to taste him. Giving it to him. He groaned against her lips. It was a struggle, but he kept the kiss slow and sweet, ignored the demanding throb of his cock.

167

He smoothed his fingers over her hair then lifted his head, dropping his hand away. "Car's in the garage. I put it there last night."

She blinked, the dreamy look in her eyes vanishing in an instant. "Pardon?"

"Your car. I put in the garage to get it off the road."

Her hands slid from his shoulders to his chest, and she gently pushed him back. "Oh, right. Of course."

What's going on in that head of yours, princess? He tried to tug her back, but she opened the door and pulled away. He fucking hated it. Hated that he didn't have the right to make her tell him what just extinguished the light in those gorgeous green eyes, that he didn't have the right to fix it, to make anything that darkened her world go away.

Yeah, like he could fix her life. He couldn't even fix his own.

He followed her to the garage and opened it for her, watched her open the driver's door of the Honda and throw in her bag.

She turned to him. "Maybe I'll see you later." She was back to not meeting his stare.

She wasn't coming. He'd fucked up. Somehow, he'd fucked up everything. But before he could open his mouth, before he could stop her, she climbed in and started the engine.

Shit. Maybe this was for the best. He should let her end it. It was the smartest thing to do. He shoved his hands into his pockets to stop from yanking open the passenger side door and demanding she tell him what the hell had just happened.

Instead, he watched her back out.

His phone started ringing in his pocket, and he pulled it out. Hit the call button. "Yeah."

Shay lifted her hand, gave him a small wave then drove away. His stomach clenched.

"Found the Toyota we need."

At least Joe had his priorities straight. "Can we get it tonight?"

"Yeah, parking attendant I know told me this guy is at the Cross Street parking lot every Tuesday night. Eight 'til late. It's ours."

"Good work." They had a couple guys they paid for information. Sometimes, they came through.

Joe disconnected, and Hugh went back inside. Into his empty house.

He looked around. He'd decorated the downstairs but then stopped. Not seeing the point, not with his future so unclear. Hell, he could wind up in prison if things went badly, or worse, if Al didn't get his way.

The scary thing was, for the first time in a long time, Hugh wanted to finish what he started.

Wanted to make this place a home.

Another reason to stay the hell away from Shay Freestone.

* * *

Shay pulled up outside her trailer a short time later and sucked in an unsteady breath when she saw her mother sitting on the top step. She'd lied to Hugh; she didn't have stocktaking to do for Jane. Shay wasn't due to start work for a couple hours. She'd just needed to get away. Before she caved, before she let him kiss her until she forgot all the reasons why they needed to end what they were doing. Closing her eyes, she took in a steadying breath, fighting back the unhappy grip in her belly, and reached for the door.

Her mother stared at her, eyes hard as she climbed out.

"Hey, Mom. Have you eaten? I thought I'd make us breakfast."

She took a drag on the smoke she was holding then stubbed it out on the side of the trailer. "Nice of you to show up. I came out here to see you, and you're never here."

Guilt rippled through her. Her mother was right. Shay had done everything to avoid spending time with her. Nothing good ever came from it. Maybe this time would be different? She almost laughed out loud at the ridiculous, almost desperate thought. "Well, I'm all yours tonight. What do you want to do?" Staying away from Hugh was for the best. She couldn't put herself through that again, what happened earlier. The way he'd kept her hidden away as if…as if he was embarrassed to be seen with her.

Her mother's lips lifted into a smirk. "Moved on to someone else already, has he?"

Pain curled in Shay's belly. She tried to move past and go inside, but her mother grabbed her arm, long nails digging into her skin.

"I thought I taught you not to aim too high. You're not in that man's league. It was bound to happen. Just be thankful it's now and not when you're attached."

That hurt. A lot. Her mother's low opinion of her shouldn't matter, but it did. Every time her Mom spewed her poison, it opened a fresh wound. Shay didn't bother correcting her mother and pulled her arm free. "Do you want breakfast or not?"

Her mother's eyes narrowed, grip loosening. "What are you going to do with the car?"

"What are you talking about?"

"I say sell it." She lit another cigarette and took a long drag. "He screwed you over. Screw him back. Sell it." She glanced away then back at Shay. "Maybe then you'll have something to spare for your mother."

That tiny shred of hope, the one that always snuck in when her mother showed up, shriveled and died. Really, she was surprised it took this long for her to ask for money. Still, even now, after all these years of disappointment, it was another hit, another blow. "I'm not selling Hugh's car. I'm giving it back."

Her mother's lips thinned. She threw her smoke to the dirt and stomped it out. "Don't be so stupid. You don't owe him a damn thing."

"I'm not selling his car."

"He gave it to you. You can do what you like with it."

Shay ignored her and went inside. Her mother followed.

"Don't be a doormat, girl. You won't get anywhere letting people walk all over you like that. Wise the hell up."

Shay moved into the small kitchen, hands shaking she was so angry, so full of pent-up emotion. "Like you said, it's my car; he gave it to me. And I choose to give it back."

Her mother planted her hands on the counter and leaned forward. "You're that selfish? That you'd rather give it back than help me out? What did I ever do to deserve that kind of treatment? My own daughter would rather see me on the streets starving than upset a man who used her and dumped her."

Shay threw up her hands. "What did you do? Really? You're asking me that?"

"I did my best for you, and you know it. It's that school your grandmother sent you to. Made you think you're something you're not.

171

Turned you into a stuck-up, selfish, ungrateful little bitch, just like she was."

Shay froze, anger surging through her. "Don't you dare talk about Gran that way."

Her mother sneered. "She never approved of her precious son marrying me. Never liked me. I hated that old cow…"

"Yet you dumped me on her the first chance you got, and you never looked back." Shay hung on to the edge of the counter for support, knees shaking. After everything her mother had done, she'd never, not once, confronted her about it. She'd tried to keep the peace, hoped that one day she'd be good enough, that things would change. She'd been kidding herself. And now her mom was badmouthing her grandmother. The woman who'd stepped up and raised her. Loved her. Who'd made sure Shay had gotten the best education, had every opportunity. It was the last straw. "But you know what, Mom? Bringing me here was the best thing you ever did for me. Here I was loved. I wasn't left to fend for myself while you went out looking for the next sucker to pay your rent instead of getting a job and paying it yourself. Because of her, I work hard, I pay my own way." She sucked in a ragged breath and leaned forward. "You want money? Get a goddamn job, like the rest of us. Pay your own damn way."

Her mother's mouth pinched, eyes narrowing. "You ungrateful bitch," she rasped.

Shay clung to the bench to tighter. "You didn't come here to see me. You came here to get what you could from me until you found your next meal ticket, the next poor idiot to fall for your lies. That's the way it always is. And I'm done," she said the last on a whisper, the words a surprise, even to her.

Something ugly flittered across her mother's face, then the mask lifted. "Now, Shay, baby, don't go saying something you'll regret."

She straightened her spine. "I want you to leave."

Her mother's bright-pink nails curled into her palms. "You don't mean that."

"I'm going to work, and when I get back, I want you gone." She'd actually said those words out loud, even though she'd barely heard herself over the blood rushing in her ears. She'd said it.

Grabbing her purse, needing to get the hell out of there, she walked out the door without a backward glance. She ignored the Honda Hugh had given her and kept going. Taking that car, using it, would make her just like her mother. She refused to be that. To become that. Someone's dirty secret, money and gifts thrown at her to keep her quiet—making sure she knew her place.

To not expect more.

That would destroy her.

She strode down the street, hoping the walk would give her time to calm down. Jane would ask her a million questions—questions Shay didn't want to answer. She hugged herself. Her mother was right about one thing, though. It was better to end this thing between her and Hugh now—before she got attached.

She just hoped it wasn't already too late.

* * *

Raggedy Jane's was unusually busy that day, which meant Shay didn't have much time to think about her mother or Hugh. Or the complete mess she'd made of her life.

When her shift finished, she walked home slowly, in no hurry to face what she'd done. God, she'd kicked her own mother out onto the street. *Did Mom have somewhere to go?* Did she have any money at all? Where would she sleep tonight?

Shay had overreacted, hadn't she? Taken her hurt and anger over what happened this morning with Hugh out on her mother. Nothing her mom had said to Shay was new. She'd heard it all before, many times, and she'd never lost it like that. Her mother was all she had left, her only family. That should mean something, right?

She pulled out her phone to call her. "Shoot." It was dead.

Picking up the pace, she half jogged the last couple of blocks to the trailer park. The sun had dropped in the sky by the time she got there, sweaty and out of breath, the colored lights already on for the evening. Harold called after her as she speed-walked past his trailer, but she didn't stop.

Unlocking the door, she shoved it open, flicked on the light, and stopped dead...

She reached for the wall to support herself.

No.

Anything not bolted down or too heavy to carry was gone. Her TV, her stereo, crappy as it was. Her CD's. Little knick-knacks that had belonged to her grandmother. The miniature cat figurine collection her gran had loved, each piece painfully selected. Even Shay's books were gone.

"I tried to stop her." Edna's voice drifted in from the door behind her, the sharpness usually there, gone. Her voice was shaky, broken.

Shay turned and lifted her hand to her mouth. Edna stood there,

174

Harold supporting her. She had a cut on her cheek…another on her hand. "Oh, my God. What did she do to you?"

"I'm okay, Shay, girl. She just shoved me out of the way. I lost my balance." She shuffled farther into the room. "I'm okay; don't worry about me."

Harold helped Edna onto the couch.

"You might want to see to her cuts, honey," he said gently. "I'm no good with that kind of thing."

Shay had never heard Harold use that tone in her life. Or seen that softness in his eyes. He'd certainly never called her honey before.

He gave her shoulder a gentle squeeze, and she came out of the haze she was in, the confusion, and raced to the bathroom to grab her first-aid kit. She cleared her mind; if she thought about what her mother had done to Edna, to Shay, she might shatter into a million pieces right then and there.

Pulling out the supplies she needed, she started cleaning Edna's cuts. "This is my fault. All of it. I kicked her out. I made her angry…you know how she gets when she's angry…I…I…" Hot tears scorched a path down her face. "I'm so sorry, Edna."

The warmth of Edna's frail hand came down on her shoulder, her grip surprisingly firm. "You did nothing wrong. You put up with her crap longer than she deserved. You hear me, girl?"

Shay nodded, nausea and emotion clogging her throat. "Did you call the police?"

Edna shook her head. "Left that decision to you. Figured without any money she can't get far. Gas will run out sooner or later."

"Gas?"

175

Edna gave her another squeeze. "She took your car, loaded it up and drove off without a backward glance."

She'd taken Hugh's car. "Oh, God."

"I wasn't sure what to do, so I called your young man. Big guy like that, way he cares about you, he'll sort out this mess."

No. She shot to her feet. "You called Hugh?"

"He gave me his number when he brought Rocky back the other morning, said if we ever needed anything, to give him a call. I gave him a call."

She raced to her bag, grabbed her phone and plugged it into her charger—the only thing her mother hadn't taken. Her phone blew up with messages and missed calls from Hugh as soon as she turned it on.

Her humiliation was complete.

Chapter Fifteen

Shay had dressed Edna's cuts and gotten her settled back in her own trailer with Harold for company when her phone rang.

She didn't want to answer it. How could she face Hugh after what her mother had done? Shay still couldn't believe she had actually *stolen* his car. Did she think she could just take it and nothing would happen? That she'd just drive off, and no one would care that she'd stolen it? This was a whole new low for her mother. Or was it? Shay had no way of knowing what she got up to during her months of no contact. Humiliation burned her cheeks, tension and anxiety pounding through her body, so much so she felt sick to her stomach. Then there were the feelings of betrayal.

How could a mother do that to her own daughter?

But Shay couldn't avoid Hugh forever, and she was no coward. He'd done a nice thing, given her a car to use, and thanks to her mother, it had blown up in his face.

Sucking in an unsteady breath, she hit the call button. "Hello."

"Thank fuck." He was quiet a couple of heartbeats, breathing heavily. "Why didn't you answer your phone? Are you okay?"

He was angry, but under that she could hear concern. It warmed her…it also confused her. "I-I'm sorry. My phone died. I didn't see your calls until I plugged it in."

"And you didn't think to call me back? That I might be worried?"

"I...well, I..." She frowned at the wall across from her. *Worried?* "No, I didn't think..."

He growled. Actually growled down the line. "Fucking hell, Shay."

"I'm sorry, I didn't think..."

He growled again, louder, cutting her off. *Oh, dear.* He was angry, more than angry, and justifiably so, considering her mother had driven off in his car.

She took a deep breath. She had to say this, or this sick feeling in her belly would never go away. "Um...look." She waited, and when no growls echoed down the line she carried on. "About the car...I will pay you back. I promise. It might take a while, but I'll pay you back every cent..."

"I'm with your mother."

Shay shot to her feet. "You're what?"

"Edna called while she was loadin' your shit. I couldn't get there fast enough, but I know a guy who lives nearby. He was waiting for her, followed, told me where she was."

"You're with her...right now?" The nausea intensified.

"Yeah, babe. Tell me what you want me to do? Decision's yours."

She heard a voice in the background. Her mother's. It was pitched high, which meant she was furious, and she was making sure Hugh knew it. *Oh, God.* If Shay hadn't been sure they were over before, she was now.

"You don't get to talk to her, bitch. You don't deserve to breathe the same motherfucking air," Hugh growled at her mother in reply.

Shay's throat tightened, more humiliation weighing her down. Had that woman ever loved Shay at all?

"Shay, baby, I need to know how you want to play this. You want the cops involved, you want me to get your stuff and make sure she leaves town. It's up to you, princess."

Princess.

He'd been calling her that a lot lately. She liked it. No, she *loved* it. He was such a good man. Even after everything that had happened, this nightmare of a situation, he was still looking out for her. He didn't need to do that. He didn't owe her anything.

She cleared her throat so she could speak past the lump. "I want my things back. S-she took Gran's cats. Why would she do that? She doesn't even like cats. Which means she did it just to hurt me." Shay was rambling now, but she couldn't stop, not when so many emotions were battling inside her. "What did I ever do? Why does she h-hate me so much?" Her voice broke on the word hate, and she had to bite her lip to stop the sob that was close to breaking free.

"Shay, listen to me. I need you to make a decision. Tell me what you want me to do."

"I want Gran's things back. Get your car. I don't care about anything else." She swiped her tears away. "I don't want her coming back here, and I don't want to hear from her again."

"Okay." His voice was gentle.

"Thank you, Hugh."

He was silent a few seconds. "Later, Shay." Then he disconnected.

Throwing the phone aside, she got to her feet and headed for the bathroom. She needed a hot shower, then all she wanted to do was crawl into bed and sleep.

For a few peaceful hours, she needed to forget the mess that was her life.

* * *

Hugh quietly opened the door to Shay's trailer. It was only nine thirty, but the place was dark. Shay hadn't answered at his knock, and the door had been locked—until he picked it.

He moved through the tiny living room and pushed open her bedroom door, breathing a sigh of relief when he saw her. *She's okay.* Of course she was, but when she hadn't answered the door, he'd freaked, had barely stopped himself from kicking in the damn thing.

Shay was fine, but she was out cold, her lush body curled into a tight ball, blankets tucked up to her chin. He wanted to climb in with her, pull her into his arms and tell her everything was okay, but he couldn't. Not tonight. Not with the way he was feeling.

That didn't stop the ache building steadily, the almost desperate need to wrap around her—to hold her close—from pounding through him.

Jesus.

His gut tightened.

But he couldn't do that, because staying here with her could only bring more shit to her door. That was the last thing she needed.

His phone vibrated in his pocket. It'd be Joe. They still had cars to find. They couldn't risk missing their deadline. Al was looking for any excuse to tie them in, and Hugh wasn't giving it to him.

He moved closer, couldn't help it, and stared down at her, at her face soft in sleep. Beautiful.

He'd wanted to strangle her mother today. The bitch didn't deserve

Shay. Didn't deserve her love. The way Shay had lost it on the phone with him…her pain…he'd heard it, shit, he'd *felt* it in her voice. She'd barely held it together. He'd wanted to comfort her more than anything, but he didn't want her mother to know how much she'd hurt her. The selfish bitch wasn't getting that, as well. She wasn't getting another piece of the amazing woman lying in this bed.

Which was why he struggled to leave now. That desire—to comfort her, to make everything okay, to be the one to do that for her—it was so damn strong. He reached out, brushed back her hair and grinned when she screwed up her face. She still didn't wake.

Shit.

He didn't have the heart to wake her, either. There was no point.

Without considering his actions or why he had to do it, he pressed his lips to her forehead. "Sleep tight, princess."

Then he walked out the door.

* * *

Hugh stood watch, while Joe strode across the lot toward a Toyota.

So far, so good. Hugh was even managing to keep his mind off Shay, tucked up in bed, all warm and soft—well, he had until right then. He tried to focus and scanned the area again.

They were close. This car, then they only needed to find one more, and they'd meet Al's deadline for that month.

Joe was half a parking lot away from the car when a figure dressed in dark clothing sprinted from the other side, stopping by the car they were there to get. There was a flash of silver—whoever it was made no effort to conceal the fact they were picking the lock. Joe obviously saw, as well, because he started running toward the person.

He didn't make it. Whoever it was, they were good. The door was open, the car hot-wired, engine firing to life within seconds. Joe reached the car as it lurched forward and squealed out onto the street.

His brother threw his hands in the air, his curse echoing into the night.

"Shit." Hugh rubbed his temples. This wasn't happening. *Jesus.* This was seriously messed up.

Joe strode back to him, expression like thunder. "What in the *fuck* was that?"

"No fucking idea."

"Al." Joe hissed out a breath. "Whoever that was, he has to be on Al's payroll. Fucker wants us missing our deadline."

They walked quickly back toward Joe's truck. "That'd be my guess."

Their only option now was to find another car, which wasn't always easy. Finding a specific make and model, no problem. Finding one in the right location, somewhere they could get to work without being seen, so they weren't taking bigger risks than they already were—that took time and energy.

"You think he had something to do with that security guard when we were casing the Merc?" Joe shoved a hand in his hair. "I mean, yeah, your phone went off, but he was scanning the lot as if he knew we were there as soon as he walked out."

Hugh nodded. Joe was right. "More than likely."

"Motherfucker."

Al gave Hugh a list of cars after each delivery, orders from his clients. Their job was to find those exact cars, by an exact date. If they didn't deliver by their deadline, Hugh was up shit creek without a paddle.

And there wasn't a damn thing they could do about it.

Chapter Sixteen

Shay walked out of her bedroom, still feeling kind of groggy. After lying awake and staring at the ceiling, feeling sick to her stomach, she'd gotten up and taken one of her gran's sleeping pills that were still in the bathroom cabinet. Shay'd been desperate to shut down her mind. It worked. The pill had knocked her out. Literally.

She had to work a shift at Woody's tonight, so it'd been imperative she get some sleep. How could she make decent tips if she looked like a zombie?

Shuffling to the kitchen, she put a pot of water on the stove to boil. Since her mother had taken her coffeemaker, Shay would be stuck drinking instant until she could replace it. Unless, of course, Hugh had managed to get hers back.

She banged a cup down on the bench and rummaged around until she found the instant in the back of the cupboard then dumped in two heaping spoonfuls. She needed to shake this haze and wake the heck up. She shuffled to the couch with her drink, taking a sip of the dark brew at the same time as she spotted her gran's cats back on their shelf.

She drew in a sharp breath, which meant she sucked the scolding mouthful down the wrong pipe. She coughed and spluttered, quickly putting the mug down on the coffee table before she spilled it all over the place.

Hugh had been here while she slept. She stared at the figurines neatly lined up in a row. He'd put away her grandmother's cats.

Her heart started doing funny things in her chest. Fluttering and warming and squeezing, all at the same time. It was a sweet thing to do. A really sweet thing.

Without thinking, she went to her phone and called Hugh's number. It rang several times, but then switched to voicemail. As if he'd cut off her call. She tried not to think about what that might mean—about why he wasn't answering and why he hadn't woken her last night—and left a quick message thanking him.

While she finished off her crappy coffee, she got ready for her day, though according to the clock, she'd slept through most of it. And as tempting as it was, she decided against going back to bed and burying her head under the covers.

She noticed the Honda outside a short time later and spent the next hour unloading and putting away her things. Hugh had gotten everything back, *including* her coffeemaker.

The hours dawdled by, and she still hadn't had a return call or text from Hugh. So when her phone did light up and start ringing, she dived on it.

But it was Kayla's voice that greeted her, not Hugh's.

"What are you up to tonight?"

Shay felt guilty for the disappointment that hit. "I have a shift a Woody's."

Kayla sighed. "That's all you ever do lately. Work."

"Tell me about it." But for once, she was happy to be busy, to not have time to dwell on everything that had happened...on the hurt that surrounded her, threatening to smother her if she let it take hold.

They talked for a while longer. Her best friend sounded a lot happier, and Shay purposely steered the conversation back to Kayla whenever it veered in Shay's direction. Kayla was Shay's best friend, but she couldn't bring herself to say it, what her mother had done. She was still too raw, and saying the words out loud, to another person, was just too damn much.

Before they said their goodbyes, Kayla agreed to come to Woody's during Shay's shift and hang out.

When her phone rang for the second time a short while later, she was in the middle of getting ready for work. She answered, positive this time it would be Hugh.

It wasn't.

"Shay…"

"No, Travis," she said before he finished whatever he was going to say.

"Honey…"

"I'm not your honey. I'm not your anything."

"The office isn't the same without you."

She couldn't deal with this, couldn't even muster the energy to tell him she was hanging up. He tried calling twice more after that, and she ignored him both times. Grabbing her bag, she locked up. She didn't want to use Hugh's car, but she was tired and angry, and the idea of walking to the bus stop later, after working her shift, made her want to cry.

She shouldn't be using it anymore. She needed to give it back. It was time to face facts. Hugh was avoiding her. He'd helped her out, got back her stuff, because he was a *good guy*. But the fact he hadn't woken her when he'd dropped off her things? It was a flashing red light with wailing sirens.

He was in this with her for fun, for the mutual pleasure they gave each other. Not to be her sounding board while she cried over her ex. Or to help out with her elderly neighbor and her *dog*. And definitely not to deal with hysterical phone calls and chasing around after her insane mother because she'd *stolen his car*.

No, she didn't blame him for running in the other direction. Not one bit. Didn't make it hurt any less, though.

Her shift went quickly. They weren't super busy, but they had a steady stream of customers. So she'd managed quick chats with Kayla between filling drinks orders, but there hadn't been time for deep and meaningful conversation. Thank goodness.

Kayla left after making Shay promise to have lunch in a couple days, and by the time she climbed back into the Honda, she was exhausted, and her feet were throbbing. She turned on her phone before she left the parking lot. Three missed calls and five texts. She quickly flicked through them. All from Travis.

Starting the car, she tried to ignore the way her heart banged, the hollow, deflated feeling behind her ribs, and headed for home.

She pulled up outside her place a short time later. Edna's lights were out. Thank God she was okay after what happened. Harold had promised to check on her and take Rocky out for her evening walkies while Shay was at work.

She went inside, and after a shower changed into her PJs. When she was putting her toothbrush away, her gaze went to the bottle of sleeping pills in the cabinet. It was tempting to take another one tonight, let it knock her out again so she didn't have to think. Didn't have to lie there awake, thinking about all the ways her life was a mess.

Her money troubles sure as hell weren't helping the situation...

A slow-ish night meant average tips. She needed to ask again if she could pick up some extra shifts.

She walked out of the bathroom. No pills. She couldn't hide from her life, from all the crap that seemed to be raining down on her. She had to find a way to dig herself out.

Sliding under the sheets, she burrowed down deep, curling into a tight ball. She would get through this.

She would.

* * *

Shay woke with a start, adrenaline spiking through her veins. But it dissipated quickly when Hugh's scent enveloped her, chasing away the fear, replacing it with happiness...excitement.

His big body lay behind her, delicious heat surrounding her. The big hand on her hip was moving in small circles, kneading and teasing her skin as he made low, soothing sounds.

"You're here," she whispered into the darkness.

"Yeah."

She opened her mouth to say more, but he rolled her to her back, and his lips came down on hers. He kissed her with a hunger that stole her breath. Deep and insistent. His hand slid up her shirt and covered her breast. Her nipples tightened into hard little peaks, zings of pleasure shooting down between her legs every time the rough skin of his palm grazed over her flesh.

He lifted his head, warm breath ruffling the hair at her temple as he exhaled heavily. "You feel so good."

Her shirt was up, exposing her belly and most of her breasts. He'd taken his off before he'd climbed in beside her, and the hair on his chest, the dark trail that led down over his abs and dipped below, was crisp and a little rough against her skin. But he hadn't just taken off his shirt. He was completely naked. *Yum.* The man felt exquisite.

And hard as steel.

Urgent hands lifted her shirt, up and over her head, then he was sliding her panties down her legs. She moaned at the feel of his bare flesh against hers.

"Tell me you're already wet, baby. Can't wait," he murmured against her lips.

She was, she was more than wet. She was soaked. One touch from Hugh and her body fired to life every time. His palms were rough and impatient as he spread her legs, thick fingers cupping her, dipping between her slick folds.

He hissed. "Fuck, Shay. Always so hot. That sweet pussy always nice and juicy for me."

She cried out. "Please."

His huge body was pinning her to the mattress, and all she could feel was Hugh.

His heavy thighs shoved hers wider, and then the fat head of his erection was pressing against her opening, stretching her, filling her as only he could.

"*Oh, God.*"

She whimpered as he slid to the root, arching into it, fingers

189

digging into his hard biceps that were flexing and bunching under her hands.

"You love it, don't you?" he rasped.

"Y-yes, I love it." *Too much.* He was an addiction, a craving she couldn't get enough of. The thought was terrifying.

She moved her hands to his shoulders, his back, the muscles shifting below his skin as he really started moving. Rolling against her like a giant tidal wave, pounding into her over and over again, relentlessly. All she could do was cling to him. Absorb every brutal thrust. He was always like this, as if he couldn't get enough of her, as if he couldn't control himself when he was with her.

He lifted his head and brought his mouth back down on hers, tongue delving deep, tangling with hers, wet and hungry. Wild.

"I needed this. Needed you," he groaned.

The last few words were said with an added growl she didn't understand, didn't know what it meant. But right then, she couldn't think; all she could do was feel. Feel the way his thick cock moved inside her, the rasp of his chest hair on her sensitive nipples.

Her inner walls fluttered, grasping him tighter.

"That's it. Let me feel it, let me see it, beautiful. Come all over my cock."

"Harder," she cried. "Don't stop."

"Not ever gonna stop, princess." He hissed and slammed up inside her, jarring her higher on the mattress.

Her orgasm hit its peak, and she shattered. She couldn't hold the feeling inside as it spread through her, so she screamed through it, clinging to him helplessly.

When her cries finally died in her throat, she hung on to his big body as he continued to pound into her, his deep grunts filling her ears as he chased his own release. She thrashed and moaned uncontrollably as another orgasm built suddenly.

She barely had time to register what was happening before it hit. "Oh…ahhh." Then she was coming again, so hard all she could do was cling tighter, crying out and shaking through it.

Hugh cursed, then he shuddered and groaned, so deep she felt it rumble through her chest. His hips started pumping erratically, cock pulsing deep inside her as he shot hot and hard.

"That's it, princess. Take it all. Take all of me," he rasped, rough and low.

She did, and God help her, she loved every minute. Loved that instead of pulling from her when he'd finished as he had to when they used condoms, he could stay where he was, planted deep. He rolled them to their sides and curled his fingers around the back of her knee, lifting it so her bent leg rested on his hip.

He tucked her in close, and she felt him bury his nose in her hair, heard him breathe her in.

"You good?"

"I'm good," she whispered.

He rubbed circles over her back, wrapping her in a warm, safe cocoon. She let it soak in, let him ease the ache in her chest. Squeezing her eyes shut, she clung a little tighter. She had to know.

"Is she…will she be okay?"

His hand stilled then started moving again. "Yeah, princess. Your mom will be just fine."

She had to believe that, needed to or she thought she might break. She shook her head against his chest. "She's never done anything like this before... I mean, she has but not to this extent. She cleaned out my wallet before she left the last time she visited. But this..." She lifted up and looked into his eyes, even though it was too dark to see his expression properly. "I'm sorry you had to deal with all of it...with my mother, having to go after her to get your car back. You didn't sign up for that. I'm just...I'm so sorry."

His hand slid around the side of her neck, thumb tracing her jaw. "Didn't go for the car. You don't need to apologize for that."

"Well, let me thank you for getting my stuff back, for..."

"Don't need to thank me for that either."

She buried her face back against his chest. Even though he probably couldn't see her, she didn't want to risk him noticing the way her eyes were no doubt glistening with unshed tears. Why the hell was she close to crying? She refused to believe it was relief over Hugh coming to her, or the fact he didn't seem to be completely horrified over the whole thing. It couldn't be that, because if it was, it meant she cared, and she couldn't afford to care. Not that much. Never that much.

"I know this sounds naive, but I just don't understand people who can take from others without a second thought. Why would she do that? What's in her that she would do that to me...to you? And not even care?"

She felt his muscles tighten. He cleared his throat. "People will do almost anything if they're desperate enough."

Shaking her head, she burrowed deeper. "No. Not desperate. Selfish. She's always been selfish."

He gave her hip a squeeze. "Had to be hard growing up with a mom like that."

"She wasn't around that much, even when I was living with her. I looked after myself most of the time. There were always different men at the house. She'd drop me off at Gran's and take off without a word…sometimes for days, sometimes weeks, with her latest boyfriend." Shay snuggled closer to him, to the heat radiating from his skin, the comfort of his massive arms. God, she'd never felt so safe. "The last time she dropped me off, she just didn't come back. I didn't see her for over a year. She didn't try to take me back after that. I was twelve years old."

"You didn't deserve that, princess."

His voice was nothing but a rasp. It skated over her skin, lifting goose bumps.

"My old man used to be gone a lot, too. Gambled nearly everything we had." His big body stiffened, arms spasming around her, as if he'd surprised himself by opening up.

She held still, hoping he'd keep going.

Finally, he smoothed his hand over her back, and his muscles relaxed. "Left school soon as I could. Got a job to pay the bills, so we didn't lose the house. He'd come crawling back when all his money was gone, stay for a while then fuck off again. Did that all my life."

She ran her hands over his chest. Aching for him, for what he'd been through. "It sounds as though I wasn't the only one with an irresponsible parent. I was lucky to have Gran. Your family was lucky to have you."

He snorted. "Try telling Lucy that."

"Lucy?"

"Baby sister and a pain in my ass. She's in college. Drama is her middle name. She's the smart one out of the three of us, though you wouldn't know it with some of the stupid shit she gets herself into."

Despite his words, there was so much affection in his voice when he spoke about his sister, it kind of made Shay jealous, which was completely ridiculous and made absolutely no sense.

"You're lucky. I wish I'd had a brother or sister. It must've been nice, having them growing up, having each other."

He was quiet for several seconds. "Yeah, it was."

He didn't say anything after that, and as much as Shay wanted to know more, she didn't push. That's not what they were about, after all. She was already in over her head with him.

***

Shay must have drifted off, because she woke again when Hugh moved. It was still dark, the middle of the night. She watched him climb out of bed and get dressed.

He isn't staying.

She squeezed her eyes closed and pretended to be asleep, hating how much she felt his loss, his heat beside her, the minute he got out of bed. This was him, defining their relationship, making sure she had no delusions about what they were doing. Their relationship was sex. That was it. Heartfelt conversations in the dark, wrapped in each other's arms, meant nothing. He was just passing time.

She knew this.

Travis had taught her well.

So why did her stupid heart ache when Hugh walked to her side of the bed, kissed the top of her head then walked out the door?

Chapter Seventeen

Hugh worked alongside Adam, switching the VIN plates on the Toyota Joe had brought in. Thank fuck. Now they only had one car to find before their deadline in a few days.

"You heard from Lucy lately?" Adam asked from under the hood.

"She texted a couple days ago, after I threatened to turn up at her place if she didn't fucking answer me and let me know she was okay."

Adam stood. "She's still pissed at you?"

"Don't give a shit. I did what I had to do to keep that fucker away from her. If he touches my sister again, he loses his job. End of story."

His friend ducked his head back under the hood. "The girl's old enough to mess around with who she likes, bro. She's not going to forgive you in a hurry."

"You think I should've stood back while she risked everything, just so she can screw some old pervert?" When Hugh had found out Lucy was seeing her psych professor, he'd nearly burst a blood vessel. Then he'd hunted the fucker down and threatened his career if he didn't back the hell off. It had been either that or beat the shit out of him.

Adam's nostrils flared, expression hard. "Hell, no. Just saying how it is. I'm with you. Only I would have messed the motherfucker up good *and* threatened his career."

Hugh shoved his hand in his hair. "He had a wife and kids."

Adam's hand curled around the screwdriver he was holding. "Did she know that?"

Hugh shook his head. "No clue."

"Shit."

Yep. His little sister didn't do things by halves—when she messed up, she went all out and usually got herself hurt in the process. "When she screws up, she does it properly."

Adam lowered the hood. "What about you?"

Hugh stiffened. "What about me?"

"Something you want to tell me?"

He crossed his arms and stared his friend down. "Can't think of anything."

Tossing the screwdriver onto the workbench, Adam stared back. "You're not fooling anyone; you know that, right?"

Obviously not. Still didn't mean he was admitting anything. Admitting it would make it real, what he was doing with Shay. And would bring home the fact that, before long, he'd lose her. "Don't know what you're talking about..."

Shoving his hands into his pockets, Adam shook his head. "Just be careful. Or it won't just be you that's getting fucked. And it won't be in a good way." Then Adam walked away.

Hugh knew Adam was right. And after the shit with her mother, the way Hugh had freaked out when she hadn't answered her phone—the emotions swirling when he thought something could have happened to her—he'd tried to distance himself. He'd lasted one goddamn day before he'd gone to her and climbed back into her bed.

Hugh covered the car; the new cloned VIN plates they'd fitted weren't any guarantee they wouldn't get caught. They just tipped the odds a little more in their favor. Joe had taken off after they brought in the car, so Hugh locked up after himself and left. And despite Adam's warning ringing in his ears, he walked past his truck—he couldn't risk it being seen anywhere near Shay—and climbed into one of their loaners.

Shay didn't work Friday evenings and he planned on taking advantage of the fact. The way he was feeling, if he had his way, he'd take her to bed and not let her out again for the whole damn weekend. But that wasn't an option. She had a shift Saturday night at Woody's, and he had a car to find. So tonight, she was his, and he was going to spend the whole damn night proving it to her.

But when he pulled up outside her place a short time later, the lights were out, the Honda still parked out front. Maybe she'd decided to go to bed early? They'd both had hardly any sleep the last couple nights.

He contemplated leaving, going home. He couldn't do it.

Fuck it... He'd get into bed beside her, wait for her to wake. Just being close to her was enough for him. Just the feel of her soft, smooth skin against his.

He squashed those thoughts quickly.

What the hell was he doing? He shouldn't be thinking like that. Warning bells should be wailing in his ears; he should he running like hell the other way. After what she'd said to him in the dark the other night, about her mother, about people taking from others. If she ever found out what he was, what he did—she'd be disgusted. She'd see him like she saw her mother. A thief. A liar. A user.

But instead of getting back into the car and driving away, he

198

quickly picked the lock to her door and walked quietly to the bedroom, desperate for a taste of her, to just be near her.

But when he pushed the door open, her bed was empty. No Shay.

He stalled in the doorway, frustration pounding him, a growl bursting past his lips. Yeah, he was acting irrationally, but he wanted her. No...*needed* her. Where was she? Grabbing his phone from his back pocket, he tried calling her. No answer. So he fired off a text, asking where she was.

Thirty minutes later, still no reply.

The feeling of helplessness surging through him was making him restless, edgy. The worry coiled around his chest made him pace the small space. Since the car was still there, she was either with someone else or planned on taking the motherfucking bus. He didn't know where she usually hung out, who her friends were. Where to start looking. And that pissed him off more than anything. He should know this shit. He should be with her, or she should have told him where the hell she was going.

She's not yours.

He paced some more, and the longer he waited for her, the more scared he got.

What if they'd been seen together? What if Al...?

The sound of a car pulling up outside ground that unwelcome thought to a halt. He walked to the window and looked out. A late-model BMW sat idling out front. It sat there for a while, then finally the door opened, and Shay stepped out. He instantly scanned her body for any signs of harm, her face to make sure she wasn't upset or afraid.

She was smiling, wide and beautiful.

He did another sweep of her body, and what he saw made his fists clench tighter at his sides, his teeth grind together. She was in that dress, the one she'd been wearing when she brought back his keys, after their first night together. The one that emphasized her full tits, small waist and round hips. She looked fucking gorgeous. Stunning. Killer heels. Her long hair in soft waves down her back.

Was she on a date? Is that what this was?

The interior light of the car hadn't come on when she opened the door, and it was too dark out to see who was in there with her. He'd been here, waiting, nearly out of his goddamn mind with worry, and she'd been out, and by the looks of it, with some other guy?

Yeah, he'd told her he didn't do relationships, but that was to keep her safe. He thought they had an understanding—maybe something special. Obviously, he'd been wrong.

She waved as the car drove away, smile still in place as she pulled her keys from her bag and unlocked the door.

Hugh stood in the center of the room, arms crossed, but only because he wanted to grab her and shake the ever-loving fuck out of her for making him feel this way. This out of control. This jealous.

This messed-up feeling of betrayal.

She walked in, flicked on the light, dumped her bag on the bench and turned around...

"Jesus Christ!" Her hand flew to her chest, and she stumbled back a step, slumping against the tiny breakfast bar. "What are you doing here? You scared the heck out of me."

Her question felt like a knife to the gut. "Have fun?" His voice sounded wrecked.

She stood a little straighter, frowned. "Yes." She crossed her arms, as well. "I had a nice time. What are you doing here?" she asked again.

"Been here the last two nights, Shay. Me showing up tonight can't be that big of a surprise to you."

Her gaze darted away from his then flitted back, locking on his chest. "But that was the middle of the night."

"I'm not welcome earlier?" There was a definite growl to his voice now, but he couldn't hold it back. "You sure as hell seem happy to see me when I visit, ecstatic, even."

Heat flooded her green eyes, and he had to fight to hold his ground and not go to her, not use her lush body to ease the pain throbbing through him. Not to take his anger out on her in a way that would leave her screaming his name in ecstasy, so she'd never forget who she belonged to.

"You should have called first, saved yourself the trouble." She was breathing hard now, full breasts heaving against the fabric barely containing the soft mounds.

"I did. You didn't answer." He wanted to tell her how worried he'd been, how fucking insane it made him that she didn't want him as much as he wanted her, but he didn't. He didn't have that right.

"Oh…" She grabbed her bag, rummaged around and pulled out her phone, turned it on. It started beeping with missed calls straight away. "I forgot I'd turned it off."

He was in front of her in two steps. "Why did you turn it off, princess? What was so important you couldn't be disturbed?"

She blinked up at him in that way she often did, all innocent and sweet. "Dinner and a movie. I always turn off my phone in the movies.

It's rude not to."

His head exploded. Just…blew up. "Who the fuck is he?" Because he was going to hunt him down and kill him with his bare hands.

She dumped her phone on the counter behind her and crossed her arms, eyes wide. "He? What are you talking about?"

The phone beeped again beside her, and his gaze darted to the screen. The name *Travis* flashed up. "Why the hell is Travis still texting you?" he gritted out.

She just stared up at him, as if he was speaking in some foreign language. He didn't blame her. He didn't know what the hell he was doing, either. Shay didn't get what she was to him, what she meant to him. He couldn't name it himself. He just knew he didn't want her seeing anyone else. When she continued to stare up at him, not answering, he grabbed her phone and clicked open the message.

She sucked in a startled breath. "You can't do that! Give back my phone."

He ignored her, holding it out of her reach, and quickly read the text. The blood started boiling in his veins. "*I miss you, honey. Please think about what I asked you.*" Hugh threw the phone back onto the counter. "You're seeing this asshole again?"

Her eyes narrowed, and she scowled at him. "How is that any of your business?"

He moved in, grabbed her hips, making her yelp in surprise, then lifted her, spun, and pressed her against the wall. "You are mine. *That's* how it's my business." He grabbed her ass so she had no choice but to wrap herself around him. "Now, I'm going to ask you again. Are you back with him?"

"Yours?" she whispered. "You're acting like a crazy person."

"Mine," he snarled. He knew he was acting as crazy as she said, but there was no chance of reining it in. "Tell me!" he barked.

She scowled harder. "No. I'm not back with him."

"Are you going to take him back, Shay?" He held his breath, waiting for her answer.

Finally, she shook her head. "No."

He kept pushing, had to. "Did you have dinner with him tonight?"

"No." Her gaze dropped to his mouth, thighs tightening around his hips.

He pushed deeper into her curves. "Then who?"

"Kayla." She arched into him, so his cock was flush against the soft heat between her legs. "I was out with my best friend."

"Why is he still texting you?"

She bit her lip, and he wanted to suck it into his mouth and soothe away the sting.

"He's still saying he…he wants me back. And that he's kept my job at TBS Designs open if I still want it."

Motherfucker.

Anger fired back to life. "Promise me while we're seeing each other, you won't see anyone else." He had no right to ask it, but he wouldn't accept anything else, not from Shay. The thought made him lose his mind.

Her fingers spasmed against his back. "I promise."

He held her against the wall with his hips, grabbed her wrists and pinned them above her head with one hand, the other going back to her ass. "Promise me you won't talk to your ex, you won't meet your ex, you won't fucking think about your ex ever again."

Her head dropped back, and she licked her lips. "I don't want him, Hugh."

"Say it," he rasped.

Her eyes held his gaze, bright emeralds, clear and gorgeous. "I promise."

"Only me."

She moaned softly. "Only you."

"That's right, only me." He shoved her dress up around her hips. "I'm going to fuck you against this wall, princess, then I'm going to take you to bed and fuck you again."

She was breathing hard, her tits almost exploding out the top of her dress. He decided to help them out and tugged down the material at the front as far as it would go, making her gasp. He growled when a puckered, cherry-colored nipple popped out over the top.

He leaned in and sucked it into his mouth, tugging and licking as he reached down and got to work on his jeans. His cock was an iron bar behind his zipper, throbbing and aching to be released.

"Hugh," she moaned softly. "Please."

"You wet enough to take me?"

"Yes."

He yanked open his jeans and groaned when he felt her against his bare skin, felt just how hot and wet she was against the underside of his dick through her panties. "You need this as much as I do, don't you, baby?"

"Yes."

She tightened her arms around his neck and pressed in, tight, pointy little nipples digging into his chest. Warm, panted breaths brushed his throat as she placed an open-mouthed kiss there.

"Please," she added.

He dug his fingers into her ass, angled back and shoved her underwear aside. Fisting his erection, he rubbed the fat head through her drenched lips, grazing her hard, little clit, dipping back down. "Now?"

She sucked harder on his skin, nipped. "Please, now," she whimpered.

He pushed inside slowly, hissing at how tight and hot she was, how goddamn good she felt. Swallowing his cock inch by painstaking inch. "This pretty pussy was made for me," he rasped. "All of you. Nothing feels this good, no one." Then he slammed up inside her the rest of the way until he completely filled her.

He held still, trying to get his shit together, but she wrapped her arms tighter around him, thighs hugging his hips and lips brushing his skin, begging him to move. He was powerless to take it slowly after that, and holding her ass in his hands, he started thrusting into her. That mouth at this throat stayed open against his skin, letting him feel every moan, every cry, every word, asking for more, asking him to give it to her harder.

"Shit, baby, you're so wet. You love it when I lose control, when I fuck you hard, don't you?"

She lifted her head and looked at him through half-lidded eyes, mouth slightly open, lush body jarring, tits bouncing each time he thrust into her brutally. He almost came.

"Yes, I love it," she whispered.

Her hand slid over his shoulder to the spot she'd been sucking and kissing on his neck then into his hair, fisting, making his scalp tingle.

"I-I can't get enough of you," she told him.

He slammed his mouth down on hers and kissed her deeply, swallowing her moans, her cries as he pounded her.

She tore her mouth away, making the sexiest sound he'd ever heard in his life, completely uninhibited, letting him know how good she felt with him moving inside her. Then she tightened around him, inner muscles clamping down on his cock repeatedly as she came. Her nails were biting into his shoulders, nipples dark cherry, straining above the top of her dress. Thighs wrapped around him so tight, he knew he'd feel them there long after they were gone.

His cock swelled and pulsed, balls drawing up so tight it hurt, and then he blew, pumping her full of him until she collapsed against his chest.

He held her close, kissed her. "Time for bed, princess," he said into her sweet-smelling hair. "I need more of you."

The way he was feeling right now, he didn't think he'd ever get enough.

Chapter Eighteen

Tonight, Woody's had a live band—they did most Saturdays—and the place was pumping, but Shay barely noticed. She'd woken up this morning early, early enough it was still dark outside, and Hugh had still been there, wrapped around her. She thought he was asleep, but as soon as she moved, he'd rolled her to her back, kissing her until her head spun, then he'd pushed inside her, making love to her, slow and perfect.

She'd tried to tell herself repeatedly that wasn't what they'd done— they hadn't *made love*—and that she was being ridiculous to even think it. But this time had been different somehow. Hugh was an intense man, always, but this morning—she'd never experienced anything like it. There'd been a fervency in the way he'd thrust into her, kissed her, as if he was trying to communicate something to her without words. As if he was trying to tell her what they were doing held significance.

God, the way he'd looked into her eyes when he'd pounded deep, the sounds he'd made as he'd pinned her to the mattress and taken her.

Taken her.

There were no other words to describe it.

He'd been jealous when she'd gotten home. Possessive. Why would he act that way if he only thought of her as casual, someone to pass the time with?

Only me.

The way he'd said it. The way he'd made her promise to see only him. His words and actions had sent her on an emotional tailspin. Confused her. Excited her.

He'd made love to her. He had. She couldn't believe anything else, but then, like the last few nights, he'd left before the sun came up.

"Shay? Your order." Branden, the barman on tonight, stared at her, eyebrow raised.

"Oh, sorry! Right." She felt like an idiot, getting caught daydreaming while the bar was pandemonium around her. "I'll just"— she smiled at him and slid her tray off the bar—"deliver these."

Her shift went fast and without a hitch after she finally got her head in the game. It was two in the morning, and the place had thinned out considerably, when the door opened and Travis walked in. He didn't bother pretending he was there for any other reason than to annoy her and walked straight over.

As soon as he stopped in front of her, she held up a hand, halting whatever it was he intended to say. "I don't know why you're here, but whatever the reason, you've wasted your time."

He wrapped his fingers around her biceps and pulled her closer. "You keep hanging up on me. You've given me no choice."

She needed this to be over, needed it to end. She'd promised Hugh she wouldn't talk to her ex, but it was the only way to make him understand it was over between them, for good. She led him down the short hall off the side of the bar, just past the toilets. Where it was quieter.

When she looked up at him, his eyes softened and he moved closer.

She placed her hands on his chest to keep him back. "Trav." Her tummy churned using the shortened version of his name, what she'd always called him, but she needed to get through to him, needed him to see she meant what she said. "You can't keep doing this. You can't keep calling and showing up. You and me, we're over, and that's not going to change."

He flinched. "You don't mean that, honey. You can't."

"I can, and I do. I cared for you once, a lot, but you destroyed those feelings, annihilated them. We're not good for each other. I'd never fit in with your family or the world you come from, and we both know it." She didn't care about his family or what they thought of her, but she'd use anything at her disposal to make her point. "It has to end. The phone calls, the texts, they have to end, Travis."

He grabbed her upper arms and yanked her forward. "I don't want it to. I made a mistake, letting you go. I messed up; you need to forgive me."

"I won't compromise myself to please someone else. You don't really want me. You want a slim, polished version of me. That version doesn't exist; she never will. This is me, and I like me the way I am."

As she said the words, she realized they were true. Hugh made her feel beautiful just the way she was, made her feel comfortable, desirable in her own skin. Hugh made her feel a lot of things she was finding harder and harder to deny…or ignore.

"Don't do this," he gritted out.

"Travis…"

He wrapped his arms around her shoulders and smashed her chest into his, then his mouth came down on hers before she had a chance to draw breath and tell him to let her the hell go. She shoved at his chest.

"Shay?" A deep voice sounded from behind her.

Travis lifted his head, and she used the opportunity to step away from him. Adam stepped forward. Hugh's friend watched her with narrowed eyes, a gorgeous, barely dressed blonde wrapped around him. He'd obviously been there for the band, because he was holding a beer tightly in his fist, but she'd missed him in the crowd.

"You okay?" he asked.

She swallowed and took another step back. "Yes, I'm fine. Travis was just leaving, weren't you?"

"Shay..." Travis reached for her again.

She shook her head. "I have to get back to work." Then she rushed away, face hot with humiliation. Would Adam tell Hugh what he'd seen? It wasn't as if she'd had much choice; she'd had to talk to him. And she sure as hell hadn't initiated that kiss. Would Hugh believe her, would he care, or had he just said those things in the heat of the moment?

Not wanting to think about it right then, she got back to work, clearing and wiping down tables. She spotted Adam the moment he walked out of the bathroom. His hair was messy, lips darker, and the top three buttons of his shirt were undone. The blonde followed, hair wild, lipstick completely gone and a small smile playing on her puffy lips. He didn't spare her a backward glance as he headed for the door. The woman didn't seem worried about him, either, and strode to a group of women across the bar.

Her stomach twisted in a tight knot. She didn't know what was between her and Hugh, but she did know things had changed, and she could admit to herself, she wanted to know where they might go. Before she could think better of it, she chased after Adam, grabbing his arm before he opened the door.

"Please, I need to talk to you."

He stared at her, no outward sign of emotion on his handsome face. He definitely didn't look like a guy who'd just gotten his rocks off with a hot babe in a bathroom stall.

He speared his fingers through his mussed hair, a bored expression now front and center. "What is it?"

Shay started to feel a little panicked. Would he believe her? "What you saw, there's an explanation…"

"There always is, honey." He crossed his arms. "Don't tell me… It's not what it looked like?"

Her spine stiffened. "It's not."

"Look, I'm the last person to pass judgment. Who you screw's your business."

She took a startled step back. "I wasn't going to…"

"Like I said, not my business."

He looked in a hurry to leave, gaze darting to the door.

"Please, just don't tell Hugh."

His eyes narrowed again.

She grabbed his arm. "Please, Adam."

He let out a rough breath. "I have no plans to rain on his parade. The man's been fucked over enough in his life." He did a sweep of her body, from head to toe. "Can't say I'm not surprised, though. Thought you might be good for him. But then I've never been a very good judge of character." Then he pulled his arm free of her hold and walked out the door.

Before she could fully explain.

She barely knew the man, but she hated that he thought badly of her, that he thought she was the kind of woman who would carelessly hurt someone else without a second thought.

The man's been fucked over enough in his life.

She pushed Adam's words from her mind. The main thing was that Hugh wouldn't find out.

The last thing she wanted was to destroy his trust before she fully had it—before she fully had him.

* * *

Shay pulled up outside her trailer and glanced at the clock. *1:15 a.m.* Another long shift. It had been exactly a week since the incident with Travis in the hallway. Since she'd begged Adam to keep what he saw to himself. Hugh had come to her every night, still arriving and leaving when it was dark. She hadn't been back to his place; he hadn't asked, and she hadn't mentioned it. She didn't know why that was and tried not to think too much about it.

At least Adam had been true to his word and hadn't told Hugh what Adam thought he'd seen.

They'd grown closer, spending all their night hours together, enjoying each other, talking quietly in the dark. She'd been disappointed she wouldn't see him tonight because she was working so late. The last thing she expected to see was light glowing from behind the curtains in her living room when she got home, the car Hugh had been using while his truck was getting work done parked outside her place.

Happy flutters started up in her belly, a smile curling the corners of her mouth automatically.

Shutting off the engine, she climbed out, opened the door to her trailer and went inside. She didn't see him, but she could hear the shower running. Stripping in her bedroom, she headed to her small bathroom, excitement curling in her belly, and eased open the door.

Hugh filled the small stall, big, wide shoulders nearly reaching right across. He had his head down, rinsing his hair. Her mouth went dry when he slicked it back, his biceps bulging.

She stepped closer, and he caught her movement. He twisted his head toward her, looking at her through the glass. Her breath seized in her throat as his gaze dropped, doing a sweep of her naked body. She had no urge to cover herself, felt no shame over the way her body looked. Not anymore. Her abundant curves no longer made her feel unattractive. How could she feel that way when he looked at her like that? Even through the steam, she could see the way his eyes darkened, the way he licked his lips as if he could already taste her skin.

Pulling open the door, she stepped in behind him. "Hey." She wrapped her arms around his waist, pressing her breasts against his muscled back.

He groaned, and his abs tightened under her palms, the ridges bunching hard. He felt amazing. Euphoria buzzed through her, and it caused equal parts excitement and terror to pump through her veins. This feeling, when she was with Hugh, it was uncharted territory. She'd never felt anything like it before. She thought she'd loved Travis at one point, but she never felt for him even a quarter of what she did for Hugh.

It scared her half to death.

But she couldn't back off, couldn't push him away. She had no choice now but to ride this out and see where it led. If it led anywhere.

He wrapped his thick fingers around her wrists and held her there. "Hey, princess."

His deep, rough voice moved through her, over her. She pushed the fear away and kissed the smooth skin of his back, licking a trail up his spine. The man was like candy, and she couldn't get enough.

"This is a surprise. I wasn't expecting to find a big, wet, naked guy in my shower when I got home." She trailed her lips over his warm skin. "But I like it."

He chuckled, and the sound vibrated through her, teasing her hard nipples. "I was over this way, decided to save time and come straight here instead of showering at my place. I'll make sure I do it more often if this is what I get when I do."

She slid her hands lower, finding him already incredibly hard. She took his thick erection in her hand, sliding her palm along his soapy length. He throbbed and pulsed under her fingers.

"I like that idea. Getting all sudsy with you is one of my new favorite things to do."

"Yeah?" He tugged her around to his front, which meant she was pressed tight against him in the small space.

His heavy cock was trapped between them, and she shivered at the feel of how hard he was for her.

"And what else do you like?" He slid his hands down to her butt and gave her a squeeze.

She reached between their bodies and massaged his thick, heated flesh. "I like this."

His eyes blazed, burned into her. "Tell me what you like about it?"

Her heart started to pound harder. When she was with him like this, she felt a million miles away from the woman she'd been that first night he came home with her. He made her feel safe—to say what she felt, what she wanted. "I like how hard it gets. That sometimes I have to struggle to take it all. I like how full it makes me." She pushed closer, making him groan. "How when it's moving inside me, I can't think straight. All I can do is take it. Lose myself to how good you feel."

He hissed out a breath, and his cock jumped under her fingers. "What else?"

His hands moved restlessly over her wet skin.

"I like the way it feels sliding into my mouth, against my tongue… I love the way you taste."

His nostrils flared, and a rough growl escaped his lips. "You wanna taste now, princess?"

"Yes."

He placed his hands on the wall, arms outstretched, supporting himself, and widened his stance. "Show me."

Her mouth went dry, her skin flushing hot with hunger. There was something so empowering about making this huge man tremble and groan. It turned her on, excited her. Made her feel beautiful. Dipping her head, she did what she'd wanted to do since she first saw it and traced the cross on his ribs with her tongue. His fingers tangled in her hair, and she felt his chest expand on a sharp, indrawn breath when she sucked and licked.

"I love this tattoo."

Finally, trailing her hands down his sides, she dropped to her knees in front of him, between those spread, muscled thighs, and looked up. He stood with his wide back to the spray, blocking it with his body. Rivulets cascaded down his sides and long legs. He looked magnificent.

But it was the dark hunger in his gaze that had her squeezing her thighs together. That she could do that to this man made her hotter than she'd ever been in her life.

His hand dropped to the side of her face, cupping her so tenderly her heart squeezed. He was huge and powerful, all muscled strength. Strong enough he could lift her, carry her, move her body any way he wanted. He had full command over his body, could take her hard, seemingly without restraint. He could also be extremely gentle, treating her as if she was a delicate piece of china, as if she could break if he wasn't careful.

But she knew he'd never fully let loose with her. He always made sure to hold a little back. She didn't want that; she wanted to watch him let go, to release all that desire she saw burning in his eyes now.

He slid his thumb over her jaw, across her bottom lip, tracking the movement with his predator's stare. She reached up and held his hand there, taking his thumb into her mouth and sucking, nipping. That gaze got darker still, his cock, only a few inches in front of her face, jumped. He was so hard now it stood straight up, resting against his tight abs.

He bared his teeth like a hungry lion and hissed out a breath. "Shay..."

She nipped the tip of his thumb then let him drag it free. "Hmm?"

She ran her hands up his thighs, one hand moving to his tight ass, the other skimming close to his achingly hard cock, but not close enough. It pulsed and jumped again, liquid leaking from the tiny slit in that broad head.

"I can't wait to taste you," she whispered.

She'd never said things like that to anyone before, but watching the way it affected him, the way his wide chest pumped rapidly, the way his abs and thighs were so hard he looked carved from marble, gave her the confidence to keep going.

"Do you want me to suck you now?"

Another hiss then his hand moved to the back of her head, fingers spiking through the wet strands of her hair. "Yeah, I want you to suck me."

She leaned in, tongue darting out, tasting the salty pre-come now leaking steadily down his thick length. "Mmm, delicious."

His growl echoed around the small space.

She tilted back her head, eyes locking with his. "More?"

"More."

His voice rumbled so low she felt it in every shaky limb.

Instead of taking him into her hand, her mouth, she held on to his hips and leaned in, kissing the underside, nipping and lapping the thick, pulsing vein there. His fingers tightened in her hair, almost painfully. She loved it.

"More," he growled again.

Still not giving him what he wanted, she dragged her lips along his shaft, sucking gently as she went, all the way to the base, nuzzling and kissing, dizzy from his musky scent. The muscles under her hands somehow got harder still, a rough moan filling her ears and turning her on even more. He was shaking, close to losing it, to unleashing all that heat on her. She wanted it…more than she'd ever wanted anything in her life.

He grazed his thumb across her temple, then cupping her chin, tilted up her face to him. "Princess…"

She lapped at the head again, and his pupils dilated. His expression grew fierce, so intense it burned right through her.

"Princess…I need you."

Oh, God.

She shivered all over.

Another swipe of his thumb…across her cheek this time. "Please, baby, I'm hurting," he rasped.

His words destroyed her. The look on his face even more so. There was a vulnerability in his stark expression that she didn't understand—and *need*—so much need.

Her already swollen breasts grew heavier, her nipples so sensitive one scrape against the hairs on his legs had her shuddering—but that plea, it almost had her coming without him even touching her. She took him in her hands and squeezed, sliding upward, milking more liquid from the tip. His groan was low and long, almost pained. She leaned in and sucked the fat head into her mouth, not wasting time, done teasing. She rubbed her tongue along the underside and took him as deeply as she could.

He jerked forward, cock pulsing, and started coming instantly. His shout, followed by his uninhibited moans, filled her ears. His hands went to the wall behind her, holding himself up. Hot come filling her mouth, while he shuddered and pumped his hips uncontrollably.

All control completely gone.

He pulled out, and she stared up at him.

He was still hard as steel.

Before she had a chance to take a breath, he dragged her to her feet. She was up, lifted against the wall. A second after that, he was inside her, thrusting like a man possessed. Mouth attached to her throat, sucking and biting her skin.

"Fuck," he rasped. "Look what you've done to me. Dammit, Shay." Then his fingers dug harder into her hips, and he started slamming her down onto his cock, meeting each thrust with jarring force. Filling her, each slide of his incredibly hard flesh over her inner walls taking her higher and higher until that was all she was, that point where they were joined—and the dirty, sweet things he was growling in her ear.

"So tight, baby. Always so wet and ready for me. Mine. All mine. Isn't that right, princess?"

"Yes," she cried, then on a wanton moan, threw back her head and screamed as her orgasm tore through her. Her body tightened around him, spasming, clenching rhythmically, milking him.

She felt him stiffen, felt the heat of his come pulse inside her, filling her, and all she could think was that she'd made a mistake. She'd pushed, and now she'd gotten what she'd wanted.

Hugh had lost control, and it was—it was glorious.

She'd tried to tell herself she could handle it if he walked away. That she didn't want anything more from him. That what they were doing was just sex.

But tonight confirmed what she already knew deep down. What they'd just done, what they were doing—it wasn't just sex. It wasn't just physical.

It was so much more.

Chapter Nineteen

Hugh lay in the dark, Shay curled into his side. He couldn't sleep. Shit, he could barely fucking breathe. The walls in her tiny trailer felt as if they were closing in, and he was slowly suffocating.

An image of Shay, curled around him, tongue darting out, worshipping the ink on his ribs, flashed through his mind. He gritted his teeth. He'd gotten the tattoo after he'd stolen his first car, his Catholic-raised soul racked with guilt. As if it would somehow bring him closer to God, to forgiveness for his sins. He didn't believe that anymore. Fuck that. There was no higher power in the driver's seat of your destiny. Shit happened, then you dealt with it the best you could.

The cross just made him feel like a hypocrite these days.

He curled his fingers into a fist. He didn't know what was causing it, the unease, the twisting, gripping feeling in his gut. He couldn't work out what put it there, what had him in knots. He was still seeing Shay, and he'd managed to keep her a secret, out of the line of fire.

They were one car from meeting their deadline in two days. Four more cars to deliver the following month and they were free. But something had him lying there, studying the dark ceiling. Had him clinging to the woman at his side as if she would be torn away from him at any moment.

He squeezed his eyes shut as that tight feeling started to unfurl, uncoiling faster and faster until he struggled to draw a breath, on the verge of a goddamn panic attack. In that moment, it all became clear.

He couldn't let Shay go.

He'd been lying to himself. Lying to her. She meant something to him—fuck, she meant everything. He'd been too afraid to admit it, even to himself. The risk of losing her, of having to let her go if things didn't go to plan, was still a very real possibility.

But tonight, after the way she'd gone to her knees in front of him, how she'd driven him past the last shred of his control—the wall had dropped. He couldn't pretend anymore. Shay was his. He didn't want casual, didn't want an end date. He wanted it all.

And as soon as Al was in his rear-view mirror, Hugh was making her his, and he was never letting her go.

He'd tried desperately to ignore the way he felt about her. To deny he'd claimed her as his almost from the moment he'd seen her standing in that parking lot dressed in that barely there costume and looking adorable as hell. He'd been determined to keep her at arm's length until he could come to her without the constant risk hanging over his head. Sneaking into her place and leaving again under the cover of darkness. Too afraid to have her at his place again because he knew, *he fucking knew*, if he had her there again, in his bed, among his things, he wouldn't be able to do it any longer.

He wouldn't be able to let her walk back out his front door.

Wouldn't be able to pretend this wasn't so much more than an affair.

When they'd first started she'd been wary. She'd been burned, wasn't ready to jump into anything, but that changed last night, maybe even before. He'd seen it in her eyes, felt it when he'd dried her off and carried her to bed. When she'd wrapped around him and hung on. Staying that way even after she'd fallen asleep.

How could he continue to treat her as if she meant nothing, when in a short time she'd come to mean every fucking thing. Jesus. He had another month of this, this sneaking around, pretending what they had was only physical.

The only other option was telling her the truth. Telling her what he was. A thief.

He couldn't do that, couldn't risk losing her, not when he'd only just found her.

Which meant, as much as he wanted to, he couldn't stay here with her until morning. He couldn't eat breakfast with her then kiss her goodbye at the door.

Still, knowing all this, he lay there for ten more minutes, smoothing his hand over her skin, her soft belly, the dip of her waist, running the tips of his fingers along the sexy crease below each ass cheek.

Shit. He needed to leave before he rolled her onto her back and took her again.

Easing from under her, he climbed out of bed, and after tucking the covers around her shoulders, he started dressing. He pulled on his jeans and yanked his shirt down over his head with more force than was necessary.

"You're going?"

Her voice, husky from sleep, drifted from the bed, soft and sweet, and he wanted to climb back in with her so badly it hurt. He shoved his feet into his boots.

"Yeah, princess. I gotta go."

The covers rustled then she flicked on the lamp. She was sitting up, sheet around her chest, the smooth, creamy skin of her bare shoulders and arms damn near glowing. Her gorgeous, shiny red hair was mussed and sexy as hell. He remembered fisting it while she sucked his cock, how silky it felt. She looked beautiful all rumpled and recently fucked.

His dick surged behind his zipper to the point of pain in an instant.

"Do you have to go?"

She bit down on her bottom lip, and Jesus, he nearly lost it. One word from her and he'd throw everything out the window, just so he could be inside her again. He'd risk it all.

"I mean...you can stay if you like. I could...I could make you breakfast later..."

His gut tightened painfully at the hopeful expression on her face, the wariness in her beautiful green eyes. This wasn't easy for her, asking him to stay. She was going out on a limb, had seen in him exactly what he'd seen in her last night. Was trusting her instincts. Something she hadn't done in a long time. And now he had to make her doubt them, make her believe she was wrong.

He wanted to punch a hole through the goddamn wall.

"Can't, princess." The words felt tight in his throat, a struggle to get out. "Don't think that's a good idea." He wanted to go to her, pull her onto his lap and bury his nose in her hair, say he was sorry. But he couldn't. If he did, he'd stay, and he wouldn't put her in danger like that.

He wanted to tell her how much he wanted to stay, more than anything, but he couldn't do that, either. Because the next time he came to her the same thing would happen. How many times could he reject her before she gave up, before she gave up on him? He had to do his best to keep things as they were, just for another month. Four fucking weeks.

She drew her knees to her chest and tightened her arms around them. "Right. Of course."

Of course.

What did that mean? What was she thinking? He wanted to know desperately, but he couldn't ask her that, either. He palmed his keys. "Tonight?"

She nodded and rested her chin on her knees.

His feet felt rooted to the damn floor. Everything had changed between them last night. Everything. He wasn't the only one feeling this thing between them anymore, and he knew what a big deal that was for her. He wanted to reassure her more than anything because he'd hurt her just now. He could see it. And there wasn't a thing he could do about it if he wanted to keep her safe. If he wanted to keep *her*. "Later, princess."

"Later," she whispered.

Then he forced one foot in front of the other and headed for the door. He heard the lamp in the bedroom click off as he opened the door and stepped outside.

Just four more weeks.

He just hoped he didn't lose her before he was finally free.

* * *

"You need to tell him how you feel," Kayla said, leaning against the counter.

Kayla often stopped by Raggedy Jane's on Mondays and usually brought in morning tea for the three of them. Today, she'd brought muffins and coffee. It smelled divine, but Shay's belly had been churning for the last two days, and she'd barely been able to eat a thing. Ever since she woke to Hugh leaving after what happened in the shower.

After what followed.

She'd thought things had changed, but then he'd left, as he always did.

He'd come by again last night, late, and again, he'd left while it was still dark. Only this morning, when he thought she was still asleep, she'd felt him come to her side of the bed and just stand there. He did this for what felt like forever, then he'd kissed her hair and left.

Which was why she'd finally opened up to her friends about her relationship with Hugh. She was in desperate need of some advice.

Jane took a large bite out of her lemon and cream cheese muffin. "So he just stood there?"

Shay leaned over the counter and rested her chin in her hands. "Yes." Then she shoved away her muffin and started to pace back and forth. "God." She threw up her hands. "I'm so confused."

Kayla washed down her mouthful with coffee. "Are you happy with the way things are?"

Was she? She had been. More than happy, but now…

"It's not a hard question, girl. Either you are or you aren't. Which is it?"

Kayla's all-knowing gaze was locked on Shay, not giving her an inch.

"No." Saying it out loud, that one little word, it finally sank in, how she felt about Hugh, what she wanted. What she had to do.

She'd stupidly convinced herself that she was safe, that her heart was safe because he wasn't her "type". That because he was the complete opposite of the men she'd been attracted to in the past, that casual would be all she'd want from him. Could she have been more naive?

Kayla grinned. "You know I've got your back. Anything you need, I'm there. I'm bound. It's in black and white in our handbook. *Anything in the pursuit of love.*"

Love? An uneasy feeling squirmed behind Shay's ribs.

"So you'll tell him?" Jane asked.

What choice did she have? Shay couldn't go on like this. Every time he left, a tiny piece of her self-respect went with him. Every time she woke up alone, it—hurt. She was no coward. A few days ago, she would have been certain asking him for more than casual would have sent him running. Now? She wasn't as sure. These last few nights, the tender way he held her, the way he watched her sleep, the way he kissed her goodbye even when he didn't know she was aware of it. All those things had to mean something, right?

They finished eating, and Kayla left, telling Shay to call after she'd talked to Hugh. She had no idea what she'd even say. Was she willing to lose him completely? Because that was what could happen.

But she couldn't do this anymore. She wanted him too much, and if he didn't feel the same way, she needed to know now before she got in even deeper.

Though, with the way she was feeling, she didn't think she could get any deeper.

She'd fallen for Hugh Colton, completely and utterly.

Maybe he had the same worries? She'd told him she didn't want a relationship...several times. Maybe he thought if he asked for more she'd end it?

Gah! This was making her crazy.

After she finished her shift, she headed home. Edna was waiting for Shay on her front step, so she took Rocky out to do his business then helped Edna with her dinner. Afterward, Shay went back to her place to shower and change. Of course, now, whenever she got into the shower she thought of Hugh. Thought about how his big body filled the small space. About the sounds he'd made, the way he'd let go.

She changed into dark jeans and a soft, black, boat-neck sweater with a cute bow to the side. She finished off the outfit with her favorite black boots, the ones with the spiked heels. After she'd dried and styled her hair, she applied light make-up and her favorite cherry lip gloss. Then she stared at herself in the mirror. She felt good. The look was casual, but the dark sweater made her eyes and hair seem more vibrant.

Nerves zinged through her. *You can do this.*

The talk they needed to have couldn't happen here, in her trailer, where every corner reminded her of Hugh. Of the things they'd done. She'd crumble or chicken out if he came to her. He dominated her small trailer, turned her to mush the instant he walked into a room. They needed to have this talk somewhere else. She'd texted him earlier to see what he was up to. He'd said he was working late. So the garage it would have to be. There were plenty of places they could have privacy, but with Joe and Adam more than likely there as well, he couldn't sidetrack her with sex.

Grabbing the keys to the Honda—which he'd refused to take back when she'd mentioned it again—she threw her bag over her shoulder and headed out the door. She hadn't told him she was coming. This was a sneak attack. Probably the wrong move but she had to do this now, before she had the chance to think too deeply about it and back out. She couldn't wait another night. She'd misunderstood Travis's feelings for her, had thought they were something more, something real, and she'd been completely wrong. She didn't know what her ex felt for her now, but it wasn't love. You couldn't love someone and want them to change everything about themselves. Hugh liked her the way she was. At least, that's the way he made her feel. But then her history with men, with her own family, was a red flashing light that she was a crappy judge of character.

She just hoped she hadn't misjudged Hugh.

* * *

It was just after seven when she pulled up outside the garage. The main doors had been pulled down, but there were several cars out front. Hugh's truck was one of them. There were also a couple of others she assumed were Joe's and Adam's or maybe a customer's. She didn't know anything about cars, but one was high end, expensive looking, all shiny black. She faltered for a moment. Could she do this?

Before she changed her mind, she shoved open her door and headed to the side entrance, her only way in with the main roller doors closed. It wasn't locked, so she pushed it wide and stepped inside. Florescent lights lit up the vast floor area and standing in the center of the room was Hugh.

Adam was off to the side a little, and he didn't look happy. In fact, neither of them looked happy—except for the guy wearing a suit. The owner of the expensive car, she guessed, and some other big man with him. He was side-on to her, but she could see his teeth, he was smiling so wide.

She took several steps closer, the heels of her boots clicking against the concrete floor. Adam's head lifted at the sound, gaze locking on her, then he closed the space between him and Hugh, his elbow connecting with Hugh's side. Hugh's head twisted toward her, as well, his eyes flaring for a split second before his expression went blank.

The guy in the suit was looking at her now, too, giving her a head to toe, then he grinned. "Don't tell me, you got me a gift?" His gaze moved over her again, landing on her chest and stayed there. "Not my usual taste, but hey, I can work with it."

The way he continued to stare at her made it obvious she was the "it" he was referring to. She hated him instantly.

"Come here, sweetheart," he said in an oily voice that made her skin crawl. "Let's have a good look at you."

"What the fuck are you doing here?" Hugh barked, so loud his voice echoed around the room.

She jumped then just stood there, heart smacking against the back of her ribs, vocal cords suddenly tight. What the hell was going on? What was this? "I-I wanted to talk to you."

His face turned cold, hard. An expression she'd never seen on him before. "I'm busy. We meet when I fucking feel like it; what part of that didn't you understand?"

She stumbled back a step. "What?"

"Are you deaf?"

Humiliation burned her face, her limbs feeling shaky and weak. "No…I…"

"Leave," he barked. "Now."

Adam, the creep in the suit, his friend they all stood there staring at her, making the whole scene ten times worse. Anger welled up, her only defense right then, making her breathe harder and, thankfully, holding back the tears threatening to escape. "I-I don't ever want to see you again; do you understand me? Not ever again."

He crossed his muscled arms over his chest. "Shit, whatever, babe. You finished?"

She didn't bother answering and raced from the garage. But she didn't get far; dizziness washed through her so fast, she thought she might actually faint. She leaned on the wall, sucking down deep breaths.

"Let's get back to business."

She heard Hugh's deep voice echo through the door.

There was a chuckle. The man in the suit maybe. "She seemed a little upset."

"Fuck 'em a few times and they get clingy. Was time to cut her loose, anyway," Hugh said.

"Give me her number. I don't usually go for women with so much meat on their bones, but I'll try anything once."

She didn't recognize the voice so assumed it was the big guy standing beside the suit.

"You want my sloppy seconds, Don? Be my guest. I'm not a huge fan of desperate and clingy…"

Shay brought her hand up to her mouth to stop the sob burning the back of her throat. She bolted for the Honda, not staying to hear the rest of what Hugh had to say about her, but stumbled to a stop before she got to it.

No way could she use that goddamn car. Pulling the keys from her pocket, she tossed them on the front seat and walked away, dialing for a cab as she went, one she couldn't afford.

She could call Kayla, but her friend would probably go to the garage and make another scene, and Shay wasn't ready to talk about what happened, not yet. *She* didn't know what the hell just happened. And no way could she endure the long ride home on the bus. She was struggling to hold it together as it was. She stood waiting for her ride, mind racing, so hurt by his words, she was in physical pain. This was so much worse than what had happened with Travis.

God, what an idiot.

She'd gone and fallen in love with Hugh.

And as much as she'd tried to convince herself otherwise, she was more like her mother than she wanted to believe. She jumped from one man to the next, just like her mom did, letting them use her then dump her. Humiliate her.

He'd made it perfectly clear she meant absolutely nothing to him. Nothing.

With a few words, he'd destroyed her, had broken her, and she'd let him.

After the cab dropped her home, she went inside and kicked off her boots, climbed into bed and burrowed under the covers. Desperate to shut down her mind. Somehow, she must have fallen asleep, because when she woke it was the middle of the night. She almost expected to feel Hugh lying beside her.

Then she heard it, the rattle of the security chain on her door.

She scrambled into a sitting position, then she heard it again. She stumbled out of bed and raced to the window, peaking out behind the curtain. Hugh's truck was outside.

He came.

She hadn't been using the chain, not with Hugh coming to her so late every night. Thank God she had tonight. She couldn't face him. Not now. Never again.

She wrapped her arms around herself. Why would he do that? Why would he come here after what he'd said, the way he'd treated her?

"Shay, please. Let me in. Let me explain."

His voice was muffled, but she heard every word. She walked out to the living room and stared at the door. It rattled again.

"Please...princess. Open up, baby."

She slumped to the floor, hugging herself tighter. Why was he doing this? What did he hope to achieve by coming here? The first hot tear streaked down her face a second later.

He was breathing heavily, so much so, she could hear him through the small opening the chain allowed. He growled, then there was a bang, as if he'd kicked the door.

"Shay. I can explain. Come on, sweetheart, let me in."

He was quiet for the longest time, but she knew he was still there, could feel his presence as she always did. Larger than life, like the man himself. A part of her wanted to unbolt that door, open up and let him tell her whatever lies he'd planned just to have him back. The weak part of her, the part of her that let people walk all over her. She ignored it.

She was stronger than that. Stronger than her mother.

She deserved better than to be treated like a piece of trash, spoken to as if she was worthless, as if she didn't have feelings.

"Princess?" he said again.

God, it hurt. So much. She couldn't take much more.

There was another bang, higher up, his fist.

Then a second later, she heard him walk away. Heard his truck fire up and tear out onto the street.

He was gone. It was all over.

Chapter Twenty

Hugh squeezed the bottle of beer in his hand so tight he was surprised it didn't shatter.

They were fucked.

A car short on their delivery to Al.

They'd been skating the wire as it was. Adam had found what they needed on the last night. They'd been down to the last goddamn hour before they were due to deliver. And the motherfucker had been stolen right out from under them. That same dark figure had appeared out of nowhere, had cracked the lock and hot-wired the thing before Joe or Adam could reach it.

They'd failed. They hadn't met the terms of their agreement, which meant Al had added on interest. A year's worth of it. Four more cars every month for another fucking year. He'd gotten what he wanted.

And Shay had walked in right in the middle of the whole mess.

He'd lost her.

No, he'd fucking destroyed her.

He speared his fingers through his hair, fisting it. He'd had no choice. Al and that asshole Don had seen her. Hugh had seen the interest in the men's eyes. His only thought had been to get her the hell out of there as quickly as possible. Out of harm's way.

What was she doing there in the first place? Why the hell had she come to the garage, looking like that—and not just what she'd been wearing—but the look on her face. Open and sweet. Hopeful.

That look was for him.

Shay was his, and Jesus, he'd nearly lost his mind when Al had turned his weaselly fucking eyes on *his* woman.

"*Fuck.*" He fired the bottle in his hand across the room. It shattered when it met the wooden doorframe, exploding all over the floor.

"Can you yell duck next time you start throwing bottles?" Joe stood by the door, expression wary.

"You wouldn't have to duck if you knocked instead of walking right the fuck on in." His words came out a goddamn snarl, the anger throbbing through him, making his voice rough as hell.

His brother stared at him. "Can't ever see that happening."

"I'm not in the mood for your shit right now." Shoving his fingers through his hair again, he stood and paced to the other side of the room. "And glad to see you're still alive. Since you blew off the meet with Al last night, I could only assume you had something more important to do."

Joe shrugged. "You know me, always in hot demand."

Hugh scowled. "Seriously? While we were losing everything...you were what? Drinking? Fucking?"

Joe opened his mouth to answer, but Hugh wasn't in the mood to hear it.

"Do me a favor and take your fucking court jester routine somewhere else."

The attitude vanished, Joe's gaze going hard. "Promise, no

236

juggling."

Jesus Christ. He was being a dick, but shit, he was angry. So goddamn angry. "Joe…"

"Forget it." His brother shook his head, crossed his arms. "I can't believe we're stuck for another goddamn year, but we can…"

"I don't give a shit about Al or his fucking cars," Hugh fired back. That wasn't the reason he was lashing out, acting like an asshole.

Joe pushed his hands into his pockets, head tilting to the side, studying Hugh. "This is about Shay?"

"What the fuck do you think?"

Joe's brows lifted. "She's that important to you?" There was no sarcasm or humor in his voice for once.

No point hiding it anymore, it was over between him and Shay. "Yes."

"Okay. So you'll talk to her, apologize. Maybe she'll…"

"No offense, little brother, but I'm not taking relationship advice from someone who's never taken it beyond one night with a woman."

Joe's brows lowered. "You make a good point, I guess."

Hugh planted his hands on his hips, stared at the floor, trying to calm the hell down, then looked back at Joe. "Anyway, it's too late. You don't know what she's come from, what she's been through, why she doesn't trust easy. I was winning that trust, thought I only had to keep her a secret for four more weeks. Just four. Now we're stuck for another *year.* I won't expose her to that. I won't risk her being used as a pawn."

Joe rubbed the back of his neck. "Shit, I'm sorry, bro." His expression turned dark, hard. "Al set us up. I'm positive of it." He stared out the window. "Now that fucker has us exactly where he wants us."

"Yeah." Hugh shook his head. "And we can't prove shit."

Joe turned back to Hugh. "If Shay's yours, if she feels the same…"

"I've lost her."

He'd told himself it was for the best. She was better off without him. Still, he hadn't been able to stop himself from going to her after the meeting, goddamn begging her to hear him out. He'd been prepared to tell her everything. In that moment, he hadn't cared. He'd just wanted her not to hurt. Didn't want to be the cause of that hurt.

And yeah, he'd wanted her back.

But he couldn't have her. Not now. Now, they were tied in for another goddamn year.

Joe hung around for a while longer, but Hugh wasn't in the talking mood, and his brother finally left.

Hugh stared out the window for a long time after, didn't know what to do with himself. If his father was there right then, Hugh would wrap his hands around the motherfucker's neck and kill the bastard. Hugh had messed up—had given the old bastard the benefit of the doubt one time too many—and now he'd taken Joe and Adam down with him. He wasn't doing that to Shay, as well.

She was lost to him…forever. He'd made sure of that.

He turned away, took in his living room, remembered all the stupid shit he'd been imagining ever since Shay had walked in there. Since she'd spent that night with him in his bed. Of them being together.

A life with her.

With a roar, he kicked the coffee table, flipping it, sending it across

238

the floor. He scrubbed his hands over his face, breath puffing in and out of his lungs as if he was on the verge of hyperventilating. He was going out of his mind, felt close to exploding out of his skin. He didn't want to be in this house on his own. If he couldn't have her here with him, he wanted to be with Shay in that tiny pink fucking trailer, lying in her bed, her soft body wrapped around him.

He couldn't have it. Any of it. Would never hold her in his arms again.

With nowhere to go, nothing to stop this restless feeling, the non-stop throb in his chest, he walked to the kitchen, boots crunching on broken glass, and grabbed another beer.

Right then, getting drunk, making himself numb so he didn't have to think or feel anymore, sounded like a pretty damn good idea. But he'd need something a hell of a lot stronger than beer for that. He put back the beer and grabbed a bottle of Jack Daniels from the cupboard, instead.

He'd screwed up everything, but getting drunk, that was one thing he could do right.

* * *

"Wake the hell up."

The voice banging away in Hugh's head wouldn't shut the fuck up. He didn't want to wake up. He wanted to stay asleep. Someone shook him, and he kicked out with his foot.

"Piss off."

"Either wake on your own or I get creative."

Adam. Hugh recognized his friend's voice. He also knew what getting creative entailed. And if Adam dumped a bucket of water in his

239

bed, Hugh would have to beat the shit out of the man, and that would take energy he didn't have. Dragging his eyes open, he forced himself to sit up, swinging his legs around so they hit the floor. He rubbed his hands over his face, head pounding.

"What the fuck do you want?"

"Bender's over. Three goddamn days is long enough. In case you've forgotten, we have a garage to run."

Hugh didn't give a shit about the garage. Didn't give a shit about anything. "I'm sure you and Joe have it covered."

"Your brother's been MIA for the last two days. I can't do this on my own. Get in the goddamn shower, and get your ass to work."

That got his attention. "Joe hasn't been at his place?"

Adam shook his head. "He sent a couple texts, so I know he's not in a ditch somewhere. Probably holed up with his latest piece."

Even as Adam said it, Hugh could see the concern in his friend's eyes. Joe had his fun but never at the expense of the business or their deal with Al. Never. "Give me fifteen."

"Make it ten."

* * *

Hours later, well after closing, Hugh was head bent, trying to focus on what he was doing under the hood of a Cadillac, when Joe strode in. Thank fuck.

The prick looked perfectly fine.

Straightening, Hugh wiped off his hands, relief riding him hard. "Where've you been?"

"Sorting out a few things."

"Yeah? What things are those?"

240

Joe stopped several yards away and feet braced, arms crossed, he locked eyes with Hugh. The look on his brother's face was one he'd never seen before. There was no grin, no smirk. No wicked glint in his eyes right before he nailed Hugh with some smartass, sarcastic comment. He was stone cold. Serious as a heart attack. Not something Joe was very often.

Hugh's gut tightened, spine like a damn steel pipe. He threw the rag in his hand on the workbench. "What is it?"

Adam strode out of the office right at that moment, gaze darting between Hugh and Joe, and pulled up short. "Shit. What in the hell's going on?"

Joe ignored Adam, kept his eyes on Hugh and something flickered through them he had no hope of deciphering, but that look, it made his gut clench into a tight knot. *Fuck.*

"Mom? Lucy?" he rasped

Joe shook his head. "Jesus. No. It's nothing like that."

Hugh crossed his arms to hide the way his goddamn hands shook. This was big, whatever Joe had to say. "Spit it out."

Joe uncrossed his arms, hands dropping to his sides. "What's going on is that we're free of Al. Dad's debt, you don't have to worry about it anymore."

What the fuck? Hugh felt his fucking knees go weak. "What?"

"It's over," Joe choked out.

"How the hell did you pull that off?" Adam rasped.

Joe's gaze darted away, then slid back. "When we lost the Nissan, the night of our meeting with Al...I followed her."

Hugh's brows shot up. "Her?"

"The woman working for Al, the one stealing shit out from under us."

Adam cursed.

Shit. "That's why you weren't there, at the meeting?" Hugh said gruffly.

Joe's lips lifted on one side, not quite a smile. "Not the big screw up you thought, huh?"

"Joe…"

His brother shook his head. "Doesn't matter now, you had no way of knowing what I was doing." He shrugged. "The only thing that matters now is we're free. She led me straight to her place. Been watching her the last few days, waiting for something, anything to prove Al was behind it. She had the Nissan stashed not far from her place. I watched her get in it, followed her to Al's warehouse for the drop off. She's his niece, on his payroll, boosts cars for him, as well." He shrugged. "Next day, same thing, only this time there were cops. They were on to her, closing in. Probably watching her on and off for weeks, waiting to get the evidence they needed. I saved her ass before she could give it to them, then I kindly offered her a ride to her uncle's warehouse, so I could fill him in on her close call." Joe shrugged again. "Al decided to show some gratitude."

"That's not like Al," Hugh said into the stunned silence.

Joe held his stare. "What can I say; he loves his niece."

Hugh shoved his hands in his hair. "So what…we owe him nothing? We're free and clear?" Every muscle in his body was rock solid, as if he was waiting for the punchline, the hit that knocked flat the hope building behind his chest.

Joe nodded, rubbed the back of his neck, looking uncomfortable as fuck. "It's over, bro. You don't need to stick out your neck for us anymore. Mom, Lucy, me. We're good."

Fuck.

Hugh planted his hands on his hips. "That's not how it was. I never thought that…"

Joe shook his head, shutting him up. "It's done. Over. Go get your girl. Tell her whatever the hell you've got to tell her to make her forgive you."

Hugh was still struggling to process what had just happened. They were finally off the hook. He could be with Shay, he could go to her, he could… He sucked in a rough breath. "I hurt her."

"Make her understand."

Shay had been through hell with her bitch of a mother, had been walked all over by that fucker she'd been seeing. Hugh would rather walk over broken glass than hurt her again.

What had him repeatedly lifting the Jack bottle to his lips had been the image of Shay, of her face a second before she walked out of the garage. The pain etched into her lovely features.

I'll only hurt her again.

Hugh rubbed a hand over his dry lips, shook his head. "I'll mess it up, let her down. Shit, like I let you all down…"

"What the hell are you talking about?" Joe growled.

Hugh lifted his gaze to his brother. "I should have known. I should have *known* how deep the old man had gotten. I should have stopped him years before it got so bad. It's my fault we were in this situation to begin with."

Joe stared at him, hard. "You can't really believe that shit…"

The side door crashed open, and their heads swung toward it.

His heart squeezed as if it was in a goddamned vise.

Lucy stood in the open door, lower lip trembling, cheeks glistening, eyes blazing. Then she pointed at him. "Don't be a dick."

Hugh froze. "Nice to see you too, little sister." He swallowed hard. "What the hell are you doing here?"

She didn't answer, because she was flat-out running toward him, her small frame hitting him two seconds later. He lifted her off her feet, and she wrapped her arms around his neck. "Shit, Luce."

She lifted her head, slapped his shoulder. "I heard what you just said, numb-nuts, and…" Her breath hitched. "I'm pissed *way* the hell off."

Lucy had always had the ability to melt him into a goddamn puddle at her feet, ever since she was a baby. He'd taken one look at her and known he'd protect her with his life. She'd kept him busy. "Yeah?"

She placed both hands on his cheeks. "I know you've been trying to protect me, but I'm not a goddamn kid anymore." She gave him a squeeze. "I know, Hugh…I know everything."

His eyes drifted shut. Jesus, he wanted to throw up. "Luce…"

"No. It's my turn to talk." Her hand cupped his cheek. "If it wasn't for you, we would've lost our house. If it wasn't for you, some days we wouldn't have had any damn food to eat. You paid for my school books, made sure I went every day." She swiped away a tear. "You paid for my prom dress…you…"

He gave her a squeeze to stop her, couldn't hear another word. She was killing him. "Scared the shit out of your date, too."

She chuckled. "Yeah, you scared him so bad, he wouldn't even hold my freakin' hand."

"Good to know."

She snorted then buried her face against his shoulder, tightening her arms around his neck. "I'm sorry for being a pain in the ass."

"I know, shrimp."

"Love you," she whispered. "Nothing could change that, ever."

"Love you, too."

He put her back onto her feet, and she stared up at him.

"You're a good man, even if you are my annoying big brother who can't stay the hell out of my business." She socked him in the biceps, a small smile playing on her lips. "What Dad did is on him. You were the one who manned up when you shouldn't have had to, when you were just a kid. You made sure we got by. You did that, Hugh." She shook her head. "I don't give a crap how you did it. The only thing that matters is that you did."

His little sister still had the ability to destroy him, to make him fucking melt. "Lucy…"

"Do you believe me?"

"Shrimp…"

"Do you?"

Deep down, he'd known what happened with their father was out of his control. That he'd just been a kid trying to be a man. And because of that, he'd made some fucked-up decisions to provide for his family. Still, he couldn't just let go of the guilt. Couldn't be absolved of it just like that. He'd been carrying it around too long.

He couldn't change the past, but maybe, eventually, he could make peace with it. Because the decisions he'd made, he'd make again in a heartbeat. He hadn't been capable of making the kind of money they needed. As for their old man…

"There's no way you could have known what Dad was doing," Joe said, as if he could read Hugh's thoughts. "He was a goddamn snake. You'd have to be a mind reader to know the shit he was involved in. Give yourself a break, man. You were a kid. He was our father. Despite everything, we loved him. Those times he came back, we all wanted to believe he'd changed, that it was for good. All of us."

Joe was right. About all of it. Hugh had been too caught up in the mess with Al to see through the fog. He'd only been able to focus on his failure when it looked as if his brother and sister had a different view of the situation completely.

Lucy reached up and gave his beard a tug. "You gonna go get your girl or what?"

Adam, who had been standing quietly on the sidelines, leaning against a car, pushed off and crossed his arms over his faded T-shirt. "You sure Shay's in this as deep as you are?"

"No," he admitted.

Lucy cursed under her breath and turned to Adam. "For once, would you keep your trap shut? No one wants to hear the negative crap you love to spew. Some of us have feelings. Some of us want a connection. Unlike you, Hugh isn't a manwhore, looking to shove his dick in every woman in the goddamn country."

Adam's brows lifted, blue eyes boring into Hugh's sister. "Manwhore?"

"You're a slut," she fired back.

"Why don't you tell me how you really feel, baby girl?"

Lucy's face went red, body stiffening, eyes narrowing. Her lips parted, about to let him have it, but Joe clapped a hand over her mouth.

"Calm down, shrimp. You're like an emotional whirlwind. My goddamn head hurts. Ow!" He pulled his hand away, shaking it. "She bit me!"

She scowled up at Joe. "You deserved it." Then she turned her angry gaze to Adam. "And as for how I really feel about you? You sure as hell wouldn't want to know."

Adam stared at her, expression blank except for the muscle ticking at the side of his jaw. "Think you're right there, sweetheart."

Lucy's face went red again, but instead of ripping their friend a new one, she turned to Hugh. "Ignore him. Go get her." Then she looked at Joe and held out her hand. "Keys. I'm crashing at your place."

Joe handed them over then patted her on the head. "We're gonna have so much fun. Can we do makeovers? I always thought I'd make a hot blond."

She socked him in the gut, and they walked away, bickering.

Just like old times.

Hugh watched them go, feeling lighter than he had in a hell of a long time.

Adam's boots scraped on the concrete floor as he stepped forward. "Need to tell you something."

Going by the look on the guy's face, the warm, fuzzy portion of the day was over.

Adam crossed his arms. "I saw her the other night at Woody's."

"Shay?"

247

Adam dipped his chin, and something tightened in Hugh's gut.

"She works there. This isn't a newsflash."

"She was with a guy." Adam let out a rough breath, something a lot like sympathy hitting his eyes. "And they weren't just talking."

"What?"

"Shay asked me not to tell you." He shoved a hand through his hair. "I didn't think she was the type to be so shady, but…"

Hugh was on Adam in two steps, shoving him against a car. "You kept this from me…"

"I didn't know you were so into her. How the fuck would I know what kind of arrangement you had going on?"

"The fact she told you to keep that shit from me was probably a heads-up that I would not be okay with it." Hugh got closer, so they were nose to nose. "You should have told me." He yelled the last, giving Adam another shove before backing off.

Rage so raw it clouded his vision exploded through Hugh with enough force he shook from it. "I'll kill the motherfucker."

"Shit," Joe murmured at his side.

Hugh was so pissed, he hadn't even seen his brother walk back into the garage.

"You don't even know who it was," Joe added.

"Yeah, I do."

Joe pointed at Adam. "This is your damn fault." Then he spun back to Hugh. "Don't do anything stupid. This is not how this day was supposed to go, dammit."

"You telling me I should've kept it to myself?" Adam fired back.

"You already did that," Hugh growled.

"At least count to ten before you hit the guy," Joe said, then mumbled, "Maybe then you'll only go down for assault."

"I don't know," Adam added. "Way he's looking right now, he could plead insanity."

Hugh ignored them both and headed for the door.

Chapter Twenty-One

Shay stood at the counter in her kitchen, staring at the statement she'd received from Landon Private Lenders a little over a week ago. She tightened her fingers around it.

She still didn't know how she'd managed it, but she'd scraped together just enough in tips and the small wage she earned working for Jane to cover this months installment. Shay had over five hundred dollars in the back of her cupboard in a cookie jar. She usually banked her tips every week, but with Hugh occupying her time—and her mind—then her mother's visit and all that followed, she had completely forgotten to do it.

Pain seared through her. Just thinking about Hugh hurt more than she thought possible. Her mother's betrayal, though awful, was not totally unexpected. But Hugh, she thought she knew him. Knew his character. That he was a standup guy. Direct when he needed to be. Sometimes sweet. Sometimes protective. Always kind.

That she'd gotten it so wrong, that she'd misjudged him so completely…it threw her. Like nothing else ever had. Despite her past, the amount of times she'd misread a situation, she'd decided to follow her heart, trust her instincts. She should have known better.

And to top it off, she'd fallen for him. Completely. Wanted him still, even now, after everything.

She was so damn blind. Travis was proof of that. Her mother, too. She'd let her mom stomp all over her. Let the woman come and go as she pleased, using Shay repeatedly. Even when her mother had shown her time and again she didn't give a crap about her. Shay had opened the door to her every time, hoping *this visit* would be different, that she might actually be with Shay because she cared. Not for what she could get.

The truth was, she couldn't trust her own judgment. She'd been hurt by her inability to see what was right in front of her face one too many times. She was better off alone.

Moving around the counter, she opened the cupboard and reached toward the back to get her cookie jar. Once she'd paid off the loan, she'd finally be able to save some money. Get the car she needed, maybe really try at getting more graphic design clients, working for herself. It was definitely an option. She popped off the lid and reached inside...

Nothing but cool, glazed china touched her fingers.

Empty.

"No. *No, no, no.*" She stared inside. It was gone. All of it. Every last dollar. Why hadn't she checked after her mother ran away?

On shaky legs, she walked to the living room and stumbled back onto the couch. What was she going to do? How would she make the payment? She had bills mounting, another installment to save for after this one.

Nothing she owned was worth that much. Even her laptop was several years old. Worthless.

She was completely and utterly screwed.

Life doesn't have any hands, Cupcake, but it can sure give you a slap sometimes.

She'd had more than her fair share. God, she wished her gran was there.

Her gaze moved to the coffee table, to her phone sitting there. The light flashed, announcing an unread text. It was from Travis; she'd purposely ignored it.

Hand trembling, she reached out and picked it up. She was out of options. She needed a job that paid more. She needed money, and she needed it now. Her pride meant nothing in the face of losing the only thing she valued. Her gran's trailer was her home. She'd do anything before she was forced to give it up. And that's what she'd have to do if she missed this payment.

She read the text. Nothing new. He wanted her back. Her job was still open.

Hitting the call button, she put the phone to her ear.

Travis answered after the second ring.

"Can we meet?" she said.

He was quiet for several seconds, and when he spoke his voice was low. "Dinner tonight. I'll pick you up at seven thirty."

Her belly clenched unhappily. "See you then."

* * *

The restaurant Travis picked was one they used to frequent often. The food was exceptional, the decor cozy, romantic. Unfortunately, the present company ruined the lovely atmosphere.

Travis stared at her over the top of his menu, eyes crinkling at the corners.

252

"Let's just start," she said again. She wanted to cut to the chase, not sit there pretending they were on a date. "What I have to say won't take long." She'd tried to talk him into taking her to a coffee shop instead, but he'd refused.

He put down the menu and smiled at her. "Sweetheart, let's just enjoy our meal first, then we'll get to what it is you want to discuss with me."

Stress made her hungry, always had. And since her stress levels were currently through the roof, by the time the waiter came to take their orders, she was starving. "I'll have the steak, please. Medium." Her dining companion wasn't very pleasant, but at least she knew the food was great.

"You're having the steak?" Travis asked, pointing out the obvious.

"Yes."

His lips thinned. "The chicken salad looks good," he not-so-subtly suggested.

She forced a smile, knew it looked frozen on her face. "Does it? You should get it then."

He glanced back down, clearing his throat. "Potatoes? All those carbs…it's not very healthy."

She ignored him and ordered another glass of wine. He claimed to want her back; if that were the case, you'd think he'd keep his jibes about her losing weight to himself, at least for a little while.

Her wine arrived, and she took a healthy sip, though she felt like chugging the whole damn thing right then. Anything to make this hellish dinner less painful.

He was watching—okay, openly staring at her breasts—when she reached the end of her patience. "Travis, I want to come back…"

"I had a feeling that's what this was about." He reached out, took her hand. "It won't be easy, but we can make this work. I'll hire a fitness trainer, anything you need. I'm so happy you changed your mind."

She fought not to yank her hand away, but she didn't want to make him angry. She also wasn't there to play with his affections. That wouldn't be fair, even after the way he'd treated her. She just wanted her job back "No. I mean I want to come back to work." She turned her hand in his, though it cost her to do it, and gave his fingers a squeeze. "I know you regret the things you said, but I can't go back. I…I think we're better off as friends, Trav."

"You don't want to get back together?" he said quietly.

"No." She gave his hand another squeeze. "We started off as friends, colleagues; we can be that again, can't we?"

He didn't answer, just stared at her.

Her face heated, and she shifted in her chair. "You said my job is still open? I've…I've found myself in a bit of financial trouble, Travis. I'd like to come back to TBS if you'll have me…but…well, I was wondering if there was any chance of a small advance…"

"An advance?" he repeated. His mouth tightened, eyes narrowing.

She sat a little straighter. "Yes. You know I'm good at what I do. I single handedly brought in half our client list."

The grip he had on her wrist tightened, no longer friendly. "I think you have me mistaken for some gullible chump." He leaned forward, yanking her closer. "You want your job back?"

"Yes." She was close to flipping out completely. Her pride was a shriveled mess on the floor, and the more she sucked up to this creep, the more she hated herself for it, for being so damn weak, for being stupid enough to get in this situation in the first place.

Travis sat back suddenly but kept hold of her. "Fine. You want your old job…you've got it."

She was stunned into silence. Maybe he'd finally seen the error of his ways?

"You want an advance, it's yours…"

"Thank you, Travis. Thank you so much…"

"You didn't let me finish." He gave her wrist another bruising squeeze. "You can have your advance, but you're going to have to work for it, honey."

"Of course. I will, I promise…"

"Not at TBS." His gaze slid back to her chest, and his lips tipped up at the sides.

"I don't…I don't follow." Though, she kind of thought she did. She just didn't want to believe it.

His gaze lifted to her mouth. "You want your job back; you're going to make yourself…available to me."

Shay froze, nausea racing through her. "You can't be serious?"

"I want you back in my bed, Shay."

"That's going to be a major fucking problem for me." A deep voice growled beside them.

She twisted, looking up, all the way up, and swallowed hard, stunned.

Hugh.

"What are you doing here?" she whispered. She hadn't meant to whisper; it was just at that moment, her voice wouldn't quite work.

Hugh's hard gaze slid from hers to the center of the table, where Travis still had hold of her wrist.

"Let go."

That was all he said, voice rougher than she'd ever heard it.

Travis's fingers loosened then slipped away. She glanced at her ex-boyfriend across the table. His eyes were narrowed, mouth pinched.

"I don't know who you think you are, but if you don't leave, I'll have you thrown out."

Everyone in the restaurant had stopped eating, were watching the spectacle in the center of the room.

Hugh stayed where he was, towering over them, eyes now fixed on her, ignoring Travis completely. "You're back with this guy?"

"What...? No." *What is he doing here? What on earth is going on?*

"This is who you were kissing at Woody's?"

She froze. Adam had obviously broken his silence. Not that it mattered now. Anger and confusion pumped hot through her veins, unlocking her limbs. "He kissed me, not the other way around. I did *not* kiss him back." She drew in a shaky breath, annoyed that she was explaining herself to this man. A man who had thrown her away, who cut her deeper than anyone else could. "What are you doing here, Hugh?"

He shook his head. "What are you doing here with him?" he rumbled. Yes, rumbled.

She bristled. "I asked you first."

He just stared at her, and she got the feeling if he didn't get the answers he'd come for, they'd be there all night.

"Fine. If you must know, I came here to ask for my job back. I have bills to pay, a loan installment…"

"I paid it," he said. "I saw the statement on your counter last week and took care of it. I cleared it. You don't owe a thing anymore. There's no need for you to work with this asshole."

"What?" she whispered.

"I paid off the loan. It's done."

"I don't understand…" She felt dizzy all of a sudden. Head spinning so fast, she was having trouble thinking clearly. "You paid it? Why would you do that?"

His dark gaze slid to Travis, expression terrifying, and just when she thought Hugh might lunge at him, he looked back at her. "Because I hated seeing you killing yourself working three jobs when I could take care of it for you."

She ignored the warmth his words stirred inside her, and shook her head in denial, still struggling to understand what any of this meant. "I don't…I'm not…" What? She didn't know what to say, what to think.

"We need to talk, and we're not doing it here. Let's go," Hugh said.

She jolted in her seat, the shock of seeing him, of learning he'd paid the rest of her loan, had momentarily stunned her. But now, all the anger and hurt surged back, full force. He didn't get to come here asking her questions. Ordering her about. How goddamn dare he?

She had no idea what he was playing at, but she didn't want any part of it. She wasn't doing this anymore. Wasn't letting people walk over her, push her around, as if her feelings didn't matter. Never again.

"I'm not going anywhere with you. And as for what you did, paying my loan…well, I didn't ask you to do that, so if you expect me to fall at your feet, groveling and thanking you for it, you have another thing coming. As soon as I can, I'll pay you back every cent." She wasn't her mother, she didn't need or want a man taking care of her, regardless of his motives.

He shoved his fingers through his hair, sucking in a deep breath through his nose, as if he was trying to calm himself down. "I don't want your money." He mumbled a curse. "We need to talk, princess." His voice had grown softer, more intimate. "There are some things, things I need to tell you."

Princess.

"Hang on a minute," Travis interrupted.

Shay had forgotten he was even there.

"I don't know who you think you are..." Travis continued.

"I'm Shay's."

His words slammed into her, battered her, had her frozen in her seat. Hugh kept his eyes locked on her, no longer dark and pissed but that soft brown she'd grown to love. The way he was looking at her, it sent tingles skittering across her shoulders, down her arms, lifting goose bumps on her skin. Then he fired another shot, this one hitting even harder.

"And she's mine."

Hope unfurled in her chest, even as disbelief and anger socked her so hard, her limbs felt weak from it. Shay stood on shaky legs, fingers curled into fists at her side, heart pounding. "No. I'm not," she rasped.

Hugh reached for her, but she took a step back.

Travis shot to his feet, as well. "If you leave with him, you're not getting your job back, do you hear me?"

She turned to him. "I don't agree to your terms, Travis. I won't be manipulated, not anymore." She turned to Hugh. "And I won't be used, either, not by you, not by anyone. I sure as hell don't want to talk to someone who treated me as if I'm nothing, as if I'm worthless."

"Shay…"

The way Hugh growled her name made her shiver. She took another step back. "Both of you just…leave me the hell alone." Then she grabbed her bag and raced from the restaurant.

Chapter Twenty-Two

Hugh pointed at the asshole across from him. "You contact her again, you fucking *look at her*, I'm coming after you." Then he strode out of the restaurant after Shay.

The street was crowded, but he saw her moving quickly away. No way was he letting her go, not tonight, not ever. Hugh pushed through the people in front of him, not giving a shit. Shay was too polite for that, which meant he caught up with her easily.

He grabbed her arm, and she gasped, spinning to face him.

"Let me go."

"We're talking, princess."

She tried to yank her arm away. "Like hell we are."

He didn't give her a chance to argue and tugged her to the side, lifted her off her feet and carried her down a narrow alley. It led to the back of the restaurants in front of it. Which meant it was quiet and, thankfully right then, besides a few cars, deserted.

She fought hard, but he held her tight so she didn't hurt herself. Her teeth sank into his forearm.

"Jesus Christ."

"Let. Me. Go." She kicked out with her legs, trying to get his shins.

"Not happening. Not until you listen to what I have to say." He spun and pressed her against the concrete wall, ducking his head so they were eye level.

"I don't care what you have to say."

Her eyes were spitting fire, but they were bright, and even though the light was shit back here, he could see her lip tremble.

"I heard what you said to those guys. After you...the way you..." She sucked in a sharp breath. "I heard all of it. You're just like Travis, just like my mother." Then she started struggling again.

He pinned her lower half with his body then grabbed her chin, so she didn't crack her head against the wall, and forced her to look at him. "Stop this and listen to me."

"Go to hell." She jerked up her knee, trying to get him in the balls.

He dodged the blow, shoving a thigh between hers, holding her more firmly in place and stared down at her.

Jesus, she was beautiful. Even when she was pissed off. Shit, especially when she was pissed off. "There she is," he said. "My feisty girl, she doesn't take any shit."

She swallowed hard. "I'm not your girl."

"Yeah, you are, princess."

"Stop calling me that."

He shook his head. "Not gonna happen." He dipped his head, rubbed his nose against her soft red hair, taking in her sweet scent. "I tried," he said. "Every damn night, to just walk out the door. But it got harder and harder. I'd go to leave, but I'd find myself by the bed, watching you sleep. Fucking gorgeous hair spread on the pillow, smooth, pale skin, glowing in the moonlight. As if you shouldn't be real. As if you were just a figment of my imagination. Like some beautiful fairy princess. I had my own fairy princess." He ran his thumb over her trembling lower lip. "And I hurt her. I fucked up."

Her whole body was shaking now. "Please stop," she whispered.

He wouldn't lose her again. The time apart from her had been the worst of his life, and considering the shit he'd been through when he was younger, in recent years, that was saying a lot. Not just about him but about his feelings for this woman. After what she'd been through with her mother—losing her when he spilled all his secrets, told her what he was, was a strong possibility. But he had to tell her. Everything. He had no choice.

"Those guys, the ones you walked in on with me at the garage…they're not good guys." He slid his thumb across her cheek. "It fucking killed me to say that shit to you." He repeated the caress, couldn't get enough, desperate to touch her. "I did it to protect you."

She stilled, blinking up at him. A single tear streaked down her cheek, and the sight of it nearly destroyed him.

"I don't believe you."

He brushed the moisture away with his thumb. "I'm telling the truth, princess. The way they looked at you. Shit, Al wanted you. That's a fact. You do not want to draw the attention of a man like Al Ramirez. I promise you that. I needed to get you away fast, before he set his sights on you. Before he worked out you mean something to me. No way was I going to let him use you to get to me."

"What are you talking about?"

Her breasts were smashed up against his chest now, and he could feel her heart pounding rapid fire, could see the pulse fluttering like crazy at the side of her throat.

He held her wide-eyed gaze. "You want to know the reason I only came to you at night, why I left when it was still dark?" His own heart was racing; what he was about to tell her could put him in jail for a long time, but that wasn't what had his palms sweaty and his mouth dry. No, it was how Shay would see him after she knew the truth. If she'd despise him as much as he despised himself. "Those men, they wanted me tied to them, to keep working for them, and they would have done anything to make that happen. That's why I had to send you away. I panicked. I didn't know what else to do."

She was still frozen in his arms. "Working for them?"

He didn't want to tell her, so much so his jaw ached from clenching it, but if he didn't at least try to get her to understand, he'd lose her, anyway. He drew in a shaky breath. "I stole cars for them." He held her gaze. "I'm a thief, Shay."

Her whole body jerked in his arms. "You stole cars?" She exhaled loudly. Her confusion, her disbelief shone clearly on her face. "No, you…" She shook her head. "No…"

"It's true."

She gave his chest a shove, but he held on tighter.

"You're just saying this, to…to…"

"To make you understand why I did what I did. It's the truth, Shay." Shit. He forced the next words past his lips. "When I first met you, I was…I was in the middle of boosting a car. I should've let you go that night, but after I chased that guy away, I couldn't leave you. I knew I should, but I wanted you like I've never wanted anything in my life. So I took you with me."

"No." She turned away. "You're making this up."

There was only one way to make her believe what he was saying.

He released her, hating the loss of her softness, her gentle warmth pressed against him when he stepped back. She stood statue still, but her gaze darted to the alley. He moved to the side, so she'd have to go through him if she wanted to make a break for it. Then pulling out his wallet, he slid the lock-pick he always carried in it free.

"What are you doing?"

"Proving it to you." He approached the car. "You know I can pick a lock, Shay, you've seen me do it...and that first night, you sat there and watched me hotwire that car." He slid the pick in the lock and had the door open and the alarm deactivated in fifteen seconds. He released a rough breath and shut the car door again, looking up at her, fucking sick to his stomach. "Yeah, any mechanic can do what I just did, but not that fast. You need a lot of practice to be as fast as me...so you don't get caught. So you can get in and drive out as fast as possible."

She stumbled back a step until her back hit the wall.

"That first night, that car, the one you drove me to your garage in? You'd just stolen it?"

He put away the pick and shoved his wallet into his back pocket. "Yeah." Then he strode toward her before she tried to run. Kept coming until he had her pinned between him and the wall again.

She jerked back, and he shoved his hand between her and the concrete wall, protecting her head. Then scooping her up, he lifted her so they were eye level again, so she had no choice but to wrap her legs around his hips. "Now do you believe me?"

"I want you to let me go."

"No."

Her jaw dropped. "No?"

"Not until I tell you everything. If you want to walk away after that? I won't stop you." What felt like every damn muscle in his body tightened. The idea of letting her walk away went completely against all his protective instincts. Against the fact that as far as he was concerned, Shay was his, would always be his.

She didn't answer, stayed stiff in his arms. But she didn't tell him to fuck off, either. Right then, he was counting that as a win.

"I told you the old man's a gambler. Gambled as long as I can remember. When we were kids, he'd disappear for months at a time, like your mom used to leave you."

Her wide green eyes started getting bright again. He forced himself to carry on, to tell her the whole ugly story.

"Just when we were getting back on our feet, guaranteed, every damn time, he'd come crawling back and screw everything up again. He did that our whole lives. Mom loved him, so she kept taking him back. She was a cleaner. Her wage didn't cover the bills…the debt he'd leave behind every time he'd run off again. So I left school as soon as I was old enough, got a job, supported the family. I took care of my mom, my brother and sister."

He felt her body relax a little, but she was still tense, fingers digging into his shoulders.

"I cleaned up his messes, paid off his debts whenever the people he owed came knocking on the door." He gave her a squeeze. "But I was fresh out of school. I wasn't making enough to keep our family afloat. So to do that, to keep the roof over our heads, I stole cars." Him and Adam had been a good team, even then. But Shay didn't need to know Adam's involvement. This was about him and him alone.

She stared up at him. "You've been a car thief since you were just a boy?"

He shook his head. "Stopped when I got a little older. Opened the garage with Adam and Joe. Kept my nose clean for a lot of years. I didn't do that shit for a thrill. I did it to feed my family. To pay the old man's debts."

Her fingers went from drilling holes in his shoulders to sliding restlessly over his shirt. "What happened?"

"The last person my father fucked over was Al. Al isn't the kind of man to let that shit go. He wanted back what he was owed, and he was owed a hell of a lot. More than me and Joe had. He threatened my mom and my sister. He knew about my past, used it to get me to fall in line. I had to pay him back, with interest, but he wanted me to do it by supplying him with cars."

He kept talking when all he wanted to do was take her mouth and kiss the fuck out of her, make her promise she was his, that she wouldn't leave him. "We were coming to the end of our arrangement with him, but Al wanted to lock me in, keep me working for him. If he worked out you were mine, he would have used you to keep me where he wanted me. He could have hurt you. I couldn't…fucking *wouldn't* allow that."

She looked at him for the longest time, emotions moving behind her eyes, too many to name, until his gut was nothing but knots, his heart close to exploding out of his chest. Her arms didn't fall away like he thought they would after hearing all that shit, seeing it with her own eyes; no, they tightened around his neck.

"Hugh," she whispered, just that one word, just his name, but the pain in her voice, for *him*, completely shredded him.

"I said those things to protect you, princess," he rasped. "Kept my distance for the same reason. The last thing I ever wanted to do was hurt you." He was shaking now, with relief that she'd stopped fighting, from the fear that he might lose her still. "But it's over now. As of a few hours ago, and in a way that's permanent." He held her gaze. "No more hiding, no more leaving in the middle of the night. You're mine. No matter what happens from this minute on, you'll always be mine."

"You're telling the truth...aren't you?" She bit her lip, eyes glistening, bright like emeralds.

"Yes," he rasped. "Jesus, what you said back at the restaurant, I can't bear that you thought I was using you. Walking out every night, leaving you...I fucking hated it, it fucking *killed* me." He gave her a squeeze, shaking so hard there was no way she couldn't feel it.

Her hands dropped to his biceps, her hold light. "It's...It's hard for me to trust...not just you but myself...after everything I've been through. I don't know...I just don't know."

Oh, fuck, he was losing her. He was going to lose her. "You have to believe me, princess. Shit. Please, baby."

She blinked, and more tears streaked down her cheek. She turned away. "This is too much. I can't think with you this close, I can't...please let me down, Hugh."

"Shay..." he croaked.

She shook her head. "I don't know what to think, what to believe anymore." She turned back to him. "Please, Hugh, let me go."

"No, baby. Don't do this."

Her face crumpled as she pushed at his chest, giving him no choice but to do as she asked. She slid out from between him and the wall, and the loss of her warmth, her softness, physically hurt, like knives or razors, a fucking anvil to the chest.

"Shay, please…"

"I need to go. This is too much. It's just…too much," she said again. Then she turned and walked quickly away.

* * *

The alarm blaring from Shay's phone made her jump, and she quickly turned it off. She hadn't slept a wink. Three nights she'd barely slept. God, she felt as if she was coming down with something, maybe the flu. Her entire body ached but mainly the center of her chest. Maybe she was about to have a massive heart attack. It hurt enough, it hurt so damn much.

But it was none of those things…she wasn't sick. She was heartbroken. The look on Hugh's face when she'd asked him to let her go, when she'd walked away. It was seared into her memory, had haunted her the last few nights.

She didn't know what to think, what to feel anymore. How many times had she listened to her mother's lies and believed every one? How many times had she allowed the woman back into her life, only to be let down? Travis was a major asshole, a complete jerk…she'd had no clue. Had been so damn gullible. It was only after she'd broken it off, after she'd left her job, that a couple of her co-workers had come forward and said how surprised they were that she'd been seeing him, that he wasn't a good guy.

She hadn't seen it.

Not until it was too late.

She wanted to believe Hugh, desperately. But what if she was wrong again? What if it happened all over again? How would she survive another blow like that?

He said he'd been trying to protect her.

That he'd been forced to steal, to break the law, all in an effort to take care of his family. If what he said was true, how could she condemn him for that? He'd shown her repeatedly what a good man he was, hadn't he? Still, those doubts niggled in that back of her mind. Tormenting her, telling her she'd be stupid to listen to her heart again. Her heart always got it wrong.

Shoving back the covers, she climbed out of bed, dragged on her robe and shuffled out of her room. She couldn't stay in bed all day. Rocky needed to go out.

Edna was waiting, her door opening before Shay got the chance to knock.

"You look like crap," Edna said as soon as she laid eyes on Shay. "You still not sleeping?"

Shay took the dog from her neighbor. "I'm fine." She ignored the question and took Rocky to do his business then picked him up and walked back to Edna.

Her neighbor was still standing at the door, beady eyes locked on Shay, pack of smokes in one frail hand. "You're pining for your man."

"I'm not pining."

"Yeah, you are. Your eyes look as if they're about to fall out of your head. And I may be old, but I'm not deaf yet." She reached out and touched Shay's arm. "I've heard you crying, girl. Why're you punishing yourself like this? Go to him, patch things up."

"You don't understand…"

"Bullcrap." Edna pointed a boney finger at Shay. "Don't tell me I don't understand."

"It's complicated."

"Do you love him?"

The pain in Shay's chest got worse, but it didn't just stay there; no, it twisted and coiled down low in her belly, knotting like a fist. "Yes," she whispered. "But I don't know if I can…I don't think I can…" She bit her lip.

"What is it, girl?"

"If I can trust my own judgement. If I can believe him, allow myself to *believe in him*… I want to…"

Edna shook her head, pulled a smoke from the pack and lit up. "You've been burned by a lot of people in your life; you're gonna be wary. But trust me on this, Hugh isn't like your mother, and he sure as hell isn't like that weasel you used to date. I know a good man when I see one. Reminds me of my Albert, God rest his soul. Strong, protective, hardworking…and so damn randy, a woman never got a full night's rest."

Shay choked out a laugh.

Edna carried on before Shay could answer. "I loved your grandmother; you know I did. But she didn't exactly set you a good example when it came to romantic relationships. Her man up and left, and she never recovered, never trusted enough to let anyone else in. That old coot, Harold, he loved your grandmother, but she never let him get too close. She could have been happy with him; they could have been happy together." She took a drag of her smoke. "Don't want you to end up like her. Don't let what happened in the past dictate your future, or one day, you'll wake up old and alone, living in this damn trailer park, and realize it's too late, wishing you'd been brave enough to take a chance.

* * *

Hugh glared at the computer screen. Working on this month's accounts was not his idea of a good time. But then, all he'd done so far was stare at the stupid thing, hoping it would spontaneously catch on fire or blow the hell up. He hated office work with a passion, but Adam had shoved Hugh in there ten minutes after he showed up for work...after he'd flipped out on one of their customers.

Turned out, he wasn't handling the situation with Shay all that well. And everyone around him was getting the brunt of it.

He got why she'd walked. Didn't make it hurt any less, though.

Leaning back in his seat, he rubbed his hands over his face. Every day that passed felt like an eternity without her. Nothing felt right anymore. Nothing. He should be celebrating. They were finally free of Al, but Hugh couldn't muster the energy. It didn't matter, not anymore. Not without Shay.

Someone knocked on the office door.

"Go away," he muttered.

"I'm going to open this door," Joe said, voice muffled. "Is it safe? Or are you going to hurl the filing cabinet at me or something?"

Hugh grunted.

The door cracked open, and Joe poked his head around the edge. "I'm gonna do a lunch run; you want something?"

"Not hungry."

"Dude, you need sustenance."

Hugh opened his mouth to answer.

"And no, I'm not talking about alcohol."

That scratched that idea. The urge to get wasted was at an all-time high. But after last time, Joe and Adam weren't having any of it. They'd been on him like a pair of festering hemorrhoids. Pains in his fucking ass.

Joe shook his head. "Sandwich, it is."

"Whatever." He turned back to the computer. Trying to get the thing to print the damn invoices was more complicated than launching a motherfucking space shuttle.

"You need a hand stuffing envelopes"—Joe piped up from his spot, lurking behind the door—"ask Adam."

"Fuck off."

"Well, aren't you extra charming this morning."

Hugh smashed his finger down on a few keys and cursed, ignoring his brother still hovering like a bad smell behind him. He hated computers.

"Bro, you wanna talk about it? Hulk-smashing the keyboard isn't going to make things better."

"Nope."

"Let's make a night of it. We can braid each other's hair, watch chick flicks, stuff our faces with chocolate…"

"Get lost, Joe."

Joe was quiet for a few seconds. "Come on, Hugh, talk to me."

Joe actually sounded serious, which meant he wasn't playing anymore. Hugh didn't want to talk about it. He relived the moment

Shay pushed him away and walked out of his life twenty times a damn day.

"Not in the mood to talk. Not to you, not to any-damn-one."

Someone cleared their throat, a feminine someone. "Not even me?"

Nope, not Joe.

Hugh spun in his seat in time to see his brother step back, revealing the woman he wanted beyond reason, a woman he'd thought he'd never see again.

Shay stood there, expression wary, gaze sliding between him and Joe.

Hugh shot to his feet.

She looked pale. Her hair, loose, tumbling down her back. She was wearing one of those dresses she liked, the kind that showed off her small waist and full breasts, flaring at the hips. Her hands were clasped in front of her, so tight her knuckles were white.

She was the most beautiful sight he'd ever seen.

Joe said something, Hugh had no idea what, and Shay gave his brother a tentative smile before Joe walked away.

Her eyes came back to Hugh and locked on.

He sucked in a sharp breath. Jesus, he'd missed her. He tried desperately to think of what to say but had nothing. Not a damn thing. His reaction to seeing her was a physical blow, his brain turning to freaking mush. Every muscle bunched tight as he fought not to rush to her, heart pounding, cock stirring. His body recognized her as his, even as his mind told him she wasn't, yelling at him to stand the hell down.

"Do you…do you have time to talk?"

Hugh dipped his chin, swallowing, trying to get moisture back in his mouth. "Yeah, of course."

She walked into the office and shut the door behind her. She looked unsure, nervous, releasing a shaky breath before she spoke. "It's good to see you. I've...I've missed you."

His heart started smacking against the back of his ribs. "Missed you too, sweetheart."

She started blinking quickly, eyes getting glassy.

He took a step toward her. "Why're you here, Shay?" Seeing her again was heaven and hell, all rolled into one.

She moved closer, as well, and now only a few feet separated them. He wanted to close the space, drag her into his arms and never let her go. But he held his ground, waited for her to tell him why she'd come. Afraid to believe it was for him.

She dropped her hands to her sides. They were trembling. "To apologize."

Shit. His heart sank. He'd tried not to get his hopes up, but they'd skyrocketed as soon as he'd seen her. "Don't need to do that," he rasped. It was a struggle to keep his voice even, to hide how much this fucking hurt. "I get it. You don't want to be with a thief. Don't blame you, princess."

She shook her head and took another step closer. "No...that's not...that's not why I'm apologizing."

"No?"

She closed the gap then, the soft mounds of her breasts pressing against his abs. Reaching up, she cupped his jaw. "No." She shook her head, soft hair slipping over her shoulder. "I'm sorry, Hugh, for walking

274

away."

He dragged a breath in through his nose.

She moved a little closer. "I'm sorry for letting my doubts and fears get in the way of us."

"Shay…"

"I didn't trust my judgment…when I knew…I knew all along…" She bit her lip, eyes closing tight.

"What did you know?" he choked out.

Her lids fluttered, thick lashes lifting, giving him her beautiful green eyes. They met his and held. "That we belong together…" Her thumb slid over his beard. "That I could trust you, that I believed you. Believed *in you.*"

"Yeah?" His legs almost gave out.

One of her hands smoothed over his back, the other sliding up into the hair at his nape. "I'm sorry," she said again softly.

His breath seized in his lungs.

"I don't care about your past, Hugh. You were looking after your family. You did what you had to do."

Her voice was still soft with a hot, little rasp behind it that sent tingles over his scalp and down his spine.

His heart stuttered to a goddamn standstill. *Jesus.* Her words had a boulder-sized lump forming in his throat. Even after all the shit she'd gone through with her mother, losing her father, her gran, that big heart of hers still shone through.

This woman, shit. She blew him away. He tucked a loose strand of hair behind her ear, finally touching her. She blinked up at him, gaze locked on his, and in that moment, it was as if she'd reached into his chest and had taken possession of his heart. It wasn't his anymore. "You telling me you're mine?"

Chapter Twenty-Three

Shay swallowed the emotion heavy in her throat and stared into his soft brown eyes, relief coursing through her limbs, making them weak. "Yes, I'm yours."

He pressed his forehead to hers. "Thank God." He cupped her face in his wide palm, his rough, callused thumb smoothing over her cheek, her jaw. "Christ, I don't know what I would've done if you'd walked away again."

She shook her head. "How could I do that…when you're all I've ever wanted? I've been waiting for you my whole life."

His entire body jolted against her, then his eyes slid shut. "Fuck, Shay."

When he looked at her again, his gaze blazed hotter than she'd ever seen. He brought his mouth down on hers, kissing her hot and hard and deep, steeling her breath until they were both shaking.

"I need to take you home," he said against her lips. "I need you in my bed where you belong. I need to show you how fucking sorry I am for hurting you. I thought I'd lost you for good, princess. I thought I'd lost you forever, and it was tearing me up inside. I need to feel you under me. I need to wake up beside you in the morning."

Everything he'd just said, she needed to hear, so badly, tremors slid through her. "I want that, too. Please, Hugh, please take me home."

He took her hand, opened the office door and led her back through the garage. Adam and Joe stopped what they were doing, watching Hugh stride through, Shay beside him, half jogging to keep up.

"When should we expect you back?" Joe said, but there was humor in his voice.

Hugh ignored his brother and kept walking.

Joe chuckled, and she heard Adam join in as they headed out the door and toward his truck.

They both climbed in then they were headed for his house.

The drive was quiet, neither one able to find the right words after what just happened, the air thick, crackling with so much emotion, she struggled to breathe evenly.

A short time later, they pulled to a stop in his driveway. Hugh climbed out, came around and opened her door, then he took her hand again and led her to the front door. His fingers shook when he unlocked it and pulled her inside after him. He still hadn't said a word when they moved farther into the house and carried on upstairs to his bedroom.

She turned to him when he shut the door behind them, breath seizing in her lungs as he reached back, gripped his T-shirt and pulled it up and off.

"Come here, baby," he said gruffly.

She went to him, that magnetic pull of his in full force.

He moved around behind her, sliding her hair to the front before he drew the zipper of her dress down slowly. His breath was heavy, choppy. The sound of his need for her increased her own. When the zipper was all the way down he pushed the fabric resting on her shoulders forward, so the sleeves slipped down her arms. The dress dropped, pooling at her feet.

He made a *hmm* sound that sent shivers skittering over her bare skin. His palm smoothed down her spine, from the base of her neck all the way down to the top of her bottom. He made another rough sound then snapped open her bra, pushing that off her shoulders, as well. He moved in closer, so the hair on his chest, the heat of his skin pressed against her back. His mouth came down against the side of her neck, and he slid his hands around her waist.

"So beautiful," he said roughly, kissing her shoulder. "All mine."

Her head dropped back against him as he worked the sensitive skin below her ear with firm yet soft lips. His hands roamed over her belly, up over her ribs. Then those beautiful, big hands cupped her breasts, kneading almost roughly, possessively. A contrast to the tender way he rubbed his lips against her, gentle and teasing.

She felt hot, feverish and wet, so very wet. The fingers tormenting one of her breasts released her, moved back over her belly, sliding down the front of her panties.

"Spread your legs for me, princess."

She did as he asked, knees so weak, she was afraid she might collapse in a heap if he kept touching her like that.

"That's my girl."

A thick finger lightly traced her folds, and she gasped.

"Please."

"Jesus, so wet." He shoved down her underwear. "Step out."

He held her hands as she kicked off her shoes, followed by her panties.

"On the bed, hands and knees."

She crawled onto the bed and looked back over her shoulder. Hugh gaze was locked on the aching heat between her thighs, and when he cursed again she knew he could see how much she wanted him. How desperate she was to have him inside her. He moved up behind her, feet still on the floor, and smoothed his hand over her bottom, down between her legs.

"This pretty pussy, these sexy thighs"—he dipped between her legs, skimming her folds, caressing her inner thighs—"fuck, baby, they're slick and glistening with how much you want me."

"Yes," Shay gasped. "I need you. Only you."

There was a rustle of clothes, then he was behind her again, the head of his cock, hot and insistent, pressing against her butt cheek.

"Wanna taste you so bad, but"—he sucked in a ragged breath, one hand going to her hip, fingers digging in—"gotta fuck you now, princess. Need to feel you wrapped around me."

Shay whimpered, unable to speak, so desperate for him, she couldn't form the words to beg him to push inside her. She didn't have to beg, though, because a second later, the fat head of his cock was slicking up and back, through her folds, then he was where she needed him, against her opening.

Both of his hands moved to her hips, his thick, strong fingers holding her where he wanted her, and he started pushing inside.

"Shit," he barked out. "So hot, baby. So wet and fucking tight."

He kept up the pressure, sliding in one slow inch at a time. He felt impossibly big in this position. God, he went so deep, filled her so thoroughly, all she could do was moan and gasp.

He smoothed his hand down her spine, up and back, not moving his hips, letting her adjust.

"So perfect, sweetheart. You feel so good. My girl. My beautiful fairy princess."

His praise, the tender way he spoke to her, made her heart swell, made tears prickle the backs of her eyes.

Then finally, *finally* he started moving. He kept that firm grip on her hip with one hand, the other caressing her as he thrust in and out of her grasping body, slowly and easily.

Her head dropped, hanging from her shoulders, lips parted, whimpers and moans all she could manage. He felt so good. *So good.* Nothing felt this amazing. No one.

"Watching you stretch around me"—his roaming hand slid up to her shoulder and wrapped around it, then holding her in place, he took her by surprise and slammed up inside her—"can't go slow. Not watching you take my cock like that. You make me lose control, sweetheart. Only you do that. Can't get enough. Never get enough."

He started thrusting into her then, hard and fast. Pleasure pooled low in her belly, sparks of light behind her lids. Fire between her legs. Her inner muscles started convulsing around him. Hugh growled and pulled from her body suddenly, then he flipped her onto her back. But before she could cry out in protest, he lifted her higher on the bed and came down on top of her. She wrapped her legs around his waist, and he jerked his hips forward, filling her hard and fast once more.

She cried out, back arching, mouth dropping open.

"Look at me, princess. Look at your man while he's fucking you."

She forced open her eyes. His expression was fierce, gaze intense.

"Wanna watch my girl come. Wanna see her face when I make her scream my name."

His hips pumped into her, his massive body straining above hers, filling her, surrounding her. Everything inside tightened almost painfully then released, like an explosion. Unbelievable pleasure radiated from her core, light sparking behind her eyelids. She hung on, screaming his name as he continued to thrust in and out of her body, drawing out her orgasm.

He quickened his strokes. "That's it. My girl feels so fucking good," he gasped out.

Then he slammed up inside her, and shuddering, came hot inside her, setting off dizzying aftershocks that had her squirming and moaning, clutching him tighter.

She held him in her arms when he collapsed on top of her, until finally, he rolled, taking her with him. He dragged her up over his body, holding her to him as if she was the most precious thing in his possession. Stroking and soothing her, hand moving up and down her back.

He kissed the top of her head. "I want you here with me," he finally said.

She smiled against his chest. "I am here with you."

He shook his head. "Look at me, Shay."

She lifted up, then because she couldn't help it, she leaned in and kissed his firm lips. One of his hands slid up into her hair, the other tight around her waist. His tongue moved with hers, deep and hungry. She only pulled back when she was desperate for breath. His lids were heavy when she looked down at him, and though it should be impossible, his cock was starting to harden again.

"Sorry." She grinned. "What were you saying?"

He blinked up at her slowly, an adorable, befuddled expression on his face.

"You want me here?" she prompted him.

The confusion cleared, replaced with intense determination. "I want you to move in."

She did some blinking of her own. "What?

His arms tightened around her. "I love you, Shay." He brushed her hair back from her face. "Never felt about anyone the way I feel about you." His fingers flexed against her side. "Move in with me."

"You love me?" she whispered.

"More than anything," he rasped.

Warmth filled her, like a light shining from within, bright and beautiful. The feeling so overwhelming, she knew Hugh could see it, too, could see the affect his words had on her. His soft brown eyes moved over her face, then he swallowed hard, throat working, and his already-tight grip on her got even tighter.

Then he smiled wide. Gorgeous.

She rested her forehead against his. "I love you, too…so much."

"Yeah?" he rumbled, throat working again.

"Yeah," she whispered.

His arms flexed around her. "You gonna move in with me?"

She nodded.

"You okay living with an ex thief?"

She smiled down at him, tears stinging the backs of her eyes. She didn't bother holding them back; they were tears of sheer happiness, and she wanted him to see the way she felt about him.

"You stole my heart, Hugh." She kissed his lips softly. "And I wouldn't have it any other way."

Holding her hips, he slid back inside her. "And you stole mine, princess. And I don't ever want it back."

Epilogue

Two months later.

Hugh opened the front door when he heard the Honda pull into the driveway. Shay had taken the car back; now he just had to convince her to let him buy her a better one. So far, he'd failed, but he'd wear her down eventually.

The door opened, and she climbed out. She'd taken a while. He'd left her half an hour ago to say her goodbyes. Joe had helped Hugh unload the bigger items of furniture from the back of his truck then took off, and Hugh had been waiting impatiently for her to get there ever since.

Though she'd been keeping most of her clothes at his house, all her other stuff had still been at the trailer. They'd been spending a few nights a week there. She was worried about Edna. Needed to know she was taken care of.

Now, Edna was covered, and it was time for Shay to come home. To officially move in.

He'd set up her computer in one of the spare rooms—her office— while he'd waited. Over the last couple of months, she'd managed to pick up more graphic design clients, enough she could quit her job at Woody's, start her own business. Thank fuck for that; she wouldn't take his money no matter how many times he offered, and he hated the thought of her around a bunch of drunks.

She opened the back door of her car and pulled out a box. His smile slipped when she turned to face him, eyes and nose red. She looked up at him, and her face crumpled.

Shit.

She started toward him, and he met her halfway. Took the box from her.

"Gran's cats," she managed through a sob.

He put down the box and wrapped her in his arms. She buried her face against his chest.

"Princess, don't cry."

"I just..." She pulled back. "Edna hugged me," she wailed.

Jesus. "She did?"

"I know Harold will look after her and Rocky, and I-I'll still make sure her freezer's stocked with her favorite meals...but"—she buried her face again and let out a loud sob—"it just felt so weird, you know? Driving away from Gran's trailer, knowing I'll never live there again."

Never live there again. Those words were music to his ears. "You regret moving in with me?"

She pulled back quickly, shaking her head. "Never. God, you don't think that, do you?"

Hugh smiled down at his sweet, crazy, beautiful woman and brushed away her tears. He shook his head. "I know it's hard to say goodbye to that part of your life, to those memories, but, baby, we're gonna make some good ones of our own right here. You and me."

She smiled through her tears and nodded enthusiastically. "You and me."

"And the dog."

She frowned. "What dog?"

"The one we're gonna get."

The smile was back. "Oh, I'd love that."

"And the kids."

Her eyes went big, and her mouth dropped open. Fucking cute as hell.

"Kids? You want children?"

"Yeah, we've got plenty of room. You want kids?"

"Y-yes." Her eyes started to get glassy again, as if she was seconds from letting loose more tears.

Nerves gripped him low in the gut. "We're shacked up, getting a dog, talking about kids"—he cupped her precious face in his hands—"I'm thinking, though, before we move to the kids part, we need to get hitched."

"W-what?" Her watery gaze searched his.

He dropped to his knee in the front yard, took her hand in one of his and dug the ring out of his pocket with the other. "I want to make beautiful memories with you, Shay, here in our house. I want to have babies with you, grow old with you, spend the rest of my life with you. Princess, say you'll marry me?"

Her face crumpled again, a second before she flung her arms around his neck, knocking him on his ass. She pushed his shoulders, so he was lying flat on his back in the grass, and straddled him. The tears were flowing again, a bright, breathtaking smile lighting up her entire face.

"Yes. Yes, I'll marry you."

His heart filled to bursting, and he threw back his head and laughed. Shay laughed with him, in between kisses.

SPIN

Boosted Hearts #2

by Sherilee Gray

He never planned on falling for the enemy…

Indebted to a local crime boss thanks to their father's gambling debts, mechanic Joe Colton and his brother have been forced to steal cars for three soul-killing years. But when Joe saves the man's niece from police – the same deliciously hot-blooded woman sabotaging their efforts to clear the debt – it's time to negotiate new terms. And discover why, that one night, she burned him with a kiss then ran…

Darcey Connors will do anything to get her baby brother away from the criminals in her family – even screw up a good man's life. Yet in the midst of tailing Joe, she somehow falls hard for the sexy tattooed car thief. Nothing can happen between them, but she owes him big time, and if he's going it alone, she is going to help. As long as no one ever finds out – not Joe, her family, the police – or she could lose everything.

Chapter One

Darcey Conners tightened her long dark ponytail, tugged her baseball cap lower, then keeping to the shadows, edged along the brick wall.

She scanned the parking lot again. All clear. Then returned her focus to the reason she was skulking around in the dark.

A little sigh escaped her lips.

Good freaking God, the man was a picture of male perfection, even while he was in the middle of committing grand theft auto. His big shoulders moved in a way that advertised the muscles under his shirt as he picked the lock, thick veins bulging along his tattooed forearms. Head bent in concentration, strong jaw covered in a thick beard, lips peeled back to reveal straight white teeth as he worked. She wanted to touch that beard. He'd grown it thicker recently, and all she could think about was how it would feel against her skin. Soft? Bristly? Would it tickle?

Ack! *Concentrate!*

The lock popped and he slid straight into the driver's seat, quickly disabling the car alarm. The engine turned over a second later. He didn't hang around, pulled the door shut and drove away .

She checked her watch. Fifteen seconds.

He was good. Really good.

Joe Colton was one of the best.

He also hated her guts, and that was a damn shame, since she couldn't even look at him without getting highly turned on—without imagining all kinds of fool things, things that involved white picket fences and happily ever after's.

What made it ten times worse? She knew what it felt like to have his lips on hers. How he tasted. The dirty, hungry sounds he made when he kissed a girl.

The man kissed like she imagined he fucked. Deep, hard, and in total control of the woman on the receiving end.

She gave herself a mental slap upside the head. She had to stop thinking like that. He had a damn good reason for despising her.

It was her fault Joe was still stuck boosting cars for Al. Al Ramirez was a complete and utter asshole. He was also her uncle. Well, that's what he liked to be called. Len, Al's bastard of a brother married her mom seven years ago, when her brother Noah had only been a few months old. That's when Darcey had been brought into the Ramirez fold—whether she wanted to be there hadn't been up for debate.

Now her mom was gone, and Al owned her—like a pair of shoes or a pet that he didn't really like all that much but kept around anyway just so he could put the boot in every now and then.

Which meant when he'd ordered her to make sure the Colton brothers didn't meet their deadline, so he could add interest to their debt—she had to obey.

But following them, watching them, it quickly became a bit of an obsession. Okay, Joe became her obsession.

So much so she'd taken to following him other times, times he was obviously not about to, or in the process of, boosting a car. This became a problem for Darcey when she followed him into a bar about a month ago, watched him pick up some random and take her home. She'd hated it with every fiber of her being. Which was irrational. Completely ridiculous.

But the next week, when he'd gone to that same bar to get himself some action, she hadn't been able to merely stand back and watch. No, instead of sticking to the shadows, she'd followed him right on in. The idea of watching him go home with someone else had been unacceptable, because as messed up as it was, Joe Colton had somehow become hers. A man she'd never once spoken to, had never even been within touching distance.

A man she'd been screwing over.

He had been standing at the bar when she walked in, elbows resting on the surface, thick, long fingers curled around his beer. Those jeans he always wore hugging his ass and long legs, t-shirt stretched over his wide shoulders. She'd wanted to walk up to him and pull him down for a kiss, stake her claim. Had wanted to be the one to run her hand over his cropped hair, feel his beard against her skin. After watching him for weeks, she'd felt as if she knew him, could feel this…this connection between them, and he didn't even know she existed.

She'd wanted that more than anything, for him to *know* her, to *see* her.

So she'd taken a stupid risk, and approached him.

He had looked down at her when she'd taken the vacant space beside him—while her heart pounded like a frightened rabbit's in her chest—unmistakable interest in his extremely dark eyes. They'd talked, laughed. Something she hadn't done in a long time.

The dream became reality.

And when she'd grabbed his hand, he'd let her lead him outside, had followed her down behind the bar, those intense, hungry eyes never leaving her. Had been completely on board when she pushed him against the wall and climbed that long lean body like a tree trunk, wrapping herself around him the way she had been dying to since she first saw him.

He'd growled in her ear, spun her around and taken over. Taken her mouth and owned it. Owned her. Joe had been everything Darcey imagined. More. Perfect.

But then she'd remembered why she shouldn't be there, why she *couldn't* be there, what was at stake—right when the tips of his rough-skinned fingers slid under her shirt. They'd ghosted over the bare skin of her belly, while his erection had pressed deliciously between her thighs.

And she'd had no choice but to shove him away...leave him high and dry.

To walk away from the man of her dreams, away from his exquisite kisses. The addicting scent of pine and motor oil that filled her head making her dizzy. His worried, "What's wrong? Are you okay?" still ringing in her ears. As if he'd done something wrong. As if he'd somehow hurt or upset her and would do anything to make it right.

But there was nothing he could do. It was all her fault.

Everything. All of it.

Still, even then, she hadn't known just how good a man he was. Not until he'd saved her ass.

A week after the make-out session to end all make-out sessions, he'd turned the tables on her. Followed her after she beat him to the punch, stealing a car he marked, a car he needed desperately to get free of Al.

Joe had no idea who she was, and he'd saved her from being caught in the act by the cops, anyway. God when he'd shoved back her baseball cap and seen her face, recognized her as the head-case from the bar. The chick who'd come on strong, gotten him hard then flipped out and ran off...

Shit, she'd never forget the expression on his face.

She forced the image away.

Yeah, he'd used her carelessness to get his brother out of the arrangement with Al. But then he'd taken that debt on himself. Al was grateful he'd kept Darcey out of police custody, but only because he didn't want any blow-back on him. He didn't care about her. And he certainly wouldn't let a debt go unpaid just because of what Joe did for her. But Al had agreed to Joe's conditions, because the guy had dirt on her, and Darcey had dirt on Al. Al knew she hated him enough that if she went down, she'd take him with her.

So no, Joe Colton hadn't saved her ass because he gave a shit what happened to her. And why would he? If she hadn't gotten in the way, he'd be free of Al by now. But whatever the reason, he'd saved her from a stretch in prison, from being away from Noah for months, and she was determined to repay the favor.

Even if he didn't know she was doing it.

Since he'd taken that debt on himself, he had no one at his back.

Well, Darcey had just taken it.

She just had to make sure that Joe—and Al—never found out…

Shoving her hands in her pockets, head down, Darcey headed back to her car. But instead of going to her crappy apartment, she made a detour across town.

It didn't take long to get where she was headed.

A nice neighborhood. Expensive cars, manicured gardens, big fancy houses with designer dogs peering out windows. She pulled up across the road from a three storey monstrosity, tacky pillars on either side of the glossy red front door, and glanced up to the second floor. The curtains were drawn, but she could see the light on behind them. Bright enough the racing cars printed on the fabric were visible from the outside. Noah would be in bed reading. Clutching one of his books, letting the story take him away somewhere wonderful, somewhere he didn't have to live with a prick of a step-father and an equally wicked step-mother. Somewhere Noah and Darcey could be together again.

A stray tear surprised her, streaking a hot path down her cheek and she dashed it away.

Tears were pointless.

Until she could think of a way to get Len to let her have regular visits with her little brother, she had to rely on Al and the control he had over their step-father. She had to stay under Al's thumb.

She blew a kiss toward his window and started her car, got out of there before Len saw her and lost his shit completely.

"Night, Noah," she whispered.

* * *

Joe Colton could feel those melted chocolate eyes burning into the back of his goddamn head. Like two laser beams trying to burn their way into his skull and fry his brain. She was doing a fucking good job of it, too. How the hell was he supposed to concentrate with her parked across the damn street, watching his every move?

"Ow! Motherfucking shit!"

Adam turned to him and snorted. "You're supposed to use a wrench to undo bolts, not smash your thumb to pulp." The prick took the wrench from Joe's hand and held it in the air demonstrating. "See it's easy."

"Eat shit, asshole." Joe snatched it back and ignored the irritating bastard.

In the last few weeks Adam had become more annoying than normal, while his brother Hugh had been walking around like he had fucking clouds for shoes. Shay, his new fiancée, had his brother whipped and the idiot loved every second of it.

Joe's feelings on love and relationships aside, he was ecstatic for the guy. Everything had worked out. Hugh got the girl, and Joe had taken on their father's debt. His brother and Adam were none the wiser. They could live in ignorant bliss. No debt. No more boosting cars, and no more being tied to Al Ramirez. And that's the way it needed to stay. Hugh had put himself on the line enough for their family. And Adam…well, this wasn't his fight. It wasn't his useless, waste of space father that left his family drowning in gambling debts.

Joe glanced over his shoulder and gritted his teeth. It was thanks to the deceitful little saboteur sitting a short ways down the street, watching him from her beaten to shit Toyota, that he'd been able to convince Al to lay the debt on him and him alone. Ironically, it was also her fault he still owed that fucker in the first place. Well, Joe had turned the tables on her, had tailed her for several days, and when the police had been closing in, minutes from catching her red-handed, with her ass in someone else's car, he got her out.

Al had agreed to his terms. The prick didn't care how he got what he was owed, as long as he got it, and Joe intended to deliver.

It would be a lot easier without his fucking shadow, though. The woman sucked at stealth. Every job he'd done since, she'd been there, watching him. Why Al still had her following him, he had no idea, but it was starting to make him bat-shit crazy.

The tingle at the base of his neck intensified. Shit. He could fucking *feel* those dark eyes sliding over his back. He growled, pissed at himself.

Pissed that her gaze wasn't the only thing he was feeling when it came to her. The memory of her soft body flush against his hadn't let up since he'd had her pressed against that wall. Neither had the sound of her husky moans when he'd thrust his tongue in her sweet as candy mouth and fucking devoured it…

"Jesus." He threw the wrench in the tool box beside him and scrubbed his hands over his cropped hair.

Adam slid out from beneath the car he was now working under. "Yes, my disciple,"

"Shut it."

"You realize talking to yourself is the first sign of madness, right?"

"You realize if you say one more smart-ass comment, I'm going to shove my foot up your ass, right?"

Hugh strode out of the office, brows hiked high. "When the fuck did this happen? Is it Freaky Friday or some shit? It's like you've switched brains." He crossed his arms, shaking his head. "I don't like it. Adam's supposed to be the grouchy, broody one and Joe's the smart-ass." He pointed at Adam. "Get fucking brooding would you. And it'll be my foot in your ass, baby brother, if you don't crack a goddamn joke in the next—" he glanced up at the clock on the wall. "—five minutes. Go."

Adam scowled. "You can talk. You're the one walking around like fucking birds and butterflies and little girly hearts are floating around your fat head."

Joe snorted. "You're whipped, bro. It's a fucking disgrace." Joe didn't mean a word of it of course. He loved Shay. But he couldn't ignore his duty as a brother. Giving Hugh shit was all part of the gig.

Hugh grunted. "Bullshit."

"No shit." Joe shut the Subaru's hood. "You're an embarrassment to men everywhere."

"You assholes can mock me all you like, but just you wait. The right girl will come along and knock you on your ass. Then we'll see who's whipped."

Adam shook his head. "Never happen."

Right then Shay walked into the garage behind Hugh, but he hadn't noticed her yet. Joe fought back a smirk. "So you wear the pants at home, huh, Hugh?"

His brother looked smug as hell. "My woman does as I say. I'm the man of my house."

"Is that right?" Shay said from behind him, hands planted on her round hips.

Hugh winced, big shoulders lifting before he turned to face his